Zack rose from his chair and offered Jeremy his hand. "This all sounds very interesting, Jeremy. Good luck with your new business venture."

Jeremy's smarmy grin sprang to his lips as he pumped Zack's hand. "I'm always on the lookout for new investors if you're interested."

He'd now gone from *we* to *I* in referring to the startup travel app, giving rise to another red flag in my already crowded cerebral cortex.

Zack and I exchanged a quick look, which Jeremy misinterpreted as interest. "Why not discuss it with your wife and get back to me?"

Before Zack had a chance to answer, the front door opened. Four men stormed into our living room. All wore bulletproof vests with FBI blazoned across the front, and all had their guns trained on Jeremy Dugan.

Acclaim for the Anastasia Pollack Crafting Mysteries

Assault with a Deadly Glue Gun

"Crafty cozies don't get any better than this hilarious confection...Anastasia is as deadpan droll as Tina Fey's Liz Lemon, and readers can't help cheering as she copes with caring for a host of colorful characters." – *Publishers Weekly* (starred review)

"Winston has hit a homerun with this hilarious, laugh-until-your-sides-hurt tale." – *Booklist* (starred review)

"A comic tour de force...Lovers of funny mysteries, outrageous puns, self-deprecating humor, and light romance will all find something here." – *ForeWord Magazine* (Book-of-the-Year nominee)

"North Jersey's more mature answer to Stephanie Plum. Funny, gutsy, and determined, Anastasia has a bright future in the planned series." – *Kirkus Reviews*

"...a delightful romp through the halls of who-done-it." – *The Star-Ledger*

"Make way for Lois Winston's promising new series...I'll be eagerly awaiting the next installment in this thoroughly delightful series." – *Mystery Scene Magazine*

"...once you read the first few pages of Lois Winston's first-in-series whodunit, you're hooked for the duration..." – *Bookpage*

"Fans of Stephanie Plum will love Lois Winston's cast of quirky, laughable, and loveable characters...clever and thoroughly entertaining—a must read!" – Brenda Novak, *New York Times* bestselling author

"What a treat—I can't stop laughing! Witty, wise, and delightfully clever, Anastasia is going to be your new best friend. Her mysterious adventures are irresistible—you'll be glued to the page!" – Hank Phillippi Ryan, Agatha, Anthony, and Macavity award-winning author

"You think you've got trouble? Say hello to Anastasia Pollack, who also happens to be queen of the one-liners. Funny, funny, funny—this is a series you don't want to miss!" – Kasey Michaels, *USA Today* bestselling author

Death by Killer Mop Doll

"Anastasia is a crafting Stephanie Plum, surrounded by characters sure to bring chuckles as she careens through the narrative, crossing paths with the detectives assigned to the case and snooping around to solve it." – *Booklist*

"In Winston's droll second cozy featuring crafts magazine editor Anastasia Pollack...readers who relish the offbeat will be rewarded." – *Publishers Weekly*

"...a *30 Rock* vibe...Winston turns out another lighthearted amateur sleuth investigation. Laden with one-liners, Anastasia's second outing points to another successful series in the works." – *Library Journal*

"Winston...plays for plenty of laughs...while letting Anastasia shine as a risk-taking investigator who doesn't always know when to quit." – *Alfred Hitchcock Mystery Magazine*

Revenge of the Crafty Corpse

"Winston peppers the twisty and slightly edgy plot with humor and plenty of craft patterns. Fans of craft mysteries will like this, of course, but so will those who enjoy the smart and snarky humor of Janet Evanovich...." – *Booklist*

"Winston's entertaining third cozy plunges Anastasia into a surprisingly fraught stew of jealousy, greed, and sex...and a Sopranos-worthy lineup of eccentric character..." – *Publishers Weekly*

"A fun addition to a series that keeps getting stronger." – *Romantic Times Magazine*

"Chuckles begin on page one and the steady humor sustains a comedic crafts cozy." – *Library Journal*

"You'll be both surprised and entertained by this terrific mystery." – *Suspense Magazine*

"The book has what a mystery should...It moves along at a good pace...Like all good sleuths, Anastasia pieces together what others don't." – *The Star-Ledger*

Decoupage Can Be Deadly
"*Decoupage Can Be Deadly* is the fourth in the Anastasia Pollock Crafting Mysteries. And the best one yet." – *Suspense Magazine*

"What a great cozy mystery series...Every single character in these books is awesomely quirky and downright hilarious. This series is a true laugh out loud read!" – Books Are Life–Vita Libri

"This adventure grabs you immediately delivering a fast-paced and action-filled drama that doesn't let up from the first page to the surprising conclusion." – Dru's Book Musings

A Stitch to Die For
"If you're a reader who enjoys a well-plotted mystery and loves to laugh, don't miss this one!" – *Suspense Magazine*

"This is one of the best books in this delightfully entertaining whodunit and I hope there are more stories in the future." – Dru's Book Musings

Scrapbook of Murder

"...a perfect example of what mysteries are all about—deft plotting, believable characters, well-written dialogue, and a satisfying, logical ending. I loved it!" – *Suspense Magazine*

"I read an amazing book recently, y'all — *Scrapbook of Murder* by Lois Winston, #6 in the Anastasia Pollack Crafting Mysteries. All six novels and three novellas in the series are Five Star reads." – Jane Reads

"...a quick read, with humour, a good mystery and very interesting characters!" – Verietats

Drop Dead Ornaments

"I always forget how much I love this series until I read the next one and I fall in love all over again..." – Dru's Book Musings

"I love protagonist Anastasia Pollack. She's witty and funny, and she can be sarcastic at times...A great whodunit, with riotous twists and turns, *Drop Dead Ornaments* was a fast, exciting read that really kept me on my toes." – Lisa K's Book Reviews

"...such a fantastic book...I adore Anastasia! She's clever, likable, fun to read about, and easy to root for." – Jane Reads

"I love this series! Not only is Anastasia a 'crime magnet,' she is hilarious and snarky, a delight to read about and a dedicated friend." – Mallory Heart's Cozies

"It is always a nice surprise when something I am reading has a tie in to actual news or events that are happening in the present moment. I don't want to spoil a major plot secret, but the timing could not have been better...Be prepared for a dysfunctional cast of quirky characters." – Laura's Interests

"*Drop Dead Ornaments* is an enjoyable...roller-coaster ride, with secrets and clues tugging the reader this way and that." – Here's How It Happened

"...a light-hearted cozy mystery with lots of energy and definitely lots of action and interaction between characters." – Curling Up By the Fire

Handmade Ho-Ho Homicide

"Merry *Crises*! Lois Winston has brought back Anastasia's delightful first-person narrative of family, friends, dysfunction, and murder, and made it again very entertaining!" – *Kings River Life Magazine*

"Once again, the author knows how to tell a story that immediately grabbed my attention and I couldn't put this book down until the last page was read.... This was one of the best books in this delightfully lovable series." – Dru's Book Musings

"The story had me on the edge of my seat the entire time." – 5 Stars, Baroness Book Trove

"Christmas, cozy mystery, craft, how can I not love this book? Humor, twists and turns, adorable characters make this story truly engaging from the first to the last page." – LibriAmoriMiei

"Take a murder mystery, add some light-hearted humor and weird characters, sprinkle some snow and what you get is *Handmade Ho-Ho Homicide*—a perfect Christmas Cozy read." –5 stars, The Book Decoder

A Sew Deadly Cruise

"*A Sew Deadly Cruise* is absolutely delightful, and I was sorry when it was over. I devoured every word!" – *Suspense* Magazine

"Winston's witty first-person narrative and banter keeps me a fan. Loved it!" –*Kings River Life Magazine*

"The author knows how to tell a story with great aplomb...this was one fantastic whodunit that left me craving for more thrilling adventures." – Dru's Book Musings

"Overall a fun read that cozy fans are sure to enjoy." – Books a Plenty Book Reviews

"Winston has a gift for writing complicated cozy mysteries while entertaining and educating." – Here's How it Happened

Stitch, Bake, Die!
"Lois Winston has crafted another clever tale...with a backdrop of cross stitching, buttercream, bribery, sabotage, rumors, and murder...vivid descriptions, witty banter, and clever details leading to an exciting and shocking conclusion...a page-turner experience to delight cozy fans." – *Kings River Life Magazine*

"...a crème de la crème of a cozy read." – Brianne's Book Reviews

"...a well-plotted mystery that takes the term 'crafty old lady' to new heights." – Mysteries with Character

"...fast-paced with wacky characters, a fun resort setting, and a puzzling mystery to solve." – Nancy J. Cohen, author of the Bad Hair Day Mysteries

"Lots of action, a bevy of quirky characters, and a treasure trove of secrets add up to another fine read from Lois Winston." – mystery author Maggie Toussaint/Valona Jones

Guilty as Framed
"Engaging and clever!" – *Kings River Life Magazine*
"This is another great entry in the Anastasia Pollack series." – Dru's Book Musings

"Winston not only combines (New) Jersey, well-crafted characters, and tight plotting, but she adds her own interpretation and possible solution to a factual museum art crime." – Debra H. Goldstein, author of the Sarah Blair Mysteries

"Author Lois Winston deftly frames the fast-moving investigation...with a dollop of mother-in-law hijinks, mama drama, home renovation, and doggie intervention." – mystery author Maggie Toussaint/Valona Jones

"Reading a book in this series is like visiting an old friend." – Nancy J. Cohen, author of the Bad Hair Day Mysteries

A Crafty Collage of Crime
"Rich in descriptions of the countryside, and alive with characters you'd recognize if you saw or overheard them, this book held my interest throughout and gave me more than one chuckle. It's a delightful read." – *Kings River Life Magazine*

"Winston imbues her story with current references, an appealing setting, layered plotting, and an unsinkable sleuth. Well done!" – Muddy Rose Reviews

"*A Crafty Collage of Crime* is yet another terrific cozy mystery featuring reluctant amateur sleuth Anastasia Pollack." – Lynn Slaughter, author of *Miss Cue*

"*A Crafty Collage of Crime* was a cute, fun, and entertaining read with independent, engaging, and delightful characters, and the mystery was outstanding, too!" – 5-stars, Novels Alive

Sorry, Knot Sorry
"If you like your mysteries with a healthy dose of humor, Winston delivers... A delightful read whether you're at the beach or in your favorite recliner with a glass of wine." – Kings River Life Magazine

"A twisty-turny plot spiked with red herrings and a double shot of moxie." – award-winning author Maggie Toussaint

"Lois Winston serves up another fast-paced cozy mystery that will have you chuckling through to the end. Add to your beach

reads basket for a fun escape!"—Nancy J. Cohen, author of the
Bad Hair Day Mysteries

"5 out of 5 stars. Another great read!" Cozy Review Crew

Seams Like the Perfect Crime

"I found myself unable to put the book down until I'd read the
very last sentence." 5-Stars, Kim Davis, author of the Cupcake
Catering Mysteries and the Aromatherapy Apothecary
Mysteries

"Wit and humor abound in this crazy cozy caper as Anastasia
and her husband aid their detective friend in hunting down a
killer. The tips for memory quilts at the end are a bonus.
Highly entertaining!" 5-stars, Nancy J. Cohen, author of the
Bad Hair Day Mysteries

"Cozy mystery lovers will devour *Seams Like the Perfect Crime*! It's
an entertaining and amusing mystery that shines through with
authentic characters." – 5 Stars, Novels Alive

Books by Lois Winston

Anastasia Pollack Crafting Mystery series
Assault with a Deadly Glue Gun
Death by Killer Mop Doll
Revenge of the Crafty Corpse
Decoupage Can Be Deadly
A Stitch to Die For
Scrapbook of Murder
Drop Dead Ornaments
Handmade Ho-Ho Homicide
A Sew Deadly Cruise
Stitch, Bake, Die!
Guilty as Framed
A Crafty Collage of Crime
Sorry, Knot Sorry
Seams Like the Perfect Crime
Embroidered Lies and Alibis

Anastasia Pollack Crafting Mini-Mysteries
Crewel Intentions
Mosaic Mayhem
Patchwork Peril
Crafty Crimes (all 3 novellas in one volume)

Empty Nest Mystery Series
Definitely Dead
Literally Dead

Romance, Romantic Suspense, Chick Lit
Love, Lies and a Double Shot of Deception
Lost in Manhattan
Someone to Watch Over Me
Talk Gertie to Me
Four Uncles and a Wedding
Hooking Mr. Right
Finding Hope

Novellas and Novelettes
Elementary, My Dear Gertie
Moms in Black, A Mom Squad Caper
Once Upon a Romance
Finding Mr. Right

Children's Chapter Book
The Magic Paintbrush

Nonfiction
Top Ten Reasons Your Novel is Rejected
House Unauthorized
Bake, Love, Write
We'd Rather Be Writing

Embroidered Lies and Alibis

LOIS WINSTON

Cover design by L. Winston

ISBN: 978-1-940795-82-9

DEDICATION

To Alexandra Bitton-Bailey for bringing Anastasia and the rest of the Anastasia Pollack Crafting Mysteries cast of characters to life with her wonderful audiobook narrations.

ACKNOWLEDGMENTS

As always, I'm indebted to the expertise of Crimescenewriter members. Former FBI agent and current security consultant John J. Robinson answered my questions regarding hackers, scammers, and FBI procedures and educated me on security systems. He even offering me the use of a few real-life scenarios he'd employed.

Along with John, Bob Mueller, Mindy Kinnaman, and Stacey Pearson offered their expertise on tracking down missing persons.

To Margy May, the winning bidder at the First Unitarian Universalist Church of Nashville's FUUNtastic Fall Auction, for the right to have her name as a character in *Embroidered Lies and Alibis*.

To Jody Tanis for reminding me of those infrequent events where New Jersey shakes, rattles, and rolls and suggesting it was time Anastasia experienced one.

And as always, to Donnell Ann Bell and Irene Peterson for their editorial expertise.

ONE

"Conflicted?" Zack eyed me with concern as we exited the Union County Courthouse.

"Why do you ask?"

"You're frowning."

Was I? I considered his question for a moment before answering. "Not conflicted so much as sad. And disappointed. It never should have come to this."

He looped his arm across my shoulders and offered me a side-hug. "You tried your best to make the situation work. I hope you're not blaming yourself."

Myriad clichés bounced around in my brain. I'd bitten my tongue. Silently counted to ten (Although, I doubt even ten thousand would have worked.) And bent over backwards. All with the goal of making the best of an untenable situation. Nothing had worked.

After heaving a sigh, I explained, "I don't feel guilty. I'm at peace with my decision."

Until a few months ago, my name was Anastasia Pollack. When Zack and I married, I became Anastasia Barnes. Last month, after my former mother-in-law defaced my property, then called a press conference to accuse me of elder abuse, I'd finally—and reluctantly—reached my limit. The woman had never had a kind word for me from the moment her son, my deceased first husband, had introduced us.

When Karl Marx Pollack dropped dead at a casino in Las Vegas nearly two years ago, he'd left me and our teenage sons, Alex and Nick, with an unwelcome surprise—gambling debt that rivaled the GNP of many a Third World nation. Yet another cliché that has infiltrated my life: The wife is always the last to know.

Through moonlighting and a series of unusual circumstances, I'd whittled down my Uzbekistan-sized debt to a more manageable Djibouti-sized number in the debit column. However, Karl had also stuck me with his semi-invalid communist mother. I still haven't decided which was more of a shock.

Some ex-daughters-in-law would have tossed the harridan out to fend for herself on her meager pension and monthly Social Security check. Maybe I'm too nice. Perhaps, I'm a glutton for punishment. Either way, I couldn't kick Lucille Pollack to the curb. I had gritted my teeth and continued to put up with her ongoing verbal abuse, as well as the constant home invasions from the twelve other members of the Daughters of the October Revolution, a group of geriatric commies with the annoying habit of descending on my pantry like a horde of locusts.

However, even the most accommodating daughter-in-law will eventually reach her breaking point if pushed far enough. With her latest stunt, Lucille had shoved me too far. Her son had left me with little more than my reputation, and I refused to let his mother hijack that. I immediately filed a temporary restraining order against her.

Court hearings in New Jersey are normally held within ten days after a TRO is issued. But thanks to a combination of summer flu running rampant through the ranks of county personnel, an already jam-packed docket, and my usual bad luck, we'd had to wait four weeks for our court date.

Moments ago, with Lucille failing to appear in court to defend herself, the judge had issued a final order that declared the TRO permanent. It didn't hurt that I had produced affidavits from many witnesses, including members of both the Westfield and Union County police departments.

In the three years since Lucille had moved in with us, she'd acquired an extensive rap sheet that included demonstrating without a permit, filing a false police report, destruction of private property, and assaulting a member of law enforcement. Her failure to show today was also not the first time she'd defied a court order, all of which explained why there is no love lost between the local men and women in blue and my mother-in-law.

I inhaled a stress-free deep breath of air that teased the pending arrival of autumn. For the first time in a long time, my cortisol levels were dipping back toward normal range. Sixteen days ago, I'd unexpectedly received the means to pay off Djibouti, and today, I'd freed myself of one huge Bolshevik thorn in my tush. Amazingly, only one of those events had involved yet another murder.

Did I mention that shortly after Karl's untimely death, I'd stumbled across my first murder victim, forcing me into the role of reluctant amateur sleuth? Or that ever since, the dead bodies continue to pile up?

"You're still frowning," said Zack.

I forced a smile, even as my brain warned me against getting too cocky. I'm all too aware of what they say about Karma.

~*~

Not knowing how long the court proceedings would take, I'd opted to work from home today, but Zack had a meeting scheduled in New York this afternoon. After grabbing brunch at a local diner, I dropped him off at the Elizabeth train station and headed home.

When I turned onto my street ten minutes later, I was surprised to find a large box truck parked in the driveway of the house across the street. Two men were carrying a sofa out the front door. After pulling into my driveway, I watched from my rearview mirror as they placed the sofa inside the truck, then headed back into the house.

I'm not a nosy neighbor, but their actions looked suspicious to me. Gloria Forester and her son Billy had flown to the West Coast two weeks ago, shortly after the arrest of her husband's killer.

The last I'd heard, she hadn't decided whether they'd return to the mini-McMansion she'd only recently purchased. Logic suggested perhaps a realtor had hired Joe's Junk Removal to cart away the furniture before staging the house prior to listing it.

Still, scammers didn't limit themselves to cybercrime. For all I knew, Joe's Junk Removal was cover for a ring of thieves who targeted empty homes in upscale communities. But if so, unless they suspected the sofa cushions were stuffed with hundred-dollar bills, I would have thought they'd take one look at the secondhand furnishings in the home, turn around, and leave.

Perhaps Gloria had decided to return to Westfield and planned to buy new furniture. She no longer needed to worry about her deceased husband's volatile personality and penchant for breaking various household items when his temper got the best of him.

To be sure, I decided to text her: *Are you aware a junk removal service is carting away your furniture?*

A minute late I received a thumbs-up emoji. No further explanation. Not that she owed me one. Satisfied that I'd done my civic duty to protect the neighborhood from would-be thieves, I entered my blissfully commie-free home.

Before releasing Ralph, our Shakespeare-quoting African Grey parrot, from his cage, I clipped Leonard's leash onto his collar and ushered him outside for a doggie pitstop and some much-needed exercise—for both of us.

Leonard, formerly known as Manifesto, is proof that you can teach an old dog new tricks. Once my mother-in-law's constant companion, even he had reached his limit with her. He issued his own doggie restraining order by switching allegiance to Nick. Lucille responded by abdicating all responsibility for the French bulldog.

As we reached the sidewalk and turned toward Unami Park, both of Joe's Junk Removal men exited Gloria's house. While Leonard stopped to sniff out a suitable spot to pee, I watched the two men lug a battered bookcase down the front steps and slowly make their way toward the truck. As they shoved the bookcase inside, I noticed the truck was completely jammed with assorted furniture and dozens of stacked cartons.

Once one of the men rolled down and latched the truck's door, he hopped into the driver's seat. The other man bounded up the front steps of the house and closed the front door. After he returned to the truck and settled into the passenger seat, the driver backed out of Gloria's driveway and drove toward Central Ave. Leonard and I continued toward the park.

Half an hour later, after several loops around the walking path, Leonard made it clear he'd had enough exercise for the day. He sat back on his haunches and refused to budge.

I once had to wrestle Leonard into my arms, then haul him a few yards across a paw-burning blacktop parking lot to my car. No way would I survive lugging the overweight pooch back to the house. I yanked on his leash and gritted my teeth. "Get up, Leonard."

He swiveled his head, issued a low growl, and shot me the French bulldog equivalent of the evil eye. Ignoring his attempt to make me cower, I pulled a doggie treat from my pocket and dangled it just out of his reach before tossing it in the direction of the spot where we'd entered the park. Leonard scurried to his feet and took off, yanking me through the wooded area as he raced off in search of the bone-shaped biscuit. Luckily, his short stubby legs allowed me to keep pace.

After he sniffed out and devoured the biscuit, he turned his attention back to me. It didn't take a dog whisperer to read the canine's mind. He expected another bribe.

I once again reached into my pocket. This time, though, I didn't dangle the treat in front of him. Instead, I reared back my arm, wound up, and let loose, hurling an imaginary biscuit through the break in the shrubs that led to the sidewalk. Leonard raced through the opening and down the street. When he arrived at the end of the block without having found the treat, I repeated the ruse, and he fell for it again.

At the end of the next block, he eyed me suspiciously. I pulled a second biscuit from my pocket. "Is this what you want?"

He barked.

"When we get home."

I ignored his pitiful whimper. After another standoff, he finally realized his whining wouldn't sway me. He issued a doggie huff and slowly plodded toward home.

As we turned the corner onto our street, I heard rock music and spied a different truck parked in Gloria's driveway. Its twin sat at the curb in front of her house. The signage announced the company name as *Mr. Repurposeful* with a globe in place of the "o." Underneath the logo, a tagline read *"Keeping treasures out of landfills.*

Laudable sentiment but what were they doing at a newly built home? From what I'd seen earlier, Joe's Junk Removal had already emptied all the furniture and household items from the home.

As the question darted across my mind, a man exited the garage. He pushed a heavy-duty hand truck with Gloria's brand-new stainless steel washing machine strapped to it. A second man followed behind him with the matching clothes dryer strapped to another hand truck.

Curious, I decided not to cross to our side of the street. Instead, Leonard and I headed down the block toward Gloria's house. As we drew closer, the decibel level of the music increased, and I realized it was flowing from Gloria's open windows. The unmistakable sounds of hammering, drilling, and sawing accompanied the Foo Fighters.

With Leonard channeling his inner sloth, we eventually arrived at Gloria's driveway as the two men emerged from the truck. Leonard decided nature once again called, and he began sniffing the weed-infested strip of grass at the curb. While I waited, I made eye contact with the men and offered them a friendly smile. I was dying to find out what was going on without coming across as a busybody neighbor.

Zack has often said that I wear my emotions, not on my sleeve, but plastered across my face. Most likely, my features telegraphed my curiosity because the older of the two men sauntered down the driveway toward the curb. "Morning, ma'am."

"Good morning."

"I'm guessing you're wondering why we're stripping the insides of this house."

Stripping? As in gutting? "It had crossed my mind. The new owner took possession only a few weeks ago."

"You know her?"

I wondered how well he knew Gloria. "We've met. And you?"

Before answering, he removed a black ball cap emblazoned with the truck's blue and green logo. Then, he used the hem of his matching company T-shirt to swipe the sweat from his brow before settling the cap back on his head. "We've never met in person. Darnedest job I've ever gotten, though. You have any idea why she wants the house completely gutted?"

"No, it's a newly built home."

He rolled his eyes. "I know. Crazy, right? And it doesn't even look like anyone's ever lived here."

No one had. At least not for very long. "Are you saying the owner hired you to remove everything from inside the house?"

"Everything reuseable. Cabinets, countertops, appliances, toilets, sinks, gas fireplace insert. Even the hardwood floors, doors, and windows. We're deconstructing the entire house."

My jaw dropped as his words sunk in. "And doing what? Why?"

In the short time I'd known Gloria, I'd quickly learned that she suffered from Leap Before You Look Syndrome. Had her grief over Barry's murder caused her to lose all sense of rationality?

"As for the *what*, she's donating everything to Habitat. The why?" He shook his head. "Beats me. She didn't say, and I didn't think it was my place to ask."

I stole a glance at the house. In a matter of hours, it would be reduced to nothing but a skeleton. "Then what?"

"Your guess is as good as mine. I was only hired to do what I'm doing." He followed my gaze, then scoped out the other houses on the street. "I've had jobs from people with too much money who redecorate every few years, but this..." He pivoted back to Gloria's house and indicated it with a sweep of his arm. "This is downright nuts. Besides, anyone with that kind of money, wouldn't be living on this street."

When he realized what he'd said, he added, "not that this isn't a nice neighborhood, it's just—"

"A typical middle-class neighborhood," I finished for him.

"Exactly."

Leonard had finally finished sniffing. Having discovered the ideal spot, he squatted and made his deposit. I offered the man a shrug before bending to bag the stinky poo. "I have no explanation for you. I suppose the owner has her reasons, but I'm as baffled as you."

He returned my shrug with one of his own. "A job's a job. Her check cleared. That's really all I care about."

"And you're sure you were dealing with the owner?" I asked. "With Gloria Forester?"

For years, Gloria had paid off bullies who egged Barry on, then threatened to file assault charges against him. Upon Barry's death, the lucrative cash stream had dried up. What if one of those bullies had found a way to get even?

I pulled out my phone, tapped my photos app, and scrolled to a picture of Gloria and her son Billy that Zack had taken at our Labor Day barbecue. I showed Mr. Repurposeful the photo. "Is this the woman you dealt with?"

"Yeah, that's her. We video chatted two or three times. I wanted to make sure she wasn't pulling a fast one. Maybe getting even with an ex. You never know these days. Even had her send me a copy of the deed to the house and her license so I could make sure the job was legit, and she was who she said she was."

With that he tipped the brim of his cap. "Anyway, time I got back to work. You have a nice day, ma'am."

~*~

The Repurposeful crew worked like a legion of rainforest army ants throughout the remainder of the day. By the time Zack arrived home in the late afternoon, the house across the street was reduced to a hollow carcass with gaping holes where the windows and front door used to be.

After kissing me hello, he tilted his head in the direction of Gloria's house—or what was left of it—and said, "I'm guessing you have a story to tell me."

I filled him in on what had transpired across the street throughout the day. "Given the arrival of the Mr. Repurposeful crew, once Joe's Junk departed, I would have expected a more detailed response than an emoji from Gloria."

Zack stared out the living room windows at the mini-McMansion. "Odd. Then again, in the short time we've known

Gloria, odd is an apt description of her." He turned back to me. "You're sure the house is completely gutted?"

"I can't imagine that anything is left, given the list the salvage guy rattled off to me."

Zack reached for my hand. "There's one way to find out."

A minute later we stood in the doorway of the empty shell of a house. We didn't dare step inside. I glanced down through the rafters into the basement. Not only had Mr. Repurposeful removed the hardwoods, but they'd also removed the subfloor.

"At least they left the drywall," I said.

"Only because it would have no value. It would be next to impossible to remove spackled and painted drywall for use in another home."

I hadn't meant Zack to take my comment literally. The floors were a different issue, though. "Why would they remove the subflooring? Wouldn't the contractor be able to reuse it when laying a new floor?"

Zack nodded. "Assuming the builder had installed a floating floor system. A glued floor might rip up the subflooring too much to be of any use. However, I doubt Gloria's planning to renovate."

I gaped at him. "You think she's tearing down the house, don't you?"

"I do. Don't you?"

"I suppose it's the only logical explanation for what happened today. Why else would she direct Mr. Repurposeful to remove the windows and doors?" Not that there was much logic in destroying a brand-new home. If Gloria had no plans to return, why not just put the house on the market? Then again, we were talking about Gloria Forester, a woman lacking a logic gene.

TWO

Friday morning, I recapped my court appearance of the previous day to my bestie and *American Woman* food editor Cloris McWerther. "Maybe I can stop holding my breath now. I didn't sleep a wink Wednesday night, thanks to a recurring nightmare."

We stood in the break room getting ready to start our workday with our morning ritual of coffee and whatever baked confection Cloris had either whipped up last night or received from a vendor hoping for a mention in our magazine.

"What sort of nightmare?" she asked as she poured two cups of coffee.

"The worst kind. One where the judge denied my petition. Not only was I permanently stuck with Lucille, but he ruled that I had to allow the other twelve Daughters of the October Revolution to live in my home."

She handed me a cup of coffee. "If that doesn't qualify as justifiable homicide, nothing would. Good thing it was only a nightmare. What happens if she violates the restraining order?"

"She goes to jail. I'm hoping it doesn't come to that. I can just imagine the negative publicity campaign the other commies would mount against me. They'd flood every social media site. I'd receive so many online death threats that I'd have to go into Witness Protection."

"So much for sweet little old ladies."

"Nothing sweet or ladylike about those old bats. Hopefully, they're blissfully content living together in that house they rented in Bridgewater, and I've seen the last of them."

Cloris eyed me over the rim of her coffee mug. "I wouldn't count on it if I were you."

An involuntary shudder of foreboding traveled through my core and forced a note of humor into my voice. "You're probably right, but a girl can dream, can't she?"

Cloris lifted the lid of the bakery box on the table, removed a muffin, and held it out to me. "Some girls. Your luck isn't that good. Those women are vicious. They're probably plotting their revenge against you at this very moment."

"That's what I'm afraid of." I reached for the muffin and scowled. I really needed a triple-dose of chocolate this morning, but the muffin in my hand was definitely not chocolate. I held it to my nose and sniffed. "Banana?"

"With pistachios and chocolate chips."

"There'd better be plenty of chocolate chips. I need all the chocolate I can get today, especially after your doom and gloom scenario."

"Just for you, I doubled the chocolate chips in the recipe."

It would have to do, but just to be on the safe side, I snagged a second muffin before they all disappeared.

As we headed down the hall to our cubicles, Cloris asked, "Have you finalized your idea for Monday's staff meeting?"

The *American Woman* editors and our assistants met with our editorial director the last Monday of each month to plan the issue five months down the road. In addition, we gave progress updates on the other issues already in the pipeline.

As *American Woman*'s crafts editor, I was responsible for creating elegant looking but easy to craft projects for each issue. Our readers might drool over Martha Stewart's creations, but their crafting talents didn't come anywhere near equaling hers. We catered to a demographic of mostly middle-aged and older women with limited skills and even more limited budgets. *Cheap and Easy* was my dual motto when it came to the craft projects in our magazine.

"I thought I'd come up with ways to decorate and repurpose all those heart-shaped boxes of candy women receive for Valentine's Day."

"Very retro."

"Exactly. I found examples in early issues of the magazine. I thought I'd create an updated version for the February issue and another for our book project. It will also tie in nicely with the beginnings of ecological awareness that sprouted up during that period. Imagine how many of those candy boxes wind up in landfills each year."

After our recent merger with Creativity Books, Cloris and I, along with decorating editor Jeanie Sims, were tasked with an additional responsibility. We were to create a series of books featuring updated versions of crafts, recipes, and décor from each decade since the launch of *American Woman*. First up, the nineteen-sixties.

We had arrived at our cubicles. Cloris nodded. "Always good to kill two birds with one stone." When I cringed, she turned as crimson red as one of those iconic candy boxes. "Sorry."

I waved away her apology. "Don't worry about it."

"How long has it been?"

"Since the last dead body?" I worked the math in my head. "Four weeks and a day. But who's counting?"

"You, apparently."

Even though I hadn't discovered the latest body, the victim was connected to Barry Sumner's murder, and that death had placed me in the crosshairs of a deranged killer.

Dead bodies were my sword of Damocles. I never knew when another one would fall, hopefully only at my feet and not on my head. But given my luck, eventually I'd cross paths with another corpse.

Before stepping into her cubicle, Cloris shook her head and sighed. No need to state the obvious. We both knew there'd be another dead body in my life at some point.

After settling into my chair, I booted up my computer to begin work. With any luck, I'd lose myself in the minutia of the day's tasks, taking my mind off both my mother-in-law and murder victims. At least for a few hours.

I had just finished clearing my inbox of all the work emails that had accumulated since Wednesday afternoon when my cell phone rang. I glanced at the screen and groaned.

"I heard that," called Cloris from across the hall.

I ignored her. She'd learn soon enough who had provoked such a response from me. "Good morning, Mama."

"Good morning, dear. I have the most wonderful news."

Wonderful for her, maybe. Mama's news often involved having met yet another potential husband. If so, he'd join the list as future Husband Number Seven for her, Stepfather Number Six for me.

Except for my father, who had drowned while scuba diving in the Yucatan on my parents' twenty-fifth anniversary, none of Mama's husbands had survived beyond a year. Stepfather Number One met his fate racing the bulls in Pamplona. Stepfather Number Two died from a lethal reaction to shellfish. Number Three lost his footing at the Grand Canyon, plunging to his death, while Number Four suffered a fatal cerebral aneurysm as he attempted to kiss the Blarney Stone. Mama divorced my latest stepfather after his conviction on multiple felonies, including murder.

I braced myself for this latest announcement. "And what would that be, Mama?"

"A weekend getaway. Just you and me. We never have any mother-daughter time together anymore."

I choked back the urge to remind her how last Christmas Eve, a killer had kidnapped us, hogged tied us, and left us in a storage closet while he prepared to make us his next victims. Mama never appreciates my morbid sense of humor.

Her idea of mother-daughter bonding usually consisted of her dropping in at mealtimes or guilting me into accompanying her on shopping excursions where I played the role of chauffeur and pack mule. While she roamed the aisles, I'd traipse behind her, laden with an ever-growing bundle of outfits she planned to try on and eventually purchase.

During those trips to high-end department stores and designer boutiques, she'd harangue me about my outdated and more than slightly worn-out wardrobe. Mama was so determined to get me to part with Benjamins I didn't have that she even offered to pay—with Ira's AmEx, of course.

Ira Pollack was my deceased husband's long-lost half-brother. He and his three extremely spoiled children entered our lives months after Karl's death. Like Gloria Forester, he believes no problem is so big that it won't disappear with the wave of a checkbook.

Paying off the debt I'd inherited from Karl had come with one major downside: I could no longer plead poverty whenever Mama came up with a way for me to spend money.

I love my mother, but she always has an ulterior motive, and nine times out of ten, that motive involves a search for a new husband. The woman can't live without a man in her life, but I had no desire to act as wing woman to Flora Sudberry Periwinkle Ramirez Scoffield Goldberg O'Keefe Tuttnauer on a weekend husband-hunting safari.

Instead of summoning the courage to quash the idea, I opted to punt the problem into the weekend. "Mama, I'm really swamped at work right now. Why don't we discuss this tomorrow?" Preferably when I'd have Zack by my side. After all, every good family melodrama needs someone in the supporting role of bad cop. Zack had stepped in to play the part on more than one occasion. Now that we were married, I considered it his mandatory responsibility.

"But I need to give Jeremy an answer, dear."

"Who's Jeremy?"

"He's sort of a travel agent."

Sort of?

I couldn't remember the last time I'd noticed a storefront travel agency. Hadn't they all gone the way of the dodo bird with the invention of smartphones and apps? Didn't everyone book vacations online these days? I suppose travel agents still existed for arranging corporate travel and group tours, but even those were probably now done through app-based businesses.

"Mama, I can't do this now. I'm late for a meeting." A meeting with my to-do list, but Mama didn't need to know that. Since she couldn't see my face, which always gave me away when I was less than truthful with her, she had no idea I had conjured up a white lie.

"Tell them to wait. This deal is only good for today."

That raised a few hundred red flags for me. "Mama, are you being pressured by someone?"

"Of course not, dear. Jeremy only has one more suite available for next weekend. If we don't take it, someone else will."

The way Jeremy's name rolled off her tongue sounded like they were old friends. I suspected otherwise. My mother had no defense against sweet-talking men. "Then someone else will grab it. I'm not available next weekend."

Two fibs in one phone conversation probably meant I risked eternal damnation, but I soldiered on. After taking a deep breath, my next words flew from my mouth. "I really need to go now, Mama. We'll talk tomorrow. Goodbye."

"But—"

I disconnected the call and turned to find Cloris, her arms crossed over her chest, standing at the entrance to my cubicle. I rolled my eyes. "She wanted to book a mother-daughter getaway for next weekend. *Jeremy* only had one suite left."

"Sounds like a scam to me."

I raised an eyebrow. "You think?"

"Where'd she meet this guy?"

"Beats me. The conversation never got that far, but I suspect she encountered him while out shopping."

"Because Flora is always out shopping?"

"You know my mother. I'm guessing he noticed her handing over Ira's AmEx black card at Neiman Marcus and struck up a conversation with her."

"Your mother's an easy mark for gigolos on the prowl."

I sighed. "I know, but there's not much I can do about that."

"Why not suggest your brother-in-law give her a credit card with a set limit? That way she wouldn't attract any lounge lizards looking to charm their way into her life."

"*Half*-brother-in-law," I reminded her. "Ira continues to wallow in guilt over fixing Mama up with his father-in-law. He'd never rescind the all-you-can-spend buffet. It's his way of doing penance for Lawrence's sins."

"In Ira's defense, at the time, he didn't know Lawrence Tuttenauer was in the mob."

I shrugged. "Does it matter? Ira solves every problem by throwing money at it. Look no further than Exhibits A, B, and C: his spoiled rotten kids."

"What do you plan to do?"

"Grill my mother tomorrow. I want to know who this Jeremy is, how long she's known him, and what he really does for a living because I smell a rat."

I returned to my computer screen. With so many of our coworkers hoarding their vacation days to use as long weekends throughout the summer and early autumn, Cloris and I were two of only a handful of people on the floor Friday. No one interrupted me the remainder of the day, and by four-thirty, I'd managed to make a sizable dent in my to-do list.

My phone dinged an incoming text from Zack as I put the finishing touches on my proposal for Monday's staff meeting. He'd once again spent the day in D.C. Such trips were occurring with more and more frequency, adding credence to my suspicion that photojournalism was cover for his involvement in covert government operations. It was the one bone of contention in our relationship, no matter how often he assured me otherwise.

But his text had nothing to do with having to jet off unexpectedly to photograph some newly discovered frog in the Amazon jungle or an unexpected find during an archeological dig in Ethiopia. Instead, he'd sent me a photo of what he'd found once he'd arrived home. Or more precisely, what he hadn't found.

I stared at my screen. At first, my brain refused to process the image. When all my neurons finally clicked into place, I gasped. "What in the world?"

Cloris called from across the hall. "Something wrong?"

I crossed to her cubicle and showed her the photo on my phone. She gave it a cursory glance and shrugged. "Why am I looking at a bulldozer parked in the middle of an empty lot?"

"When I left for work this morning, Gloria Forester's house sat on that empty lot."

I quickly filled her in on what had occurred at the house yesterday. "At first, I thought Gloria merely planned to replace her old furniture. That was before Mr. Repurposeful arrived."

She turned her attention back to the image on my cell phone, her eyes bugging wide. "Why would anyone in their right mind bulldoze a brand new million-dollar home?"

The second photo Zack had attached answered her question and confirmed what Zack had suggested yesterday. I scrolled to the image and enlarged a section of it before holding it up for

Cloris to see. A sign staked into the ground at the corner of the property announced, "Future Home of the Barry Sumner Memorial Garden."

THREE

With Zack having already arrived home and most of the staff taking Friday off, I decided to leave half an hour early. Since I'd finished my presentation for Monday, I saw no point in starting another task I couldn't complete in the remaining thirty minutes.

Besides, with so few people in the building today, I doubted anyone would notice if I ducked out early. Even fewer would care.

I powered down my computer and shouldered my purse and tote. Before heading to the elevator, I called across the hall to Cloris, "I'm wrapping for the week."

"Best idea you've had in months. Count me in. I still have packing to do before we leave tomorrow."

I had forgotten Cloris and her husband Gregg were flying to Italy tomorrow for a week in Tuscany. I waited as she powered down her own computer and grabbed her purse. Then, together we headed toward the elevator.

Throughout the drive home, I puzzled over Gloria Forester's decision to tear down her house. Although she had plenty of money for such an irrational act, she hadn't struck me as the sort of woman who would pull such a wasteful stunt. Since money was no object, I suppose it meant more to her to create a lasting memorial to her husband, no matter the cost.

Barry Sumner had had his flaws, chief among them his volatile temper. Even with some evidence to the contrary, Gloria had blamed his outbursts on the injuries he'd sustained years earlier from a motorcycle accident. Whether the truth or her need to rationalize his behavior, I'd never know.

What I did know was that Barry Sumner had been an easy mark. Blackmailers took advantage of his short fuse and his wife's need to keep her husband out of jail. Whenever anyone threatened to press charges after provoking Barry, Gloria pulled out her checkbook to make the problem go away.

She truly loved the man, warts and all. Maybe tearing down the house and creating a tiny memorial garden on the property was more about Gloria finding closure and moving on with her life. After all, since she apparently had no plans to return to New Jersey, she'd never find solace by spending any time in the garden.

Or perhaps the memorial garden was Gloria's ultimate revenge against the people who had bullied Barry for years. By creating a lasting in-your-face reminder of the despicable way they'd treated him, these men would be forced to confront their actions every time they drove down our street.

However, since the one-block long street was neither a major thoroughfare through town nor much of a shortcut for avoiding traffic jams on Central Avenue, few of Barry's former tormenters would ever have reason to drive past the garden.

If this was Gloria's rationale for creating the memorial, her reasoning was seriously flawed. Given Gloria, though, it wasn't beyond the realm of possibilities.

After arriving home, I first stood on the sidewalk for a moment and stared across the street. A professionally crafted sign stood against a backdrop of a battered yellow bulldozer situated at the center of a weed-strewn pile of earth.

A poet or philosopher might fashion an appropriate metaphor about new life springing from the ashes of death, but I was more cynic than poet or philosopher. No matter how many flowers eventually bloomed on the small plot of land, I'd always see the scene as a depressing reminder of a brutal crime.

I shook the morbid thought from my head, hoping to replace it with the expectation of a relaxing evening. However, as I approached the front door, my hopes shattered when I heard my mother's plaintive whine drifting out the open living room windows. "Where will I store everything?"

"I'll rent a storage unit for you," said Zack.

Years ago, Mama had transferred most of her worldly possessions into my garage when she moved into Stepfather Number One's apartment. With the death of each subsequent stepfather, the available space in my two-car detached garage had shrunk to just barely enough room for the lawncare and snow removal equipment.

After several major blizzards last winter, Zack had grown tired of digging out our cars from two feet of snow, only to find an inch or more of ice encasing each vehicle. I couldn't blame him. With Alex off at college, we were down one able-bodied shoveler. It was past time to reclaim the garage.

"But what if I need something?"

Zack called her bluff. "When have you ever stepped foot in the garage to retrieve something, Flora?"

"That's beside the point."

"No," answered Zack, having obviously stepped into his Bad Cop persona. "It's exactly the point."

I groaned. Even though I'd agreed that we needed to regain possession of the garage before the first flakes of winter fell, I wasn't prepared for a battle today, especially since I already had one with my mother waiting in the wings.

Before entering the house, I paused, my hand on the latch. After taking a deep breath and pasting a smile on my face, I swung open the door and stepped into the foyer.

Mama accosted me before I had a chance to ditch my purse and tote in the hall closet. "Anastasia, did you know about this?"

I decided to play dumb, although I was surprised Zack hadn't waited until the two of us could confront Mama together. I suspected he'd wanted to spare me her histrionics, but his decision had backfired. "Know what, Mama?"

She took one look at me and narrowed her eyes as she waved an accusatory index finger under my nose. "You did know!"

"Mama, if this is about the garage, yes, I knew. We're not going to suffer through another winter of shoveling out our cars when we have a perfectly good garage that will accommodate two of the three vehicles."

"But my things!"

"Will be fine in a storage unit," said Zack. He stepped between Mama and me and planted a quick kiss on my lips. As he drew back, he executed an almost imperceptible shake of his head accompanied by an eye roll. The man was a saint, but even he had his limits.

Mama threw her hands onto her hips and glared at him. "And to think I once liked you, Zachary."

Before Zack could respond, the doorbell rang.

"That should be Jeremy," said Mama.

Jeremy? "You invited your travel agent here?"

Mama sidestepped me and reached for the door. "Jeremy is much more than a travel agent, dear. Besides, he's taking me out to dinner this evening, and I thought it best to clear up a few things first while the suite is still available for next weekend."

I didn't have time to remind her that I was unavailable next weekend. Then again, I don't think she had believed me.

Mama swung open the front door. A glance at the guy standing on the other side of the threshold sent my Gigolo Alert blaring. I hardly considered *Jeremy* a man, even if he did look old enough to vote. He couldn't be more than a few years older than Alex.

Mama greeted him with a wide smile and looped both her arms around one of his. "Come inside, Jeremy, dear." As she led him into the foyer, she added, "I'd like you to meet my overly suspicious daughter Anastasia and her husband Zachary."

"Mama!"

My mother tossed me a smirk. "If the shoe fits, dear."

Mama often whined, wheedled, ranted, and cajoled, but she rarely resorted to sarcasm. She considered the trait unladylike, which she mentioned each time I employed it. Apparently, though, whining, wheedling, ranting, and cajoling were all perfectly acceptable ladylike behaviors in Flora's Rules of Etiquette. Go figure.

Jeremy's gaze flicked between Zack and me before he darted a glance over his shoulder at the sound of the door clicking shut. Did he suspect we were onto whatever scam he'd planned to use on my mother and now contemplated a quick escape before we called the cops?

As his attention settled back on us, he offered a smarmy smile. "Pleased to meet you both."

When neither Zack nor I responded immediately, he glanced at his watch, then turned to Mama. "We should get going, Flora. We have a dinner reservation."

"Before you leave," I said, "we'd like to hear more about this spa weekend you offered my mother. She's invited me to join her."

Jeremy once again shot a quick look at Mama. She patted his arm and smiled. "My daughter always thinks the worst of people. I wanted you to explain your new business and assure her that you have no plans to kidnap me and hold me for ransom."

Color flooded his cheeks, and he quickly avoided eye contact, suddenly extremely interested in his Air Jordans. He'd paired the expensive footwear with black jeans, and a stylish untucked aqua sports shirt, under which I suspected lurked six-pack abs and not a single ounce of fat or flab. His deliberate five o'clock shadow and rakishly unkempt jet-black hair gave off a quasi-sexy cover model vibe. I had absolutely no doubt *Jeremy* had found an easy mark in Flora Sudberry Periwinkle Ramirez Scoffield Goldberg O'Keefe Tuttenauer, a woman old enough to be his grandmother.

Mama segued into her former social secretary of the Daughters of the American Revolution persona. "Shall we all have some wine? A nice pinot grigio, perhaps, Zachary, dear."

Ever the curious African Grey, Ralph swooped into the foyer and settled on his favorite human's shoulder. Zack pulled a sunflower seed from his shirt pocket and presented it the bird.

Jeremy never took his eyes off Ralph as Mama urged him into the living room. "Ignore the vulture," she said, directing him to a seat on the couch and settling in close beside him.

Jeremy gulped. "Vulture?"

"Braawk! *Let vultures vile seize on his lungs also! Henry the Fourth, Part Two*, Act Five, Scene Three."

Leave it to Ralph to get right to the heart of the matter. Ralph not only had an uncanny knack for squawking situation appropriate quotes from The Bard, but he also had an innate sense of knowing when his presence was required. Jeremy appeared quite thrown off his game.

However, short of creating a scene, I saw little choice other than complying with Mama's wine request. I couldn't prevent Jeremy from taking advantage of my mother if I didn't know how he planned to con her.

Zack and I headed into the kitchen for wine glasses and grigio for the gigolo. "What's going on?" he asked.

I whispered a two-sentence recap of my earlier conversation with my mother. "I suspect he's trying to scam her."

"Don't worry. Whatever his game, we'll put a stop to it."

"I've a good mind to alert Ira. He needs to cut off her credit cards. I suspect Jeremy targeted her on one of her shopping sprees."

"What makes you think he hasn't already conned Ira?"

I stared at Zack. "Into what? Marrying him?"

He chuckled. "I don't think that's what's going on here."

"Then what?"

"Probably some sort of investment scheme."

I pulled four wine glasses from the shelf and placed them on the island. "But Mama doesn't have any money to invest."

As Zack filled the glasses, he said, "I doubt Jeremy knows that. Or if he does, maybe his plan is to con us. We have no idea what she's told him about you and me."

"Which is why we need to play along until we know exactly what he's up to."

I picked up two of the glasses while Zack grabbed the other two. "I suppose you're right."

After we returned to the living room and distributed the wine, Zack and I settled into the two chairs across from the sofa. Mama took a sip of her wine, then got right to the point. "Anastasia, Jeremy graciously offered us a weekend getaway, but you acted like he's some sort of hustler. Or worse."

"I never said any such thing, Mama."

She speared me with a no-nonsense look. "Do you think I can't read between the lines? I know what you were thinking."

She was right about that, but I tamped down my initial accusatory impulse and instead turned to Jeremy and asked, "Tell us about yourself, Jeremy. How did you and my mother meet?"

His expression grew puzzled. "You don't know who I am?"

"Should I?"

When I continued to stare at him, he added, "I'm Jeremy Dugan."

The name meant nothing to me. Maybe he was a former student during my brief post-graduation stint as an art teacher, but if so, how did he connect with my mother? I shook my head. "Sorry."

Mama jumped in. "Honestly, Anastasia, he's Melissa Dugan's grandson."

The name didn't ring even a single tinkle from a distant bell. I wracked my brain but again, came up empty.

Mama huffed. "You went to preschool with Melissa's son Randolph before her husband was transferred to St. Louis. Surely, you remember."

I gaped at my mother. "Really, Mama? You expect me to remember someone I knew briefly when I was three or four years old? And that he has a son named Jeremy?"

Mama sniffed. "I remember all my childhood friends. I can't imagine why you don't remember yours."

"I do remember my friends, Mama. None were named Randolph."

She dismissed my comment with a wave of her hand. "Melissa and I have kept in touch on Facebook. We exchange Christmas cards every year. I'm certain I told you about Jeremy when he was born."

Which was probably at least twenty years ago. Besides, that didn't disqualify him as a potential scammer of susceptible Baby Boomers.

I turned back to him. "Well then, Jeremy, son of a preschool classmate I don't remember, why are you pressuring my mother into paying for a vacation?"

His jaw dropped, and his expression grew puzzled. He turned toward Mama. "Didn't you explain?"

"She never gave me the chance."

He turned back to me. "There is no cost."

Free vacations always come with strings attached. Usually, hours of high-pressure sales presentations and lots of arm twisting to get people to sign up for expensive time-share resorts that are never available when they want to book a week.

"What's the gimmick?" I asked.

"None." He paused, glancing at Ralph, still perched on Zack's shoulder. Then his expression grew sheepish, and he added, "Well, maybe one."

I turned to my mother. "See, Mama?"

She sputtered. "It's nothing like that."

Zack had remained silent during this exchange, his nose buried in his phone. I suspected he was doing an Internet search of Jeremy Dugan. Or perhaps, he was texting Tino Martinelli, former member of Special Forces and current Homeland Security expert on all things cyber-related, asking him to do a deep dive into Jeremy.

Finally, he looked up and said, "Jeremy, why don't you start from the beginning and tell us exactly what you offered Flora and why?"

Relief washed over Jeremy's face as he broke into his sales spiel. "I specialize in app creation. My latest project is for a startup in the hospitality industry. Using AI, the app acts like a personal concierge. After users answer a series of questions about themselves, the app provides vacation suggestions, then books whichever trip the user chooses."

"What makes this app different from all the other travel apps I can download onto my phone?" asked Zack.

"Jurnee is tailored to cover every aspect of a vacation for each specific user, whether it's a three-month around-the-world cruise or a weekend spa getaway. Instead of having to spend hours researching online, the app does the research in a matter of seconds. After the user chooses from the menu of options generated from the questionnaire, it provides all reservations from travel to hotels, tours, entertainment, and restaurants. Once the trip is booked, the app sends updates, reminders, and daily schedules. There's also twenty-four/seven live customer service for a seamless, hassle-free vacation experience."

While listening, Zack had returned to his phone. "How do you spell that? I'm not finding anything in the app store."

Jeremy hesitated. "J-U-R-N-E-E. But the app isn't live yet."

Zack glanced up from his phone. His expression tightened, signaling that at least one red flag warning had popped up in his gray matter. "Yet you're already booking vacations?"

"We're in the beta testing stage," said Jeremy. "Part of the beauty of Jurnee is that it's geared toward all demographics, both age and economic groups. The marketing division came up with the idea of offering free weekend trips to select individuals in each demographic in exchange for posting reviews on social media to generate advance buzz."

This made no sense to me. "My mother is hardly an influencer with millions of social media followers."

Jeremy nodded toward Mama. "Few people of her generation are, but Baby Boomers do a lot of traveling, and more and more of them, like your mother, are active on Facebook, TikTok, Instagram, and other sites. We also plan to blitz the airwaves with radio and TV ads, beginning once the initial reviews are posted."

I shifted my attention toward Mama and found she had an extremely smug expression on her face.

"That doesn't explain how you came to contact Flora," said Zack.

"Everyone involved with the startup was tasked with finding people who might be interested in a free vacation," said Jeremy. "My grandmother knew Flora enjoys traveling. She offered to reach out to her and several of her other friends for me."

He flashed Mama a wide grin. "Much to my delight, I discovered Flora has quite the social media presence for someone of her age."

Knock me over with a pompom. Since when was my mother active on social media? Maybe I should ask Tino to do a deep dive into her Internet presence.

At this point several clichés had parked themselves in my brain. Chief among them: *If something is too good to be true, it usually is.* "Why the pressure to make a decision by the end of today?" I asked.

Once again, Jeremy had a pat answer on the tip of his tongue. "As a first test, we booked Rejuvenate, an upscale spa out on the Northshore of Long Island, for next weekend. Today is the last day to cancel if we don't fill all the rooms."

My mouth dropped open. "You booked the entire spa for next weekend?"

Jeremy nodded.

That alone sounded odd to me. I'd heard of Rejuvenate. It was the Hampton's equivalent to the world-famous Golden Door Spa. I found it highly unlikely that every suite at Rejuvenate had been available for next weekend.

However, if no money was expected to change hands between Mama and Jeremy, I was at a loss to pinpoint the grift. Still, I couldn't shake the feeling that a con artist had Mama in his clutches. But for what purpose?

I did notice, though, that Jeremy had switched from describing himself as hired help in his app developer capacity to *we* when referring to Jurnee, indicating he had a much bigger stake in the enterprise.

"And after the spa weekend?" I asked.

Jeremy grew puzzled. "I don't understand the question."

It's not like I was asking him to translate Proust. "What else is required of your guinea pigs after they post glowing reviews of next weekend's spa retreat?"

"We hope they'll have enjoyed the hassle-free experience so much that they'll not only continue to sing our praises about their experience but also book all their vacations through us."

I pressed further. "And?"

Mama patted Jeremy's knee. "Tell them about the VIP Platinum Club."

Then she turned back to me, excitement written across her face. "We're automatically enrolled. Isn't that exciting, dear?"

"Which means what?" asked Zack.

Mama continued to answer for Jeremy. "Platinum VIP members receive special perks on every trip they book through the app."

"How much is the annual membership fee?" I asked, the scam now coming into focus for me.

Again, Mama answered for Jeremy. "Don't be silly, dear. It's a perk."

I glanced toward Zack. Once again, he pretended to ignore the conversation, his attention on his phone screen. "What sort of perks?" I asked.

"We ...uh...we haven't exactly worked out those details yet, and again, they'll be individually tailored to the guests and the trips they book."

He then placed his empty wine glass on the coffee table, stood, and offered his hand to Mama. "We really do need to leave now, or we'll lose our table."

"I'll just dash into the little girl's room to powder my nose first," said Mama.

Zack rose from his chair and offered Jeremy his hand. "This all sounds very interesting, Jeremy. Good luck with your new business venture."

Jeremy's smarmy grin sprang to his lips as he pumped Zack's hand. "I'm always on the lookout for new investors if you're interested."

He'd now gone from *we* to *I* in referring to the startup travel app, giving rise to another red flag in my already crowded cerebral cortex.

Zack and I exchanged a quick look, which Jeremy misinterpreted as interest. "Why not discuss it with your wife and get back to me?"

Before Zack had a chance to answer, the front door opened. Four men stormed into our living room. All wore bulletproof vests with FBI blazoned across the front, and all had their guns trained on Jeremy Dugan.

FOUR

"Hands in the air," barked one agent.

Within seconds, Jeremy was wrestled to the floor, cuffed, searched, and dragged from the house. A moment later Special Agent Aloysius Ledbetter entered the living room.

When I first met the Special Agent, I had chalked up one more mark in my Zack-is-a-Spy column. However, it turned out Zack and Ledbetter have a more familial connection. He's Zack's ex-wife's cousin, and the two men have known each other for decades. Our paths have crossed several times since that first meeting, and not always crime related. Ledbetter even attended our wedding.

Although, it does pay to have friends in spy places when you're constantly tripping over dead bodies. Or trying to protect your mother from scam artists.

Zack pointed to one of the wine glasses on the coffee table. Ledbetter removed a pair of rubber gloves and an evidence bag from his pocket. After snapping on the gloves, he placed the glass in the bag. Either both men had mastered the art of mindreading, or Zack had already alerted Ledbetter about the glass while texting.

Mama returned from powdering her nose. She cast a skeptical eye on Ledbetter. "This better be a social call and not another murder."

I placed my hand on her arm. "Have a seat, Mama."

"I can't. We have dinner plans." She shook off my hand and scoped out the room. "Where's Jeremy? Is he waiting outside?"

"I'm afraid Jeremy had to leave suddenly."

Her eyes searched the room again, then, with hands on hips, she leveled her annoyance on each of us in turn. "What's going on?"

"Special Agent Ledbetter will explain everything," said Zack.

"I don't understand. Tell me you're not involved in another murder case, Anastasia. And don't try to lie to me."

"I promise I'm not, Mama."

She scrutinized my face. I watched as confusion, then panic, set in across hers. "Then why is the FBI here? And where's Jeremy? Has something happened to him?"

"Jeremy isn't who you think he is," said Ledbetter.

"What does that mean? Of course, he is. He's Melissa Dugan's grandson."

"No, ma'am, he's not."

Mama's hands flew to her chest. "Perhaps I'd better sit down."

After I led her to the sofa and settled in next to her, Ledbetter continued. "The person who contacted you is a computer hacker. He hijacks social media accounts and chooses a victim from one of the account holder's long-distance friends or acquaintances."

"How? How would he know anything about me?" asked Mama.

"He checked you out on social media and discovered you were the perfect mark for his purposes."

Mama's voice grew indignant. "Meaning what? Are you suggesting I'm a gullible fool?"

Ledbetter shook his head. "Of course not. He was looking for an older woman who lives alone and enjoys traveling. When he found you, he pretended to be Mrs. Dugan contacting you about her grandson's new business venture."

"Mama, were you expecting to hear from him?"

"Melissa told me she passed my email on to Jeremy. I certainly wasn't expecting to be contacted by someone posing as him."

Her attention returned to Ledbetter. "He didn't con me. I never gave him any money."

"Neither did any of his other victims. That's the beauty of this scam. Once he hooks a target, he waits until the last minute to hack into their accounts to help himself to their funds. His timing is impeccable, striking as the victim waits for whatever transportation he's arranged for their trip. They wouldn't suspect anything until the driver failed to show up, or they arrived at the airport or cruise line to discover they held bogus tickets. By then he'd be long gone, their accounts drained, and all the contact information he'd given them would bounce back as undeliverable or not in service."

I worried that may already have occurred. Mama had little money of her own, but she received a monthly Social Security check and a decent pension from my father. What if the hacker had rerouted her payments to untraceable accounts? Or talked her into investing in cryptocurrency and set up an account for her?

She wouldn't know until her checks stopped arriving. "Mama, did you fill out one of those questionnaires he mentioned?"

"He was going to help me fill out the form after we returned from dinner this evening."

"That makes you one of the lucky ones, Mrs. Tuttnauer."

She stiffened. "I no longer go by that name. Not after what Lawrence did. You may call me Flora or Mrs. O'Keefe."

He nodded. "Noted, Mrs. O'Keefe. But keep in mind, Americans lost sixteen billion dollars to romance scams last year. That's only one type of fraud. There are hundreds of others being perpetrated. Not to mention all that go unreported because so many people are too embarrassed to come forward to report what happened to them."

"But I—"

Ledbetter cut her off. "You should check your accounts, ma'am. Change your passwords, notify your credit card providers, place fraud alerts with the reporting agencies, and file a report with local law enforcement."

Mama shook her head. "But none of this makes any sense. Melissa contacted me about Jeremy."

"Did she call you?" asked Ledbetter.

"She sent me an email."

"You never spoke with her?"

When Mama shook her head, Ledbetter continued. "He spoofed Mrs. Dugan's email to contact you."

"He posed as Melissa?

"I'm afraid so. He then used another fake email address to pose as her grandson. The real Jeremy Dugan is a high school algebra teacher in Walnut Creek, California, not an entrepreneurial app developer."

Mama appeared to struggle to wrap her head around this new reality. "He knew so much about Melissa and her family."

"Because he'd accessed her Facebook account," said Zack. "People foolishly post all sorts of personal information on social media."

Ledbetter turned to Mama. "Their entire lives are online for anyone to see. Do you have any idea how many homes are robbed each year because their owners post live updates of their vacations for any would-be burglar to see?"

Mama's cringe led me to believe she was one of those clueless vacationers. "I'm not sure I want to know."

"Thousands," said Ledbetter. "They might as well leave the front door unlocked and set up a huge flashing neon sign saying *No one's home*."

She gasped. "But if Jeremy isn't Jeremy, who is he?"

"We don't know," admitted Ledbetter. He glanced at the evidence bag containing the glass with Jeremy's fingerprints and DNA. "We hope to find that out and much more once we interrogate him."

Mama's gaze fell on me. "How did you know?"

"I didn't, but I had my suspicions. He confirmed them when he mentioned he'd booked every suite at Rejuvenate."

"He overplayed his hand to impress us," said Zack.

I nodded. "How likely is it that a five-star spa resort in the Hamptons would have all its suites available for next weekend?"

Mama lowered her head and stared at her clenched hands. She'd twisted her fingers into a tight knot on her lap. "Why didn't I pick up on that?"

"You were too excited over the prospect of a free weekend. He's a con artist, Mama. He played you."

She heaved a huge sigh and turned toward Ledbetter. "Maybe I am a foolish old woman."

I placed my hand over hers. "You're hardly old, Mama."

"Well, no, I suppose I'm not, but I was foolish."

"Don't beat yourself up," said Ledbetter. "The FBI's Internet Crime Complaint Center has been after this guy for months. He's always one step ahead, leapfrogging across the country, changing his alias and his looks with each new scam, using different social media sites to target his victims, and switching up the type of offer he uses to lure them in. He's also extremely cautious, only hitting up one victim per hack before moving on to the next city, the next hack, and the next victim. But we've got him now."

"What changed?" I asked.

"He chose the wrong victim this time. He never counted on you, Mrs. Barnes. Or Zack."

"How?" I asked.

"Perfect timing. Your initial skepticism, coupled with Zack alerting me, was exactly the break needed to nab this guy before your mother became his latest victim."

Something didn't make sense, though. The nearest FBI field office was in Newark. Experience had taught me that an operation such as we'd just witnessed took time to coordinate and execute. Especially during Friday night rush hour gridlock. The hacker hadn't been here long enough for an FBI team to travel the twelve miles from Newark to Westfield, even with sirens blaring and lights flashing.

Besides, unless Ledbetter had recently switched jobs within the agency, he worked out of the Manhattan field office, an even greater distance to Westfield. "How did you get here so quickly?"

"We were in the neighborhood."

That answer required a more in-depth explanation, but the look on Ledbetter's face, along with the tone of his voice, indicated none would be forthcoming. At least not to me and Mama. I glanced at my husband. Whether he was a member of some alphabet agency or not, he'd also mastered the classic alphabet agency stony visage.

Ledbetter and a strike team being "in the area" struck me as too coincidental. I checked my phone for breaking news concerning a local FBI sting, kidnapping, mass shooting, terrorist attack, or some other nearby criminal activity that might result in federal law enforcement involvement. My phone showed nothing.

Of course, something still may have occurred without the Fourth Estate getting wind of it. However, in this age of cameras everywhere and reporters constantly monitoring law enforcement movements, not to mention criminals live streaming their crimes as they occurred, how likely was that?

Addressing Zack and me, Ledbetter said, "I need to get going. A flatbed is on its way to tow his vehicle."

"Those were some fancy wheels," said Zack.

"What was it?" I asked. I didn't know much about luxury sports cars, but even I had realized that was no ordinary vermillion red car parked in front of our house.

"McLaren 570S," said Zack. "They start around two-hundred grand."

"Yikes! He must be one very successful scammer."

"Not anymore," said Ledbetter. "With your help, we're one step closer to shutting down another operation that preys on g..." He paused for a split second and glanced toward Mama. "...unsuspecting citizens."

I appreciated that Ledbetter had thought to choose a more diplomatic adjective to describe my mother nearly falling for a con artist. I'm certain *gullible* had been on the tip of his tongue before he caught himself.

"You're welcome to stay for dinner," I said.

He raised an eyebrow, as if assessing my ulterior motives. "Wish I could but I've got a suspect to interrogate."

"Another time them," I said. "You're always welcome."

"Especially if you come to save me from my own stupidity," added Mama in a soft whisper.

The three of us stared at her. Still on the couch, she appeared to have shrunk into herself. Mama's youthful appearance meant she was often mistaken for my sister. Right now, though, she looked every one of her nearly sixty-six years and then some. She needed a restorative ego boost, and I knew how to dispel the funk that had settled over her.

After Ledbetter left, I pulled out my phone once again and booked two facials and massages at a local spa for tomorrow. "Mama, it's not Rejuvenate, but you and I have a spa date tomorrow morning."

She immediately brightened. "With lunch afterwards?"

"Of course."

"And maybe some shopping?"

No good deed goes unpunished. Instead of answering, I said, "I'll pick you up at nine-thirty."

Luckily, Nick arrived home before the conversation could continue. After kissing me and his grandmother, his eyes darted around the room, his brow furrowing. "Do we have company?"

"No, why?" I asked.

Instead of answering me, he turned to Zack. His voice filled with excitement. "Did you buy a new sportscar?"

Zack shook his head.

Nick deflated. "There's a McLaren parked in front of our house. Who's is it?"

"Later," I said.

That only caused a look of worry to spread across Nick's face. "Everything okay?"

"It is now," said Mama. "All's right with the world."

Given the state of the world, I found her comment overly optimistic, but Mama saw life through her own extremely narrow lens.

Nick appeared to share my assessment. The worry on his face transitioned to puzzlement. He glanced at Zack who repeated, "Later."

Nick shrugged. Like a typical teenager, he changed the subject to a far more important topic. "What's for dinner?"

~*~

Mama stayed for dinner. Afterwards, Zack and I drove her home and checked her bank accounts. Relief washed over me when I saw that Jeremy—or whoever he was—hadn't had time to wipe out her savings.

But that relief quickly dissipated. Mama had dozens of accounts that made her a hacker's dream. Along with her bank, Social Security, Medicare, pharmacy, AARP, healthcare, Daughters of the American Revolution, and the social media "Jeremy" had mentioned, she also belonged to a plethora of online communities and had subscriptions to a dozen online magazines. The A-to-Z topics included everything from ancestry searching to creating Zentangles.

Worst of all, she used easy-to-guess passwords, often the same one for multiple sites. Knowing my mother, she'd balk if I suggested she delete so much as one site. Instead, I said, "Mama, you need more complex passwords and a different one for each site."

She sat ensconced on the den sofa with Catherine the Great settled on her lap. With one hand, she stroked the cat's long white fur. Her other hand waved away my concern. "All those rules about caps, no caps, symbols, and numbers. I can't possibly be expected to remember more than a few. It makes my head spin."

Zack had settled onto the center of the sofa with Mama and Catherine the Great to his right, me to his left. Mama's laptop perched on his thighs. "Your passwords are very easy to guess, Flora."

"I don't think so."

He tapped a few keys, bringing up a site with Mama's name, age, address, and phone number. Her jaw dropped. "How did they get all that personal information about me?"

"Many sites sell user information," I said. "It's one of the ways they make money."

Mama gasped. "Isn't that against the law?"

I shook my head. "Not if you gave them permission."

"I did no such thing!"

"You did," said Zack. "Every time you clicked a box accepting an app or site's terms of service, you run the risk of having your information sold. It's often buried in all that fine print no one bothers to read."

"Are you saying some of those sites sold my password?"

"Not the legitimate ones," said Zack. "But these days, most high school kids can write a program or use AI to generate a list of possible passwords from a name, address, birthdate, and telephone number. Like you, many people use those stats to create their passwords. At least you didn't use *password* as your password or 123456."

Mama turned her head away from us and buried her face in Catherine the Great's fur.

"Tell me you didn't," I said.

She raised her head slightly and mumbled. "Only for some."

I bit my tongue. Chastising her served no purpose. I was just grateful the FBI had arrived before Jeremy had caused any permanent damage. I shuddered to think what might have happened if Mama hadn't asked him to pick her up at our home instead of her condo.

"What do I do?" she whined. "I can't remember a different password for each site."

"You won't have to," said Zack. "I'm going to create a password manager for you and show you how to use it."

"Is it difficult?"

"Not at all."

"Mama, we also need to add a fraud alert to all the credit reporting sites."

"Whatever for?"

"To keep someone from posing as you to try to apply for credit cards or secure a loan in your name," said Zack. I've also contacted Ira. He's having American Express issue you a new credit card. Until it arrives, you won't be able to charge anything."

Mama's eyes grew wide. "But—"

"No buts, Mama. This is for your own protection."

She breathed a heavy sigh. "I understand. Thank you, Zachary."

My husband was now back in my mother's good graces. She'd either forgotten about the storage unit or gotten over her anger about it.

~*~

The following Friday, Zack called me at work. "Al texted me. He wants to speak with both of us."

"About Jeremy who isn't really Jeremy?"

"He didn't say. He was pulled into a meeting and had to cut the call short. I think we can assume it has something to do with your mother and what happened last Friday."

"Should we be worried?"

Zack paused for a moment, as if deciding how to respond. "Let's not jump to conclusions. I invited him to dinner."

~*~

Ledbetter had already arrived by the time I got home from work. I found him and Zack, beers in hand, sitting in the living room. The aroma of something mouthwatering drifted in from the kitchen.

Both men rose to greet me, Zack with a kiss, Ledbetter with a nod and a smile. Afterwards, I excused myself to change out of my work clothes.

When I returned to the living room, I found a glass of Reisling waiting for me on the coffee table. Ralph kept an eye on the living room action from his perch on the back of one of the dining room chairs. Leonard had hunkered down alongside the armchair occupied by Ledbetter.

I settled in next to Zack on the sofa, took a sip of the wine, then held my breath, anxiously awaiting whatever Ledbetter had wanted to tell us.

"There's good news and bad news," he began.

Ralph squawked. "*Good news or bad, that thou comest in so bluntly? Richard the Third.* Act Three, Scene Two." He then took flight, landing on Zack's shoulder to await his sunflower seed reward.

Leonard lifted his head from his paws and yipped in agreement.

I grimaced and muttered, "Not the best way to start a conversation."

Ledbetter shrugged. "Not my favorite part of the job but it's always better than arriving with only bad news."

I turned to Zack. "I suppose your friendly FBI Special Agent has already filled you in?"

He reached for my hand and squeezed. "While we waited for you to arrive home."

I turned back to Ledbetter and braced myself. "Lay it on me, Special Agent."

He took another swig of beer before continuing. "In the good news column: Thanks to the glass of wine you served him, we now know our fraudster's real identity, Brad Jankowitz. He's twenty-three and graduated summa cum laude last year from UC Berkeley with a degree in computer science."

"He was in the system?"

"No, but we got lucky with a familial DNA match. His brother is serving time for drug trafficking."

I didn't even bother trying to tamp down my inner snark, "Their parents must be so proud. Did you charge him?"

"Yes and no. That's where the bad news comes in. Since he initially contacted your mother through email, we were able to charge him with wire fraud. Also, attempted theft and false impersonation."

I frowned into my wine. "I sense a huge *but* coming."

Ledbetter continued. "We were able to hold him for a few days while we obtained the arrest warrant and grand jury indictment. This also allowed us time to run his DNA, but he refused to talk and immediately lawyered up.

"After the indictment Tuesday, we were still able to hold him for seventy-two hours prior to his initial court appearance. During that time, we executed a search warrant of his apartment, hoping to find his computer to tie him to the other crimes across the country."

"I'm guessing you didn't?"

Ledbetter shook his head. "We found no electronic devices at his residence. Not even an e-reader."

"Given his degree in computer science, that alone raises suspicions," I said.

"Exactly. If he's our con artist, we suspect he works from a remote location and is savvy enough not to keep anything that would incriminate him in his apartment."

"What about his phone?" I asked.

"The phone he had on him when we picked him up was a burner. It only contained the email exchanges with your mother. Nothing more."

"That must have raised a host of questions," I said.

"All of which he refused to answer."

"You said you were able to hold him for an additional seventy-two hours. Does that mean he's now out on bail?"

"As of late this afternoon."

"Tell me he's at least wearing an ankle monitor."

Ledbetter scowled. "Wish I could. The prosecution requested one. The judge denied the request. He'll be monitored by a federal probation supervisor until he has his day in court. Assuming he shows up."

"And if he doesn't?"

"We put out an All-Points Bulletin and file additional charges. When we catch him, we lock him up until he goes to trial."

"I'm guessing he's already scouting his next target and making plans to leave the state. If he hasn't already."

"It's not as bad as it sounds. We have eyes on him. We're hoping he'll lead us to the location where he runs his operation."

I had a bigger worry. "What if he tries to retaliate against my mother? He may think she set him up, that she was only pretending to be naïve and clueless."

"Like I said, we have eyes on him, but I don't think you need to worry."

I glared at him. "You'd better be right. And those eyes had better be working twenty-four/seven."

"They are. We want to nail this creep before he has a chance to target anyone else."

But could the FBI outsmart Brad Jankowitz? From everything I'd learned, I had concluded he was some sort of evil computer genius. A summa cum laude from Berkeley attested to that.

I sighed. "I know I'm sounding naïve, but why do so many people with incredible skills and Mensa-level brains use their gifts for evil rather than the good of humankind?"

Zack and Ledbetter answered in unison. "Greed."

"Wouldn't they make as much money or more if they set their sights on finding a cure for cancer or Alzheimer's disease or solving the climate crisis or ridding the planet of hunger?"

"Greed exceeds both patience and altruism in people like Jankowitz," said Ledbetter. "Their goal is to amass as much wealth as possible in as little time and with the least amount of effort. For Jankowitz, that meant preying on gullible, naïve senior citizens."

"I wonder what his grandmother would think of her grandson if she knew what he really did for a living."

Then again, maybe he and his brother were part of a family of bloodsuckers, the kind that drain bank accounts rather than bodily fluids. They may have learned their lying, cheating, and stealing ways from the family matriarch.

My stomach chose that moment to pull an Audrey Two and loudly demand sustenance, yanking me out of the weeds of conjecture.

Thanks to his alphabet agency training, Ledbetter remained stone-faced as the *Little Shop of Horrors* monster plant that had sprung to life in my tummy continued to rumble. The guy didn't even blink.

Zack, on the other hand, darted a glance at my midsection and said, "Feed me, Seymour?"

"More like, 'Feed me, Zack,' but I can't be held responsible when the tantalizing aromas of whatever you have in the oven set off my stomach clock."

At that moment, the oven timer began beeping, and we heard Nick enter the house through the back door.

Zack stood. "Timing is everything."

Before Zack had entered my life, I would have thrown together a Friday night casserole comprised of the week's leftovers. He'd prepared Lobster Newburg, serving it over rice pilaf with roasted asparagus.

"Where did you learn to cook like this?" asked Ledbetter after helping himself to seconds.

I answered for Zack. "I suspect my husband was once embedded at the Cordon Bleu on one of his spy missions."

Ledbetter directed a raised eyebrow at Zack. "You told her?"

Nick's mouth gaped open as his head whipped between Ledbetter and Zack. "You really are a spy?"

I scowled at both men. "They're having a laugh at my expense, Nick."

"Are you sure, Mom?"

"That Zack's not a spy? No. That I'm being teased. Yes."

Ledbetter speared an asparagus stalk and asked Zack, "Can't get anything past her, can we?"

Zack sighed. "I don't even try. As I'm sure you're aware by now, the woman has mad sleuthing skills. I'm beginning to suspect she's the spy in the family."

Ledbetter cast an appraising eye in my direction. "Could be. I've said it before, and I'll say it again, Anastasia, you'd be a huge asset to the agency."

"And I'll say this again, thanks, but no thanks. Unlike some people," I said, eyeing both Ledbetter and Zack, "I can't lie with a straight face. Just ask my mother." Thankfully, that put an end to the spy commentary.

That, and Ledbetter's phone buzzing. He glanced at the screen, then quickly pushed back his chair and jumped to his feet. "Sorry to eat and run, but duty calls."

FIVE

"Is it my imagination," I asked Zack as we cleaned up the dinner dishes, "or did the always unflappable Aloysius Ledbetter look completely rattled by that text he received?"

For a micro-second, every muscle in Ledbetter's body had tensed, and the color had drained from his face. But his stony facade had returned so quickly that I wondered if my eyes had deceived me.

Zack finished scrubbing the rice pot, then rinsed it and handed it to me to dry. "Definitely not your imagination."

"Then you saw it, too?"

He nodded. "Something's up. Those guys are trained not to show any emotion."

Zack dried his hands, then pulled his phone from his pocket and scrolled through a news feed. "Typical Friday night crimes in New Jersey. Mostly DUIs. A few burglaries and assaults. A shooting in Elizabeth. One domestic violence arrest in Plainfield."

He looked up from the screen. "Nothing that mentions FBI involvement."

"Not even his earlier reason for being in the area?"

Zack shook his head. "Something spooked him."

"Agreed. Maybe the media hasn't gotten wind of it yet."

"Or it could be personal. *Duty calls* might relate to family, not business."

"He would have mentioned something family related."

"If you say so."

Zack's relationship with Ledbetter went back decades. Mine, only months. "Maybe he didn't want to say anything in front of me."

He grew thoughtful. "I'll call Patricia tomorrow."

"Why not now?"

"If it's personal, she may not know anything yet."

"That makes sense." I'd stifle my curiosity until tomorrow.

As it turned out, we didn't have to wait until Saturday to learn why Ledbetter had rushed out so quickly. Before calling it a night, we turned on the eleven o'clock news. The teaser at the top of the broadcast announced a suspected carjacking and kidnapping in an industrial section of Newark. Both Zack and I immediately recognized the vehicle on the screen, a vermillion red McLaren 570S.

"I suppose it could be coincidence," I said. "In a state with nine million plus residents, there must be more than one vermillion red McLaren 570S on the roads."

Zack had paused the TV. He reached for his phone on the nightstand and opened the home security app.

I shifted my gaze between the TV and his phone, comparing the two vehicles. The car that had been parked in front of our house last Friday had a New Jersey vanity plate: TEKBRO1. So did the image on the TV.

Zack hit the play button. The Eyewitness News anchor came to life. "Our top story this evening involves the disappearance of twenty-three-year-old Brad Jankowitz, a suspect in the swindling of multiple senior citizens across the country. For details, we take you to Darlene Jamison, on the scene in Newark. What can you tell us, Darlene?"

I groaned. Zack reached for my hand and squeezed it as the screen switched to the thirty-something Barbie doll reporter. She wore a sleeveless, curve-hugging aquamarine sheath with a plunging neckline that showed quite a bit of cleavage. Given that the thermometer had dipped into the forties this evening, I wondered if she'd run out on a dinner date, hoping to snag a scoop for her network.

Darlene Jamison had made it her mission to connect me to every crime within the tri-state area. She never took "no comment" for an answer, no matter how many times she'd hurled questions at me. I held my breath as she began to speak.

As she talked, she fought to keep her long, blonde tresses in check as a stiff breeze whipping around her. "Details are scant at this point, Kent. What we do know is that the suspected con artist Brad Jankowitz, an apparent computer genius, was released on bail earlier today after pleading not guilty to several federal charges stemming from the attempted scamming of a Union County senior citizen."

"Do we know his victim's name, Darlene?"

"Not yet, Kent. Because these are federal charges, the FBI is overseeing the investigation, and they haven't been very forthcoming so far. We're hoping for a statement at some point.

However, I did a bit of digging among my sources, and I can tell you that according to one, who wishes to remain anonymous, the Special Agent in Charge has a connection to Anastasia Pollack."

"Remind our viewers who she is, Darlene."

"Viewers should recognize her as the woman we've dubbed Westfield's very own Jessica Fletcher for the various cases she's helped area law enforcement solve."

"Do we know what sort of connection, Darlene?"

"Unknown at this time, Kent. We're looking into it."

I cursed under my breath. "That woman never gives up. She'll be ringing our doorbell by sunrise tomorrow morning."

"We'll deal with it," said Zack.

Easy for him to say. No one had dubbed him Westfield's very own Nick Charles or Hercule Poirot. I'm not even sure the investigative reporter knew Zack exists. Which is odd, considering he's a world-renowned photojournalist, not to mention a former *People* magazine Sexiest Man Alive, whose DNA swam around in the same primordial pool that spawned Hugh Jackman and George Clooney. But Darlene Jamison couldn't care less. Her laser focus was aimed squarely at me.

The anchor continued his questioning of the reporter. "Why do the police suspect foul play, Darlene?"

"Jankowitz's high-end sportscar..." She paused to consult her notes. "... a McLaren 570S, was found abandoned with its doors open not far from where I'm standing, just beyond the police tape that's cordoning off the area behind me. Unfortunately, it's now being blocked from view by various law enforcement vehicles, but we were able to get a shot when we first arrived on the scene."

"Yes, we have it up on split screen. Do we know who discovered the McLaren?"

"I'm told the industrial park security guard came across it while making his rounds. We haven't been able to confirm this, but one of the other networks is reporting there were signs of a struggle with blood found at the scene."

"Are we talking a ransom scenario? Was a note found at the scene?"

"Ransom or perhaps revenge. No mention of a ransom note, so far. It's all speculation at this point until we have a statement from an FBI spokesperson. With Jankowitz suspected of having scammed other elderly women, perhaps he chose the wrong victim and a relative has taken the law into his own hands to extract revenge. After all, Kent..." She paused for effect before adding, "This is New Jersey."

"Indeed, Darlene. One of his Granny victims might have been a Mafia family member. Hopefully, you'll have more information for us before we sign off this evening."

"You'll be the first to know, Kent. For now, this is Darlene Jamison, signing off from the scene of a suspected carjacking and kidnapping in Newark, New Jersey."

Zack switched off the television. "Didn't Ledbetter say they were following Jankowitz?" I asked as we lay side by side.

"He did."

I turned onto my side, propped myself up on one elbow, and leaned over him. "So where were they when all of this went down?"

"Good question."

"If this was a carjacking and kidnapping, there had to be another vehicle involved."

"Not necessarily. It could have been a crime of opportunity with Jankowitz attacked when he stopped for gas or at a traffic light. The perpetrator could have been someone loitering near the gas station or street corner, waiting for an opportunity to strike."

"Then why not throw him from the car and drive off in it? Why would a carjacker risk taking the driver with him?"

Before Zack had a chance to respond, my mind traveled to a darker place. "What if it wasn't a carjacking and kidnapping? What if it was an orchestrated escape with inside help?"

"From someone in the FBI?" Zack shook his head. "Not likely."

"But still possible."

"I'll admit to an extremely remote possibility. If he did have inside help, more likely it came from wherever he was held prior to his release. But you're forgetting about the blood found at the scene. And how did they get out of the industrial park?"

"Maybe they're still in the industrial park, hiding out in one of the buildings."

"I'm sure the FBI has taken all these possibilities into consideration and is doing a thorough investigation, including checking all area CCTV recordings between the facility and the industrial park."

"That still doesn't explain why the FBI wasn't following Jankowitz as they were supposed to."

"And I'm sure that's also being looked into."

I let loose a huff of frustration and flopped back onto the bed. "I don't like not knowing what's going on."

"I'm sure Al feels the same way right now, but I think something else is behind all this speculation. Am I right?"

"Of course."

"And?"

"Improbable or not, if Jankowitz did escape, how do we know he hasn't decided to go after Mama? Ledbetter may have discounted the possibility, but I can't. What if he's wrong?"

"Why didn't you just say so?" Zack threw back the quilt and jumped out of bed. "Call her. Tell her I'm on my way to pick her up. She'll stay with us until we have enough answers to keep you from going crazy and me from getting any sleep."

"Have I ever mentioned how much I love when you morph into my white knight?"

"Keep the bed warm. You can show me when I get back."

Mama lived in Fanwood, less than ten minutes from us. Half an hour later, when Zack still hadn't returned with her, I shot him a text: *Should I be worried?*

He replied: *She's still packing* and included an eyerolling emoji.

They finally arrived an hour later. Mama clutched Catherine the Great to her chest as Zack made multiple trips from the car to the house. He hauled in the pampered cat's high-tech litter box, a large container of kitty litter, a rolling cooler of premium cat food, and enough luggage for a month-long, multi-continent vacation.

Either Nick hadn't fallen asleep, or the commotion had awakened him. He padded barefoot into the foyer as Zack deposited the last load from the car and closed the front door. "What's going on?"

"Your grandmother is staying with us for a few days."

"Another flood?" asked Nick.

A few months ago, the hot water heater in the apartment above Mama's had sprung a leak, forcing her to camp out at Casa Pollack while repairs were made to her condo. "I'll explain in the morning. Go back to bed. It's nearly one a.m."

"Excellent idea," said Mama. "I'm exhausted and need my beauty rest." She reclaimed her cosmetics case from the pile of luggage and followed Nick down the hall.

"Good thing you took my car," I told Zack as I eyed the cluttered foyer.

"Is it?"

He had a point. If he had taken his Boxster, he wouldn't have had room for half of Mama's closet.

I lifted the litter box and set it on top of the cooler. Then I grabbed the kitty litter with one hand and the cooler handle with the other. "I'll take care of this while you deposit her luggage in the bedroom."

~*~

The next morning, the local news featured a recap of last night's carjacking and kidnapping but provided no updates other than the FBI releasing a statement about an ongoing investigation into the disappearance of a suspected scammer out on bail. The statement ended with the promise of more information to come when available.

"Not very encouraging," I muttered as I switched off the television. "Why aren't they showing a photo of Jankowitz and warning the public about him?"

"Hard to say," offered Zack.

"I think they know more but for some reason have decided to withhold the information."

"I'm sure Ledbetter will fill us in when he's able."

I studied my maybe-a-spy husband. Every time I gazed at Zack, I wondered how a former *People* magazine's Sexiest Man of the Year could have fallen for a slightly overweight, pear-shaped me.

Instead, I said, "You seem very calm about all of this. What do you know that I don't?"

"Not a thing."

"Really?"

He wiggled his little finger under my nose. "Would it help if I offered to pinky swear?"

"Couldn't hurt." I hooked my pinky onto his and sealed it with a lip kiss.

Zack then ran out to pick up fresh bagels and fixings. By the time he returned home, Nick was awake and had walked Leonard. We let Mama sleep, setting aside some breakfast for her whenever she woke up.

~*~

During the past week, work had progressed across the street as the Barry Sumner Memorial Garden began taking shape on the property that once held the house he briefly shared with his wife and son. After cleaning up from breakfast, I stood in front of my living room window, assessing the transformation as I sipped my second cup of coffee.

The plot of land had been graded, sodded, and a sprinkler system installed. Along the center front of the property stood a black wrought iron arbor entryway. A decorative plaque with a dedication inscription hung from the top center of the arch.

An assortment of flowering shrubs, alternating with ornamental grasses, extended from either side of the archway and ran around the perimeter of the property. Eventually, they'd grow tall enough to create a secret garden, but for now the entire garden was visible from my front window.

Perennial flowerbeds lined the front of the shrubs and grasses. Steppingstones ran around the property in front of the flowerbeds and created a path from the arch to a circular marble pool, approximately ten-feet in diameter and a foot-and-a-half deep, at the middle of the property. A massive fluted octagram pedestal sat in the center of the pool, gradually widening to double its diameter as it rose four feet. A solid square cap extended several inches from the fluted pedestal and rose another half a foot. Bronze spouts projected from the recesses between the star points of the octagram below the cap.

Another flowerbed surrounded the fountain. More steppingstones created a circular path around the outer edge of the flowerbed and branched off into two paths that led toward the back corners of the property.

"Strange fountain," said Zack, coming up behind me.

I scowled at the object in question. "There's certainly nothing aesthetically pleasing about it. Just goes to show that having money doesn't necessarily go hand-in-hand with good taste. It's a shame because the rest of the landscaping is quite lovely."

"It might look better if it didn't have that massive platform at the top."

"I wonder if that's meant to hold something. Maybe a huge marble ball with water shooting out of the top."

Zack chuckled. "You think that would be an improvement?"

"*Au contraire*. But it would be the cherry on the top of the most hideous fountain in Westfield."

"Maybe Gloria has ordered a giant cherry and plans to call it a soda fountain."

"Very funny. You do realize that sounds very much like a Dad Joke, don't you?"

"We'd have to call it a Stepdad Joke for accuracy, but I'll wear the badge with pride."

I turned my attention back to the fountain. "At least it's not a giant beer can sculpture."

"That would have been a more fitting memorial to Barry."

"I know. Put in that context, the fountain isn't so bad."

"As long as it's not going to hold a giant beer can sculpture."

~*~

Later that afternoon, Zack heard from Ledbetter. "Al wants to fill us in on the details from last night. I invited him to dinner."

I raised an eyebrow. "You sure he just doesn't want another one of your gourmet meals?"

"That might have something to do with it. I didn't mention we defrosted a pan of Lasagna a la Anastasia for this evening."

"I hope he's not too disappointed."

Mama choked back a sob. "How can the two of you joke at a time like this?"

She sat on the sofa with Catherine the Great clutched to her bosom. She hadn't been the same since the aftermath of her encounter with Jankowitz, but her anxiety had ratcheted up tenfold since hearing of his disappearance last night.

She glared at Zack. "I hope your FBI friend is coming to tell us he's recaptured that horrible fraudster and locked him up for good this time. I still can't believe the judge allowed him to post bail. What was he thinking? My nightmares had nightmares last night."

I settled in next to her and offered her a hug. "You're safe here, Mama."

"Am I? Are you forgetting how I was tied up and tossed into your bathtub nearly two years ago?"

She had a point. "That was before Zack installed a high-tech security system."

She glared at my husband. "Where's your gun? Why aren't you wearing it?"

"Would you feel more comfortable if I did, Flora?"

"Under the circumstances, I shouldn't have to ask."

Zack left the room, returning shortly with his Sig Sauer.

Mama eyed the gun. "Is it loaded?"

When he nodded, she released a huge sigh.

~*~

Ledbetter arrived a few hours later. He juggled two bottles of wine in the crook of one arm and held a large bakery box with both hands. After accepting the box, I said, "The last time a member of law enforcement brought me a bakery box, it contained a taser."

The ever-unflappable Special Agent quirked an eyebrow. "I'm guessing there's a story behind that."

"There is," said Nick, entering the foyer, Leonard at his heels, "and it was delicious." He then changed the subject. "Speaking of delicious, when's dinner? I'm starving."

"About fifteen minutes," said Zack. "Plenty of time for you to walk Leonard."

Nick headed out with the dog. Ledbetter kept my extremely impatient mother company in the living room while Zack opened one of the bottles of wine and I placed the garlic bread in the oven.

After Zack and I entered the living room, Mama got right to the point. She leveled an accusatory look at Ledbetter. "You said you had eyes on that man. What happened?"

He scowled into his wine glass. "A Harley cut in front of our surveillance vehicle, clipping it with enough force that the driver lost control. The car jumped the curb and plowed into a storefront."

I gasped. "Was anyone hurt?"

"The two agents sustained some injuries, but they'll both recover. Luckily, no pedestrians were in the car's path."

"And the people in the building?" I asked.

"The business was an insurance agency that had already closed for the day."

"What about the motorcyclist?" asked Zack.

"He sped off."

That certainly raised suspicions as far as I was concerned. "Are you sure it was an accident?"

Ledbetter's expression tightened. "Not anymore."

SIX

Mama let loose a strangled cry. "What do you mean *not anymore*?

She gripped Catherine the Great so fiercely that the cat yowled, sprang from her arms, and raced out of the room. Mama barely noticed. She stared wide-eyed at Ledbetter, her mouth agape, her lips trembling. "Are you saying the motorcycle deliberately ran your men off the road to help that horrible man who tried to scam me escape?"

"We don't think this was an escape," said Ledbetter.

Mama's voice rose into hysteria range. "What else could it be?"

He downed the remainder of his pinot noir before he continued. "We recovered CCTV footage that shows an orchestrated abduction. The motorcyclist continued following the McLaren. About a mile farther down the road, a panel truck and an SUV converged on the McLaren, boxing it in. Both drivers and the motorcyclist jumped from their vehicles and wrestled Jankowitz from his car. When he tried to fight back, one of them pulled a knife and stabbed him."

"Did they kill him?" asked Mama. Was it my imagination, or had her voice struck a hopeful note?

"We don't think so. At least not at that point. We found blood at the site, but the camera footage shows his assailants zip-tying him and tossing him into the back of the panel truck.

"Not much point in tying up a dead man," said Zack.

Ledbetter nodded. "Exactly."

"Were you able to identify his attackers?" I asked.

He shook his head. "They all wore balaclavas. And gloves. Nothing for facial recognition to work with and no fingerprints."

"What about the plates on the panel truck, SUV, and Harley?" asked Zack. "I'm assuming you checked MVC?"

Ledbetter answered as he poured himself another glass of wine. "The panel truck plates belong to a housepainter from Irvington. He reported them stolen yesterday after noticing them missing, but he can't be sure when or where the theft occurred. The panel truck was stolen from a used car lot in Kearny. The Harley plate came from a stolen Kawasaki dirt bike grabbed out of an unattended open garage in Chatham. The bike was stolen from in front of a dive bar in Newark. The owner discovered it missing after a night of drinking."

"And the SUV?" asked Zack.

"Stolen from a Walmart parking lot last night. The plates came from a Toyota sedan parked in a driveway in Clark. The owner wasn't even aware someone had taken them."

"Last night's news reported the McLaren was abandoned in an industrial park," I said. "Was that his base of operations?"

"Doubtful."

"Because you searched all the buildings?" I asked.

"Because Jankowitz didn't drive there. After he was tossed into the panel truck, one of the suspects ditched the McLaren in the industrial park. We have footage of the driver leaving and meeting up with the panel truck a few blocks away."

"But the reporter mentioned blood found in the industrial park," I said.

Ledbetter shook his head. "That's the rumor. It's not true, and we haven't pinpointed who first mentioned it. Whatever someone thought they saw, it wasn't blood. Jankowitz was stabbed a mile away and never set foot in the industrial park."

"What happened to the panel truck?" I asked.

"We found it abandoned at the docks in Elizabeth. A camera captured the kidnappers dragging Jankowitz onto a waiting speedboat that took off the moment they hopped aboard."

"And the other vehicles?" asked Zack.

"Both the Harley and SUV were abandoned at the site of the abduction."

"Then he did outwit you and escape," accused Mama.

"No ma'am. We strongly suspect they dumped Jankowitz out at sea."

"You have no footage of the boat returning?" I asked.

"Not so far. We're in the process of checking cameras at other piers, both in New Jersey, New York, and beyond. A boat of that size can travel about four hundred miles on a full tank."

"That's a lot of territory to cover," said Zack.

Ledbetter nodded. "My guess is we won't find anything. I suspect the speedboat is on the ocean floor along with the body."

Ralph had perched silently on Zack's shoulder throughout our discussion, as if waiting for his cue. He ruffled his feathers and squawked. "*And all the clouds that lour'd upon our house in the deep bosom of the ocean buried. Richard the Third.* Act One, Scene One." He then nudged Zack's cheek, waiting impatiently for his sunflower seed reward.

I ignored the performance, instead choosing to respond to Ledbetter's comment. "If so, a second boat had to be involved to return all of them back to shore. That makes at least five accomplices."

"Exactly," said Ledbetter. "We assume a second boat met them somewhere offshore in international waters."

"Quite a bit of involved planning went into Jankowitz's abduction and disappearance," said Zack.

"The Eyewitness News reporter speculated it was a mob operation," I added. "That he fleeced some Mafia granny and her family retaliated. But if so, why not just kill him and leave the body in the street to minimize the risk of capture?"

"We suspect they were after information," said Ledbetter.

"What kind of information?" asked Mama.

"We haven't been able to trace any of the funds Jankowitz stole from his other victims. Because there's no money trail to follow, it's logical to assume he converted everything to cryptocurrency. Chances are, they first tortured Jankowitz to get his passkey before dumping his body."

"Do you think they were successful?" asked Zack.

Ledbetter shrugged. "We may never know. Crypto is the new Wild West of finance. Legislation hasn't kept up with its rapid growth."

"At least that reprobate is dead," said my mother.

Her comment startled me. "Really, Mama? What about due process?"

Although she'd gone through her share of trauma the last few years, especially after her experience with Lawrence Tuttenauer, I'd never heard her sound so vengeful.

"There's now one less scam artist out there preying on us gullible seniors," she said. "You won't catch me shedding a tear over the death of Jeremy Dugan or Brad Jankowitz or whatever his name is."

Harsh words but I found myself agreeing. I sent up a silent prayer to whichever of the gods had intervened on Mama's behalf by raising enough red flags for Zack to alert Special Agent Aloysius Ledbetter. And for my husband having friends in spy places. Right now, I didn't care whether he was a member of their ranks. His quick action had saved the day.

I turned to Ledbetter. "Does that mean you've officially closed the case?"

"We'll continue to search for the perps. Someone might have a come to Jesus moment and 'fess up or want to cut a deal."

"And risk violating Omertà?" I asked. "If it was Mafia, anyone who talked would be signing his own death warrant."

Ledbetter raised both eyebrows. "For a magazine crafts editor, you seem to know a lot about the Mafia, Anastasia. Are you sure I can't convince you to join my team?"

I chuckled. "My answer remains the same as the last half-dozen times you asked me. But I don't know any more than anyone else whose lived her entire life in New Jersey. Call it Six Degrees of Separation, New Jersey Style. Everyone knows a guy who knows a guy. And these guys live by a strict code of honor. They don't rat out their own."

He shook his head. "We've found the younger generation doesn't adhere to that code as much as the old guard did. It's more every made man for himself these days. However, as for Jankowitz, all indicators suggest he's wearing cement shoes. It's time to move on to shutting down the next dirtbag."

"How many are there?" asked Mama.

"Way too many."

"Then I suggest you get to work, young man."

"Will you at least allow the Special Agent to eat his dinner first, Mama?"

She sighed. "If he must."

With that, the discussion came to an end, both because Ledbetter had no more information to impart, and Nick had returned with Leonard. He glanced from Ledbetter to Zack to his grandmother to me. "What did I miss?"

"We'll fill you in later," I said. "Get washed for dinner."

~*~

After a week went by without any further word from Ledbetter, Mama began to accept his pronouncement that Brad Jankowitz now swam with the fishes. She no longer worried that he'd break into her condo to murder her in her sleep.

Having received her new AmEx card from Ira, on Friday evening, when Mama asked that I take her shopping and out to lunch the following day, I knew she'd made enough of an emotional recovery to return home. I didn't even have to cajole her. With her next sentence, she added, "Afterwards, you can bring me and Catherine the Great back to our condo."

"Are you sure, Mama? You're welcome to stay as long as you want."

"I know, but I haven't had a nightmare for several nights. I think I'm over the trauma."

I don't know that anyone ever completely gets over trauma like that, but Mama only had a close call. She must have been thinking the same thing because she added, "I was lucky, dear. I sustained no permanent damage to my body nor my bank account. Unlike that evil man's other victims. I can't sit on your sofa with my cat on my lap forever. I do have a life."

Places to go, shopping to do. Mama's mantra. I gave her a hug. "Shopping and lunch tomorrow. I promise."

~*~

During the previous week, progress had continued on the Barry Sumner Memorial Garden. The steppingstone paths that led to the two back corners of the property now made sense. A brightly painted yellow and blue Little Free Library had gone up in the far-left corner. On the opposite corner, a drinking fountain had been installed, complete with separate spigots for filling water bottles and doggie bowls. Nearby stood a trash receptacle with a poop bag dispenser.

Black wrought iron benches with teak slats now circled the massive water fountain. Even though the structure hadn't yet spouted its first streams of water, many of the residents on our block, as well as those from neighboring streets, had begun taking advantage of the peaceful setting, especially during the weekend.

Throughout Saturday and Sunday, at any given time of day, I'd observed at least one or two people reading, conversing, or simply sitting quietly on a bench. As I left for work at seven-thirty Monday morning, I noticed one man had already claimed a bench to the left of the fountain, providing me with a profile view of him. His head bent toward what appeared to be a large book on his lap, his right hand clasped around a to-go coffee cup.

With the glare of the bright morning sun, I couldn't see well enough to tell if he was someone I knew. I waved anyway and called out a friendly, "Good morning." When he didn't respond, I assumed he wore earbuds, and his music drowned out my voice. I shrugged and unlocked my car to begin my morning commute.

As usual, Cloris had beaten me into work. I found her in the break room, starting a pot of coffee. "How was Tuscany?"

"Everything I'd hoped it would be and so much more."

While the coffee dripped, she went into detail and showed me pictures from her phone. When the coffee had finished brewing, she poured two cups and handed me one. "What did I miss while I was gone?"

I sighed as I added half and half to my cup. "I'm not even sure where to begin."

She opened a tin and held it out to me. "Have a cherry-pistachio biscotti and dish."

Cloris's eyes grew wider and wider as I filled her in on everything that had happened since I last saw her. When I finished, she said, "But your mother's okay, right? He never got his hands on any of her money?"

"Thankfully, no. Thanks to Zack's quick thinking and his FBI connection."

"What about emotionally?"

"She's sped through four of the five stages of grief in rapid succession. On Friday she announced she was over the trauma and went back to her condo."

Cloris looked skeptical. "Did you suggest she speak with a professional? No one gets over something like that so quickly. Which stage did she skip?"

"Bargaining." I thought for a moment. "Come to think of it, scratch that. Bargaining was involved."

"In what way?"

"She wheedled me into a day of shopping and lunch before I drove her and her cat back to Fanwood. Retail therapy is the only therapy Mama ever needs, especially when charged on Ira's black AmEx card. It was worth playing pack mule as she dragged me around Bloomie's, though."

"In what way?"

"Her near-costly experience with Jankowitz taught her a valuable lesson."

"As long as she remembers it the next time some smooth-talking guy crosses her path."

"There is that. Flora Sudberry Periwinkle Ramirez Scoffield Goldberg O'Keefe Tuttnauer is a sucker for any handsome man who looks twice at her."

"Maybe I should start a line of Sandwich Generation Cookies. Merlot ganache sandwiched between two triple-chocolate fudgy cookies."

"Add some THC and CBD, and you'll make a fortune."

I topped off my coffee and grabbed another biscotti before we headed to our cubicles.

~*~

My phone rang two hours later. Homicide detective Samuel Spader would only call me at work for one of two reasons: he either craved an invitation to one of Zack's home-cooked gourmet meals, or he wanted to pick my brain.

Spader and I first met nearly a year and a half ago at the Sunnyside of Westfield Assisted Living and Rehabilitation Center where my mother-in-law was recuperating from a minor stroke.

The detective and I didn't exactly hit it off right away. He'd set his sights on Lucille as the prime suspect in the murder of her roommate.

Although Lucille is a nasty pain in the patootie, I didn't believe she'd murdered the victim. Unfortunately, witnesses claimed hearing her shout, "If that damn woman doesn't shut up, I'm going to strangle her!" Even more unfortunately, I was one of those witnesses, and her roomie had indeed been strangled.

However, in the end, I proved the detective wrong and gained his respect for my sleuthing abilities. Albeit, begrudgingly at first. Since then, his respect for me has grown to the point where he has requested brain-picking privileges whenever he's short-staffed or short on clues. Since the Union County body count keeps growing, and his budget keeps shrinking, he's basically become part of my extended family.

Hoping this was a call more about meals than murders, I answered with a cheery, "Good morning, Detective."

He responded with a grumpy, "Says who?"

Uh-oh. "Starting the day off with a new case?"

"Mrs. Barnes, do you happen to know of any Westfield witches that were hanged or burned at the stake back in the sixteen-hundreds?"

SEVEN

Not a question I ever thought I'd hear coming from the mouth of Detective Samuel Spader. Or anyone else, for that matter. "I hope you're asking because you're investigating a really, really old cold case."

"Hardly. I'm thinking that a certain street in town is cursed. Wanna guess which one?"

I knew of only one street in Westfield where multiple murders had occurred over the last year and a half. I took a deep breath. "Please tell me you're not talking about my street."

"Wish I could."

"Is it someone I know?"

"You'll have to tell me. The victim had no ID on him. According to those of your neighbors who are currently home, he doesn't live on your block, and everyone swears they don't know who he is."

"I take it he's not in the system?"

"Too soon to tell. We only arrived on scene an hour ago. I'm texting you a photo."

A moment later, my phone dinged an incoming text. I'd seen enough dead bodies at this point to recognize the gray pallor of someone who had slipped his mortal coil. A long, jet-black hipster beard covered his face, making it hard to guess the man's age, let alone anything else about him. With no discernable acne scars, wrinkles, sagging jowls, or telltale gray hairs hiding among a straight shoulder-length mane, he might be anywhere from his early twenties to mid-forties. "No clue, detective."

"You're sure?"

"One hundred percent." Spader had sent a closeup of the man's face with no background scenery. "Where was he found?"

"On the property across the street from you. The one that's already seen two other murders in recent months."

Hence, the suggestion of a witch's curse. Perhaps a witch had been hanged on the property back in the day. I wasn't all that versed in Westfield history prior to the Revolutionary War. To my knowledge, the town had never reenacted any witch trials, which led me to believe none had ever occurred.

I've been to Salem and seen how the town capitalizes on its infamous past. Promoting Westfield as New Jersey's version of Salem, Massachusetts would boost tourism and enhance the economic vitality of the town. Westfield wouldn't pass on such an opportunity. We already make a big deal out of our connection to Charles Addams, creator of the Addams Family. A witch connection would bring in far more tourism dollars.

Anything was possible, though. The hanging or stake burning part. Not the cursing part. I didn't believe in witches with street-cursing capabilities. However, since we've never touted witch trials and stake burnings, I doubted any had ever occurred within the town's borders.

Spader continued. "I'd appreciate you checking your security camera for footage that would show any activity on the street or in the garden last night."

Zack had installed high-tech security equipment around our house after a series of break-ins nearly two years ago. He'd added to the system after two murders had occurred on the street.

I opened the app on my phone and scrolled through the footage from one of the cameras at the front of the house. "Nothing."

"You're not seeing anyone enter the property across the street from you?"

"I'm not seeing anything at all on the footage. One moment, I'm looking at an empty street. The next moment, the footage is completely blurred. I'll check the other cameras." After a few minutes, I said, "This is very odd. Same scenario for the other camera at the front of the house."

"Looks like someone deliberately took out your cameras," suggested Spader.

"Wouldn't the cameras have captured that person disabling them?"

"Not necessarily. There are other ways."

"Hacking?"

"Or lasers. An LED spotlight aimed directly at the camera. WIFI jamming equipment. Even paintballs."

"Paintballs?"

"Low-tech, low cost, and quick. The perp hides behind a tree or bush, out of camera range, and shoots off a round. All it takes is someone with decent aim."

So much for state-of-the-art high-tech equipment. "Hold on while I check the cameras at the back of the house and on the garage."

I tapped on the first of those, then the others. "All working."

Neither of my elderly next-door neighbors had security systems. We were the only house on the block that would have captured the street directly in front of our house and at least some of the Barry Sumner Memorial Garden.

Spader cursed under his breath. "Would you mind sending me the footage? Maybe our tech can get something off it."

"Happy to." After texting him the files, I asked, "Have you determined cause of death?"

"Close range bullet to the back of the head."

"Execution." It wasn't a question. No one accidentally shoots himself or someone else in the back of the head. Especially at close range.

Something occurred to me. "Was he shot within the garden? You didn't ask me if I heard gunfire last night."

"The M.E. determined the victim was killed elsewhere and the body moved."

"Unless someone is sending a message, that's a very odd place to dump a body." Especially one killed execution-style. Those guys usually wind up in the murky swamps of the Meadowlands or miles offshore.

It would be several years before the recently planted shrubs in the Barry Sumner Memorial Garden matured enough to hide a body. Only one possibility remained. "Was he dumped in the fountain?"

Spader emitted a huff of frustration. "This is where it gets really strange. The body was found sitting on a bench with a large book on his lap."

I gasped. "And a cup of coffee in his hand?"

Spader raised his voice. "How the heck would you know that?"

"Because I saw him as I left for work this morning."

"You said you didn't recognize him."

"I didn't, but I did see a man sitting on the bench this morning when I left for work."

"You didn't notice the long beard?"

"Not with the sun glare. All I saw was a silhouetted man. I wasn't even sure about the item on his lap but assumed it was a book. I only noticed the cup due to the angle of the bench in relation to my line of sight. His right arm extended away from his body. If it had been tucked against his torso, I never would have noticed him holding a cup."

Spader muttered something under his breath. All I caught was "death of me" and "until retirement." I hoped he was referring to the case and not me.

"I take it you have no leads."

"Your powers of deductive reasoning never cease to amaze me, Mrs. Barnes."

Spader sounded hangry. I'm guessing his breakfast this morning had consisted of cop coffee and a stale donut. If he'd even gotten breakfast. "I'm always at your service, Detective. Ears to listen, brain to pick, even a shoulder to cry on if needed. And you're in luck. We're running a two for one special today at Casa Pollack. Two brains and two sets of ears for the price of one."

"No shoulders?"

"I'm guessing the case is new enough that you haven't reached the point of needing those yet. Act fast, though. This is a limited time offer. Dinner's at six-thirty."

"Mrs. Barnes, I know I don't have the budget to pay you as a consultant, but I just might put you in my will."

With that, in typical Spader fashion, he hung up without so much as a *thank you* or a *see ya later*.

I shot Zack a text: *Call me when you have a minute.*

My phone rang a moment later. "What's up?"

"Spader thinks a seventeenth century witch put a curse on our street."

"Words I never thought I'd hear coming from either of you."

"Funny. I thought the same thing. What's all that banging?"

"I'm at the gallery, overseeing the exhibit installation." Zack was one of a dozen photojournalists taking part in an upcoming exhibition of endangered wildlife with all proceeds going to conservation efforts. "Hold on while I find a quiet place to talk."

The hammering grew quieter and quieter. When I could no longer hear it, I explained about the latest dead body. "Spader's coming to dinner. Maybe by this evening he'll have more information."

"This wasn't a random dead body drop," said Zack. "Someone knew details about the houses on our street. Enough to know where the security cameras are located and how to take them out without being detected."

"Yeah, both Spader and I already came to that conclusion."

"What else do you think, Nancy Drew?"

I pondered for a moment. "Gloria has tried to create something beautiful out of the ashes of Barry's murder. That body was deliberately staged in the garden. I think someone is taunting her."

"Who? Barry's killer is in prison."

"Has to be one of the blackmailers ticked off over his cash cow drying up."

"Sounds like a good place for Spader to start looking. You should mention it to him this evening if he hasn't already thought of it himself."

"I will. Do you plan to be home in time to cook dinner, or should we order something?"

"Not sure. I'll let you know."

~*~

Later that evening, I turned onto our street and caught a glimpse of Nick and Leonard heading toward Unami Park. As I pulled into the driveway, I expected to find crime scene tape cordoning off the memorial garden. Not only did I see none, but I found several of my retired neighbors congregating on the sidewalk in front of the garden entrance. When I exited my car, one of them called out and waved me over.

I approached with trepidation. No one had ever accused me directly, but I suspected some of my neighbors blamed me for the ongoing deadly crime wave on our street. Since I had a direct connection to each of the previous murders, I couldn't blame them.

Joanna Fredericks, who lived next door to the garden, got right to the point. "What do you know about another dead body showing up on our street?"

I briefly considered playing dumb, but I doubted she, her husband Brent, or Yvonne Walters would buy into a plea of ignorance. Not with Spader's unmarked car parked in front of my house. By now, everyone on the block was quite familiar with that particular county vehicle.

I sensed no hostility from the question, though. More a mix of extreme worry laced with a heaping dose of curiosity. "Not much," I said. "The detective on the case texted me a photo of the victim to see if I could identify him."

"Could you?" asked Yvonne, who lives two doors down from me.

I shook my head. "All I know is that he was on the bench this morning when I left for work. He appeared to be reading a book, but the detective said he was killed elsewhere and his body transported here."

In the waning light of the setting sun, I noticed the skepticism on Brent's face. His bushy gray eyebrows knit together as he squinted at me. "Are you saying you have no connection at all to what happened?"

"None."

After they all released a collective sigh of relief, his wife asked, "Why bring the body here?"

"I don't know, but I suspect it might have something to do with the owner of the property."

Yvonne pulled her sweater tighter across her chest, lowered her voice, and whispered conspiratorially as her eyes darted around the darkening garden. "Is it true she was paying off blackmailers?"

Did she think someone had bugged the garden? I fought the urge to execute an eye roll. "Yes."

My answer elicited collective grimaces from the group. "This used to be such a nice quiet street," said Joanna.

"Not anymore," muttered her husband.

I tamped down another urge, this time to apologize. At least this latest murder had no connection to me. I nodded in commiseration as I turned to leave.

Yvonne placed a hand on my arm to stop me. "Please let us know if you hear anything, Anastasia."

I acknowledged her comment with a nod but made no verbal commitment. Any information Spader shared with Zack and me was always in confidence.

The Fredericks turned in the direction of their house while Yvonne followed me across the street toward her house. As I headed down the path toward my front door, I sensed three pairs of eyes continuing to watch me. I was tempted to cast a quick look over my shoulder to see if the three had instead stopped to stare at me, but I tamped down that urge as well. As I entered my house, I couldn't help but wonder if the trio had lain in wait to waylay me the moment I arrived home.

"I was about to come rescue you," said Zack after I walked into the house. He strode across the living room to greet me with a kiss.

"You saw?" I asked, hanging my coat, purse, and tote in the hall closet.

"We figured they wanted the inside scoop."

"They did, but I had little information to give them. I can't blame them for worrying, though."

"What did you tell them?" asked Spader after I settled onto the sofa.

I first took a sip of wine from the glass waiting for me on the coffee table. "That I didn't know the victim, which relieved them. Ditto for me, by the way. Another dead body on the block is bad enough. I don't need another one with a connection to me."

"I ditto that," said Zack.

I then asked Spader, "Have you identified the victim?"

"Not yet. All we know at this point is that he's a Caucasian in his mid-to-late twenties. One piercing in each ear. No scars. A few tattoos scattered on his extremities and torso, not unusual for males of that age. He was dressed in Old Navy black jeans, a Fortnite T-shirt, black knit cap, and black hoodie. We have no missing persons reports for anyone fitting his description. For now, he's a John Doe."

"Any theories?"

"Only the one you've already mentioned to your husband. We're in the process of bringing in all the blackmailers for questioning."

I nodded. "I was surprised to see my neighbors inside the garden. Isn't the property still a crime scene?"

"No need with the murder having occurred elsewhere. CSI went over every inch of the garden with the proverbial fine-toothed comb. They found nothing. Whoever dumped the body knew what he was doing to avoid leaving any trace evidence."

I frowned into my wine. Zack noticed. "Something wrong with the wine?"

"The wine is fine. Something's wrong with my theory."

I turned to Spader. "When you were questioning the blackmailers during your investigation of Barry Sumner's death, did any of them stand out as rocket scientist caliber?"

He barked out a laugh. "Just the opposite. All combined, those guys don't equal one above-average brain."

"That was the impression I got." I sighed. "Which means there's a serious flaw in the blackmailer theory."

"Not if the guy wore a mask and gloves," said Spader. "We already know he was smart enough to take out the cameras without giving himself away. Even the dumbest criminal is lucky until he finally gets caught. This guy appears a step ahead of the rest, but he still might be one of the blackmailers. Maybe one of them will slip up during questioning. I'm curious to learn if any of them are into paintball."

The quick and easy low-tech method Spader had mentioned earlier. "That's how he took out the cameras?"

"He modified paintballs with a diluted solution of water-based white paint to mimic bird poop," said Zack. "I found a few birds enjoying some wild birdseed on the ground beneath one camera and more birdseed scattered near the other camera."

"Talk about authenticity and pre-planning. Are the cameras ruined?"

Zack shook his head. "The paint washed right off."

At this point, Nick had returned from walking Leonard. We tabled the conversation until we all gathered around the dining room table and began passing around a platter of roasted chicken, a bowl of mashed potatoes, and a medley of roasted vegetables.

Nick glanced from Spader to Zack to me. "What did I miss about the dead guy across the street?"

I wasn't surprised that he already knew about the body on the bench. "Not much. It looks like one of the blackmailers was sending Gloria a message."

"Why? Because she was no longer writing him checks?"

"It's a theory," said Spader. "We have no leads and no other plausible reason why someone would deliberately stage the body in a public location different from the murder scene."

"Do you have any idea where the murder occurred?" asked Nick.

Spader frowned. "Not a clue."

"What about the book on his lap?" asked Nick.

"You know about that as well?" I asked.

"Heck, Mom, the murder is all over social media. People are placing bets on whether you're somehow involved."

I groaned.

Spader brought the subject back to Nick's question. "What about the book?"

"Maybe it holds a clue."

None of us had thought of that. "What was the title of the book?" I asked.

"And what was on the pages the book was opened to?" added Zack.

Spader shook his head. "What sort of clue? Something as obvious as the author or a character sharing a name with the killer? You really think someone who was clever enough to place the body in the garden without leaving any incriminating evidence would leave such an obvious clue?"

"Probably not," I said. "But this could be the first salvo in a cunning game of cat-and-mouse. If he thinks he's committed the perfect crime, he might be toying with you, daring law enforcement to find him."

"Or the clue is meant to misdirect the investigation," added Zack.

Spader whipped out his phone and spoke as he shot off a text. "The book was a massive dictionary. I figured the perp had used it to weigh down the body to keep it from falling off the bench. You may be onto something, though."

Less than a minute later, Spader's phone dinged with an incoming message. He glanced at the screen. "Well, well, well. I guess this is why I pay you the big bucks, Mrs. Barnes."

"Hey, what about me?" asked Nick. "It was my idea."

Spader shrugged. "You can split the consulting fee with your mother."

When Nick eagerly turned to me, I said, "Happy to. Zero divided by two is zilch. Spend it wisely."

Spader then passed his phone across the table to me.

I stared at the screen. It showed a closeup of the book on the victim's lap, his finger pointing to a word on the page. "Joker?"

EIGHT

"There are multiple definitions for joker," I said. "Does the clue refer to someone who tells jokes, is the butt of a joke, or the knave in a deck of cards? And is the killer referring to himself or to his victim?"

"What if it's none of those things?" asked Nick.

We all turned to face him. "You have a different theory?" asked Spader.

"It could refer to The Joker from the Batman movies."

I'd never seen any of the Batman movies. They were always father/sons outings before Karl's untimely death. Besides, my taste in superheroes ran more toward Superman. Or Zack. "In what way?"

"I think you're right about the cat-and-mouse thing, Mom. The relationship between Batman and The Joker is like Sherlock Holmes and Professor Moriarity."

Zack nodded in agreement. "Worthy adversaries."

"Hmm..." Spader scrubbed at his jaw, studying Nick as he appeared to mull over my son's suggestion. After a long pause, he finally spoke. "If we're dealing with a cocky killer who believes he can outsmart law enforcement, Moriarity would be too obvious a choice. A word with multiple meanings is a more subtle clue to keep us guessing."

He reached over and patted Nick on the shoulder. "Nice work, kiddo. You're definitely your mother's son."

Nick beamed. "Cool."

Was it? My reluctant involvement in criminal cases had come at a price. I wondered if Nick's recent interest in murder and mayhem would lead him to major in Criminology when he entered college.

Until recently, he'd led the charge in demanding I not get involved in any further investigations. Now, he was all in, hanging on every clue, and eager to play a role in ferreting out the Westfield criminal de jour.

How would I feel about having a son on the front lines of criminal investigations? Probably the same way he'd felt prior to his about-face. Chances were good that I'd never get another decent night's sleep. Maybe I could convince him to major in Creative Writing with the hope that he'd become the next James Patterson.

Zack pulled me from my musings and back to the here and now of the most recent dead body. He addressed Spader. "That should narrow the blackmailer suspect pool. You need a paintballer who's a Batman fan and smart enough to plant a cryptic clue."

"A clue that may or may not misdirect," I reminded them. However, even as I uttered the words, my skepticism grew over any of the blackmailers having the skillset required to match wits with law enforcement or plant red herrings that would misdirect an investigation.

Then again, maybe the killer had simply gotten lucky. He hadn't left any fingerprints or other obvious evidence because he'd bundled up against the dip in the mercury last night.

Barry Sumner was not the brightest bulb in the daffodil patch. Neither were the guys who egged him into physical confrontations, then blackmailed his wife. I suspected many of them fell into one, if not both, of the first two categories. It's not much of a stretch to assume that guys who enjoyed dressing up in period costumes and acting out historical battles might also get their jollies shooting paintballs at each other.

As for the Joker connection, for all we knew, some of them might also dress up as the Dark Knight or his arch nemesis. ComiCon is crawling with guys in their twenties who dress up as superheroes and villains.

But I doubted any of the blackmailers was a criminal mastermind on par with a classic villain, whether from comic books or literature.

"The word is still a clue," said Nick. "We just need to figure out what it means."

"Or not," I said. "If one of the blackmailers had staged the scene, he may have simply opened the dictionary to a random page near the middle of the book to distribute the weight evenly on each of the victim's thighs."

Nick sighed as dejection spread across his face. "I suppose that's also a possibility."

I placed my hand over his and gave it a squeeze. "Or you could be onto something. We have more questions than answers right now. That's why Detective Spader is here brainstorming with us."

"Your mom's right," said Spader. "No idea is a bad idea. No theory gets discounted until it doesn't pan out."

Nick eyed him suspiciously. "You're not just saying that to make me feel better?"

"Heck, no. Your Batman theory gives us an additional line of questioning, and for all we know, it might crack the case."

By this point, we'd finished dinner. Spader had thoughtfully provided a dessert of apple pie and vanilla ice cream, and I rose to retrieve it from the kitchen as Nick cleared the plates.

Half an hour later, after we'd made short work of the pie and ice cream and bandied about a few more theories, Spader pushed back his chair and stood. "As always, thanks for dinner and the brainstorming session. Maybe we'll turn up that unicorn of a blackmailer tomorrow and quickly solve this latest murder."

One could only hope. As we walked with him to the front door, another thought popped into my head. I stopped short in the middle of the living room and turned to face the detective. "Which dictionary was on the victim's lap?"

He pulled his notepad from his pocket and flipped through a few pages. "Collins English Dictionary."

I did a quick search on my phone. "The Collins English Dictionary is the largest dictionary printed in one volume. It contains more than seven-hundred-thirty thousand entries and is more than twenty-three hundred pages in length."

Nick let loose a whistle. "I wouldn't want to lug that around in my backpack."

"How old was the dictionary?" I asked Spader.

"I'd have to check but relatively new, judging from the lack of wear and tear. Where are you going with this, Mrs. Barnes?"

"I can't imagine many people buy such a comprehensive dictionary. Especially with the availability of online dictionaries. You should check area bookstores for recent sales. What's the likelihood of any bookstore selling more than one or two Collins dictionaries a year? If you're lucky, the killer slipped up and paid with a credit card."

"Better yet," added Zack, "if they have store surveillance, they may have captured video of him making the purchase at the register."

"What if he bought the dictionary online?" asked Nick. "He wouldn't show up on store video."

I shook my head. "He'd need the book before he killed the victim. Either he already owned a copy, or he bought it right before he set out to commit the murder."

"If he already owned a copy," said Spader, "chances are, he used it. His prints would be all over it. With more than two thousand pages, no matter how carefully he tried to wipe his prints, he'd miss some."

"Exactly," I said. "He most likely purchased the dictionary specifically to keep the corpse from falling off the bench. Which means he had entered the bookstore and walked the aisles until he found the largest book they sold."

"Why go to the trouble of buying a large dictionary?" asked Nick. "If he needed to weigh down the body, he could have grabbed some of the concrete steppingstones from the garden."

"Did you notice the man when you left for school this morning?" I asked.

"To tell the truth, Mom, I don't remember. There have been one or two people sitting in the garden for a few days now. I haven't paid any attention."

"But you would have noticed if he had a pile of concrete steppingstones on his lap, wouldn't you?"

"Yeah, I guess so."

"Exactly. Any object other than a large book would have immediately raised the suspicions of someone walking a dog or heading to school or the train station this morning. If I had seen a pile of concrete on his lap, I would have walked across the street to check it out, found the body, and called the police. But since I saw a book on his lap, I didn't give the man a second thought. It wasn't until later in the morning that someone entered the garden and noticed the man was dead."

"Even then, at first glance the death appeared from natural causes," said Spader. "Not murder."

Nick wasn't giving up on his theory, though. "But if you're dealing with a Joker or Moriarity-level mastermind, he may have planned the murder far enough in advance to buy the dictionary online."

"Valid point," said Spader. "One step at a time, though, Nick. For an investigation to be thorough, we employ a methodical, step-by-step process. We won't rule anything out. First, we finish interviewing the blackmailers and bring the ones we already spoke with in for more questioning. See if we can tie any of them to paintball, The Joker, or an interest in cryptography. At the same time, I'll have someone checking area bookstores."

Nick continued to press. "What if none of those pan out?"

Spader pulled a face. "We're hoping for a DNA hit on our John Doe. Knowing who he is, widens our search parameters. We can interview family, coworkers, friends, neighbors. He didn't drop from the sky. This guy had a life before he was murdered. There are people out there who know something about him. We just need to find them."

"How long do DNA results take?" asked Nick.

"Anywhere from a day to months," said Spader.

Nick's mouth dropped open. "Months? Why so long?"

"Mostly backlog. Few departments across the country have the resources and funds needed for adequate staffing. Budgets haven't caught up with advances in science. We could crack more cases faster if we had an army of lab techs working twenty-four/seven, but most states don't allocate enough funds in their budgets for that."

"Can you fast-track it?" asked Zack.

"I can put in a request," said Spader. "If we strike out with the blackmailers, we could be looking at a much different scenario, and having DNA results would be crucial to catching the guy."

"What kind of scenarios?" I asked.

"Given the odd circumstances surrounding this murder? He could be a serial killer."

I didn't like the sound of that. "Are there any reports of similar murders?"

"No, but this wasn't an ordinary gangland or Mafia-style execution. Those guys aren't interest in playing cat-and-mouse with the cops. When they dispose of a body, it stays disposed. They don't create a tableau in the middle of a garden."

"But why leap to serial killer if there are no reports of similar killings?" I asked.

"Think about it, Mrs. Barnes. Every serial killer starts with a first kill. If we're looking at the beginnings of a murder spree, I want to catch this guy before he strikes again."

"Let us know what we can do to help," said Zack.

Spader nodded. "If I can't get the lab to fast-track the DNA analysis, I may ask you to pull some strings with your FBI friend."

~*~

As I pulled out of my driveway the following morning, a large flatbed truck hauling a huge wooden crate drove up to the curb of the memorial garden. My nosiness nearly got the better of me, but I forced myself to continue driving to work. If this was a delivery for the garden, I'd have to wait until I returned home this evening to satisfy my curiosity.

For all I knew, the cargo wasn't even intended for the memorial garden. The driver may have pulled over to check his GPS. Or maybe his brake light had begun flashing, and he was calling roadside assistance.

"Life is never dull in Anastasia World," said Cloris when I entered the break room nearly an hour later, thanks to the Garden State's eternal bumper-to-bumper drivetime traffic.

I moaned. "I yearn for dull. I take it you've been on social media."

She tapped her phone and showed me the screen. My mouth dropped open as I scrolled through the feed. "I thought Nick was kidding when he said people were placing bets on my involvement. This is much worse."

Draft Kings and Fanduel were both taking bets on whether I'd find the killer before the cops and how many days it would take me.

"I may have to place a bet," said Cloris, retrieving her phone. "After all, I have an inside source."

I shot her a dirty look before dropping into one of the molded plastic chairs surrounding the table. "Save your money. I'm not involved in any way with this dead body. I don't even know who the victim is. I wish the press, not to mention all those true crime bloggers, vloggers, podcasters, and influencers, would find someone else to obsess over and leave me alone."

Months ago, my sons and Alex's girlfriend Sophie had created a podcast about my reluctant amateur sleuthing exploits. Their aim was to make enough money to help pay off the remainder of the debt Karl had dumped on me when he died. Much to everyone's surprise, the podcast became a huge success among true crime junkies, and my life has never been the same.

We quickly learned that fame is not always what it's cracked up to be. It strips you of your privacy and causes the crackpots to crawl out of their holes.

Cloris pressed the button on the coffee maker to begin the drip process. "I'll wave my magic wand."

"You're a true friend."

"I know. Help yourself to a pastry, and fill me in."

I lifted the lid of today's bakery box to discover two dozen assorted mini pastries. I grabbed a chocolate croissant, taking a bite before I provided Cloris with a sixty-second synopsis of all that had occurred since I left work last night.

When I'd finished, she said, "Since you have no connection to this latest victim, why not tell Detective Spader he's on his own this time?"

I popped the remainder of the croissant into my mouth and helped myself to a raspberry rugalach. "I could, but I can't."

Cloris raised an eyebrow. "That makes so much sense. *Not*."

"Spader's more than a cantankerous county homicide detective at this point. He's become more like family, and the poor guy is understaffed and overworked. I worry about his health."

"You've morphed into Ado Annie."

When I stared agape at her, she added, "You know, the girl who can't say no. From *Oklahoma*."

"Oh, I got the reference. But Ado Annie wasn't a reluctant amateur sleuth."

Cloris laughed. "No, she wasn't exactly reluctant about anything."

I couldn't help but chuckle at that. "I like to think that I'm doing my civic duty by allowing Detective Spader to pick my brain."

"Because Anastasia Pollack has so much free time."

"Well, I am free of Lucille drama these days, and thanks to Gloria Forester's generosity, I no longer have an avalanche of debt threatening to bury me."

"Two perfectly good reasons to get involved in another murder investigation."

"Hey, sarcasm is my schtick."

Cloris shrugged. "I've learned from the best."

~*~

I'd managed to get through Tuesday without a single crisis at work. More importantly, I hadn't stumbled across any dead bodies in my office or elsewhere within the building. I took my wins where they came.

Cloris and I were heading to the elevator at five o'clock when my cell rang. After a quick glance at the screen, I dropped the phone back in my coat pocket.

"Spam?"

"Probably. I didn't recognize the number."

The moment the elevator doors closed behind us, my phone pinged an incoming voice message. I ignored it. "Probably another politician asking for a campaign donation."

"It's that time of year," said Cloris.

"No good deed goes unpunished. A few weeks ago, I gave a donation to the mayoral race. Small contribution. Huge mistake. Suddenly, I'm inundated with campaign calls from candidates all over the country. And from both parties. How is that even possible?"

"You're not alone," she said. "I suspect every campaign has at least one sleazy staffer who sells their donor list. Or the campaigns hack each other."

"Probably both." As we stepped from the elevator, I dug into my coat pocket and retrieved my phone.

"Put it on speaker," said Cloris.

I glanced around the lobby. We were the only staff in the area. The elevator had ascended back upstairs and was sitting on the fourth floor. The security guard was at his desk at the opposite end of the building, too far to hear anything. I tapped the app, and we both listened: *You think you're so smart, Anastasia Pollack, but you're no match for me.*

Cloris and I stopped short and stared and at each other. "Are you sure you have no connection to that dead body found in the memorial garden?"

NINE

"How could I?" I asked after I stopped hyperventilating, my heart ceased pounding, and my adrenaline level sank back into normal range. "The guy's a John Doe. I've never seen him before in my life."

"And you don't recognize that voice?"

I shook my head. Emphatically.

"Are you one hundred percent, absolutely, positively?"

"Of course. Besides, that voice sounded computer-generated."

She cocked her head and arched an eyebrow. "What if he was someone connected to one of the other recent dead bodies in your life?"

"Like whom?"

Cloris waved her hand in the air. "I don't know. One of the guys from that TV production company? You never had a chance to see any of them, did you?"

"No, but why would any of them have something to do with this? Or me?"

"They all lost their jobs, didn't they? Maybe one of them flipped out and blames you."

"And he did what? Decided to kill some rando and leave his body on a park bench across the street from my home? That's quite a stretch."

"Stranger things have happened in your life."

"Point taken."

Cloris continued peppering me with possibilities. "What about someone associated with that corrupt Southern politician? Or connected to Barry Sumner's killer? Take your pick. You can't rule out the possibility that someone could be toying with you."

Nick had suggested John Doe's killer might be toying with Spader. Maybe he'd gotten the toying part right but not the target. Cloris had now planted an unwelcome suggestion that amplified Nick's idea and buzzed around my brain like a persistent gnat. I had been so convinced that this latest murder victim had no connection to me. Was I wrong?

Still, I tried to swat the idea away. "There was nothing even remotely familiar about the guy found in the garden." I pulled up the photo Spader had texted me yesterday and showed her. "Does he look familiar to you?"

Cloris stared at my phone screen, then shook her head. "Not in the least. But I'm not the amateur sleuth who keeps finding dead bodies."

"*Reluctant* amateur sleuth," I reminded her.

"Whatever. You need to call your friendly neighborhood homicide detective to let him know about that message."

Cloris was right. While still in the lobby, I placed a call to Spader, but after one ring, the call went directly to his voicemail. I left a detailed message, forcing my voice to remain calm and not reveal the panic that had settled over me. I'm no actress, though. My ears told me that my efforts had produced an epic fail.

After leaving the building, I settled into my car and began the drive home. If the rush hour traffic gods were smiling down on me, I'd arrive in less than an hour.

I wasn't exactly surprised when I turned onto my street and saw Spader's standard issue unmarked sedan parked in front of my house. Truthfully, I was relieved to see the black Ford. I was also relieved to find none of my neighbors lurking nearby, ready to pounce on me as I exited my Jetta.

However, surprise didn't come close to describing my reaction to the new addition in the memorial garden that came into view as I approached my driveway. After stepping from my car, I stared transfixed.

The fountain, illuminated by a series of colorful spotlights in the surrounding flowerbed, now gushed a steady stream of water with droplets glistening like a rainbow of gemstones. However, that image came in a distant second to the sight that had drawn my eye.

I now realized the flatbed truck driver this morning hadn't been lost or in need of roadside assistance. He'd arrived at his destination with a delivery.

And what a delivery it was. Stunned, flabbergasted, dumbfounded, speechless, stupefied. All those adjectives and more, rolled up into one jaw-dropping, mind-boggling, I-can't-believe-what-my-eyes-are-seeing moment that kept my feet riveted to the driveway as I gaped at the gleaming bronze statue perched atop the pedestal of the memorial garden fountain.

"How long do you plan to stay out here staring across the street?" asked Zack, coming up behind me and looping an arm across my shoulders.

"I'm trying to decide if I'm in the middle of a hideous nightmare and will eventually wake up. Am I really seeing what I think I'm seeing?"

"You are."

Perched atop the memorial garden fountain pedestal and lit by LED lights embedded in the base, stood a life-size bronze statue of Barry Sumner in all his half-naked, beer-belly glory, pushing a lawnmower. I wondered if the artist had created the lawnmower from scratch or had bronzed an actual lawnmower. For that matter, the bronze Barry looked so realistic that my mind flashed to an image of Han Solo frozen in carbonite.

"What was Gloria thinking?"

"Beats me."

"That was a rhetorical question." We both knew Gloria never thinks before she acts.

"Come inside. It's getting cold out here, and dinner's ready."

I had been so laser focused on the statue that I hadn't noticed the gentle early October breeze of this morning had morphed into an evening of frosty, gusting wind. Tree branches swayed in the waning light, leaves swirling to the ground and whipping down the street. No chance of Indian Summer this year, and judging from the dip in the mercury, winter was nipping on autumn's heels.

Still, I didn't move. "I need a picture of this to show Cloris." Even a thousand words wouldn't come close to describing the monstrosity of the Barry Sumner fountain.

After I snapped a photo, we walked toward the front door. Before entering the house, I glanced over my shoulder and took one last look across the street. "I'll say this for Gloria, at least she found a talented sculptor. There's no mistaking who's pushing that lawnmower."

Nick and Detective Spader were setting the dining room table when Zack and I entered the house. In typical Spader fashion, he dispensed with any salutations and held out his hand. "Let me have a look at that message you received."

I unlocked my phone and handed it to him before removing my coat. "I told you verbatim what he said on the message I left you. I'm not sure what else you can glean from looking at it."

After listening, he tapped the screen a few times, his frown growing stronger with each tap before he handed the phone back to me. "Looks like he probably used a burner."

"Did you have any doubt?" I asked.

He shrugged. "Sometimes a perp is dumb enough to leave a trail of breadcrumbs. This one didn't leave so much as a single crumb."

Nick had stopped setting the table. His eyes widened. "Does this mean *you're* the mouse, Mom, and not the cops?"

"Possibly."

"More like probably," said Zack who now wore a frown that vied with Spader's.

After hanging up my coat, purse, and tote, I offered an alternate theory. "What if the text came from one of those rabid podcasting true crime junkies?"

"To what end?" asked Zack.

"To solve the murder before I do."

Zack, Spader, and Nick gaped at me. Before one of them began to challenge my theory, I continued. "Think about it. What better way to boost your cred and rake in advertising dollars for your podcast than to out-sleuth a sleuth?"

Spader turned to Zack. "She has a point."

Zack conceded. He reached out and drew me into a side hug. "I can live with that. It's a better theory than worrying a killer is toying with you."

Zack had prepared a Tuscan stew to slow cook in the crockpot before he'd caught the train into the city this morning. He'd paired it with a loaf of crusty sourdough bread that he'd picked up on his way home. As he ladled out the stew and passed bowls around the table, I asked Spader, "Have you made any progress?"

"Some. Based on our discussion about paintball and Nick's Joker suggestion, we brought the blackmailers we'd already interviewed back in for further questioning. We also interviewed the remaining blackmailers. Turns out guys who like to dress up as Revolutionary War soldiers also like to go into the woods and shoot paintballs at each other."

"What about The Joker?" asked Nick.

"These guys never matured out of their adolescence. Every single one of them has attended ComiCon for years. In costume."

Nick's eyes grew wide. "As The Joker?"

"Most saw themselves more as hero material. Only two admitted to a fondness for various DC villains, specifically The Joker and Riddler. We're checking out their alibis for the night of the murder."

"Then the killer did leave a clue by having the dead guy point to a specific word in the dictionary," said Nick.

"Maybe," said Spader.

"And maybe your killer had help," I said. "Someone who sees himself as The Joker and someone else who sees himself as the Riddler. After all, we already established that if *joker* means something, it's a riddle as to what it means."

Spader nodded. "Which is why those two blackmailers are at the top of my suspects list right now."

"What about the dictionary?" asked Zack. "Did you find any recent sales?"

"Only one," said Spader. "But it's probably a dead end." He tapped his phone a few times, then turned the screen for Zack, Nick and me to view the image. "Any of you recognize this woman?"

The bookstore surveillance image showed a twenty-something pudgy woman with a ponytail. She stood smiling at the checkout counter. The three of us nodded. Shock registered on Spader's face. "All of you recognize her?"

"She's a bagger at ShopRite," I said.

Spader whipped out his notebook and pen and flipped to a fresh page. Pen poised, he glanced up at me. "What's her name?" When I hesitated, he speared a narrow-eyed glare of suspicion at each of us in turn. "What's going on?"

"You can't pull her in for questioning," I said. "She'll freak out and shut down."

"Mrs. Barnes, I have a job to do."

"I know, but she's not exactly your run-of-the-mill witness or person of interest."

Spader slammed his pen onto the table. "You're suddenly sounding like someone withholding information in a murder investigation."

"It's not like that," said Zack.

"You should let my mom speak with her," added Nick.

"I need more than that," said Spader.

I nodded. "Her name is Dory. I don't know her last name. She's part of a program run by the state where they train people with intellectual and developmental disabilities and place them in jobs that match their level of skill."

"She's certainly not your killer," said Zack. "She has the mental capacity of a ten-year-old."

"Ten-year-olds have been known to commit murder," said Spader.

"Execution-style at close range with a bullet to the back of the head?" asked Zack.

"Point taken." Spader's features softened. Slightly. "I understand your concern for the young woman, but she may have information vital to this case."

"Agreed," I said. "But let me speak with her first. She knows me. I won't intimidate or frighten her the way you might. If it's necessary to bring her in for questioning, I'll make the arrangements with the supermarket manager, her group home, and the state agency."

Spader offered a reluctant nod. "You think she's working this evening?"

"Doubtful. Check with the store manager to see when her next shift is scheduled."

"I'll have someone contact the supermarket." He shot off a text. A few minutes later, he had a reply. "She's working from nine to three tomorrow."

"I'll make arrangements to go into work late."

~*~

Spader had notified the store manager, making sure to stress that Dory wasn't in any trouble, only that she may have witnessed something pertinent to an ongoing investigation. Even so, the manager insisted on being present when I spoke with Dory. I couldn't blame him, and I appreciated his protectiveness of his more challenged employees.

Several picnic tables were set up at the back of the parking lot for employees to take their breaks in nice weather. The manager had told Spader that's where he and Dory would wait for me.

Dory immediately spotted me when I rounded the corner of the building. Her face broke out in a wide grin as she furiously waved. "Hi, Miss Ana!" She'd never been able to master my full first name.

I settled onto the bench opposite her and the store manager, a middle-aged man with a receding hairline, slight paunch, and a friendly face that revealed the vestiges of a teenage battle with acne. "Hi, Dory. Did Mr. Gene tell you why I wanted to speak with you?"

She beamed with excitement. "About books. I love books. Especially comic books."

"I know. I thought I saw you the other day when I drove past the bookstore across the street. Did you buy some books during your lunch break?"

"Just one."

"Only one? It looked like you were carrying a bag with lots of books."

"It was one big book. A dictionary. But it wasn't for me."

"Oh? Was it a gift for someone?"

"Mr. Johnny said it was for his girlfriend."

"That was nice of you to run an errand for Mr. Johnny. Is he a friend of yours?"

"A new friend. He's really nice. He paints houses."

"Is he painting your house?"

"Nu-uh."

"Where did you meet Mr. Johnny?"

"Here last Friday. He asked me to go across the street to buy the book. He said it was waiting for him at the counter. He gave me a hundred dollars and said I could keep the change. I only did a quick favor for him, and the change was twenty-five dollars and thirty-six cents. I thought that was too much. I didn't want to cheat him. But he said he wanted me to keep all of it. Wasn't that nice of him?"

"That was. But why didn't Mr. Johnny buy the book himself?"

Dory rolled her eyes. "Because he was really, really dirty. His clothes and shoes were all covered in paint. And plaster dust. He offered to drive me across the street, but my mommy and daddy told me I should never get in a car with someone I didn't know very well. I just met Mr. Johnny."

"That's very good advice, Dory. Did Mr. Johnny walk across the street with you?"

She shook her head. "No, he waited here for me."

"Did you see what type of car he drove?"

Dory rolled her eyes again. "It wasn't a car, silly. It was his painting truck."

"Do you remember what it looked like?"

"White." She glanced around the parking lot, then pointed to a white panel truck parked nearby. "Like that one, but it had a ladder on top."

"Did it have any lettering?"

"Nope. Just all white."

"And what more can you tell me about Mr. Johnny?"

She scrunched up her face. "Like what?"

"What he looked like? Was he young or old? Skinny or fat?"

She thought for a moment. "Young. My age. Maybe a little older. And skinny." She smiled coyly and giggled. "And he was very handsome."

"You like handsome guys, Dory?"

She stared at me in surprise. "Doesn't everyone? Your Mr. Zack is very handsome, too, Miss Ana."

I chuckled. "Yes, he is, Dory. Anything else you can tell me about Mr. Johnny? Maybe the color of his hair?"

She frowned. "I'm not sure. He wore a hat. And he had thick glasses with black frames."

"Thank you, Dory. I really appreciate you taking the time to talk with me." I rose. "You have a great day."

"You, too, Miss Ana. I like talking with you."

"And I like talking with you, Dory. I'll see you soon."

I nodded to the store manager. "Thanks for your help, Gene."

"Happy to."

He led Dory toward the employee entrance while I walked around to the front parking lot and met Detective Spader where we'd agree to rendezvous.

"Get anything?" he asked once I'd settled into the front passenger seat of his car.

"Not much." I explained how Dory had come to purchase the dictionary. "We now have proof he planned the killing at least several days in advance."

"Anything else? Did she give you a description of the perp?"

I rattled off Dory's limited details of Mr. Johnny. "I suspect both the white van and paint-spattered overalls were a disguise. Probably the thick, black-framed glasses as well. She said he wore a hat that hid his hair. She was more fixated on how handsome he was. Anyway, I have to agree with you that this was a dead end except for maybe eliminating the blackmailers."

"How so?"

"Dory said she thought Mr. Johnny was around her age. Aren't all the blackmailers in their late thirties and forties?"

"They are, but can Dory accurately discern a person's age? Some of those blackmailers look younger than they are."

Dory was far from the best witness, but being developmentally challenged, she was the perfect accomplice. "Valid point. Many people, when they first meet my mother, think she's my older sister. I never met all the blackmailers. Do any of those in their thirties look younger?"

"Two come to mind. We'll do a deeper dive into them, but first, I'd like Dory to look at photos of the blackmailers. Maybe she can point this Mr. Johnny out to us."

"Would you like me to show her the photos?"

"I was hoping you'd volunteer." Some men can occasionally multitask. Spader was one of them. He'd been texting throughout our conversation. "I'm sending them to you now. I'm still convinced this murder is connected to Sumner's murder. We just need to keep digging."

"At least Dory wasn't covering for the killer. She was merely in the right place at the right time."

Spader agreed. "He either specifically targeted her, or he was aware of the program. I suspect he parked where he had a perfect view of the employee picnic area, then bided his time until one of the baggers exited the building."

I stepped from Spader's car and headed into the supermarket. After finding the manager, the two of us walked over to the checkout aisle where Dory was bagging groceries.

Dory broke out in another wide smile when she saw me. "Hi, Miss Ana! Did you forget to ask me something?"

"I did, Dory. I need your help for a minute. Mr. Gene will take over for you here."

"Okay." She handed Gene the can of tomatoes she was about to place in a bag and followed me to the small café area next to the deli department. I chose a table away from the only other occupants, two women sipping coffee.

"Dory, I'm going to show you pictures of some men. Would you tell me if you recognize any of them?"

"Sure!"

I brought the photos up on my phone. One by one, I slowly scrolled through them. "Him," said Dory. "And him. And him. And him."

She continued picking out each man. "You recognize all of them?"

She executed another eyeroll. "Of course, silly."

"How?"

"Mr. Stanley always buys a deli sandwich for his lunch, and he always offers me his pickle. I like pickles and he doesn't. Can you imagine someone who doesn't like pickles, Miss Ana? You like pickles, don't you?"

"I love pickles, Dory. What about the other men."

She continued explaining how she recognized each of the blackmailers. "What about Mr. Johnny, Dory? Is he one of the men in the pictures?"

"No. Mr. Johnny is much cuter than any of these men."

"Thank you for your help, Dory."

I walked her back to her checkout line, thanked Gene once again, and returned to Detective Spader's car. "None of your blackmailers is Mr. Johnny."

"She was sure?"

"She knew every one of the men by name."

Spader squinted at me. "Really?"

"Dory might be developmentally challenged in some ways, but she's got a great memory for names and faces. You might want to rethink your blackmailer theory."

"Not what I wanted to hear, Mrs. Barnes."

"Don't kill the messenger. One thing we know for sure, though."

"What's that?"

"Mr. Johnny took great pains to avoid getting caught by the bookstore surveillance cameras. What about ShopRite's surveillance and CCTV cameras? This is a major intersection. Any chance one of them caught a white panel truck with a ladder and no markings leaving the supermarket parking lot shortly after Dory purchased the dictionary?"

He glanced up from his phone and winked at me. "Already working on it. Keep your fingers crossed."

TEN

Spader called the next morning while I sat in rush hour traffic. As always, he launched right in without any greeting. "The good news is that one of the CCTV cameras caught the white panel truck leaving the supermarket parking lot, and we got a clear image of the license plate."

"That's great, but no one ever starts a conversation with 'the good news is' unless there's also bad news. I suspect a huge 'but' is coming."

Spader grunted. "Astute as always, Mrs. Barnes. The vehicle was reported stolen in Iselin Friday morning about an hour before Dory purchased the dictionary. The owner left the truck running while he ran into a gas station restroom."

"I'm doing an eyeroll, Detective. How long does it take to turn off an engine and grab your keys?"

"Apparently too long when you've eaten a bad breakfast burrito. By the time the poor guy came out of the restroom, the truck was gone."

"Were you able to track the panel truck after he drove out of the ShopRite parking lot?"

"Not for long. We've issued an APB, but I'm guessing our perp abandoned it somewhere shortly after leaving the supermarket Friday. Anyone who risks stealing a vehicle to keep from being spotted in his own car isn't dumb enough to keep driving around in hot wheels."

"In other words, another dead end."

"Another astute observation, Mrs. Barnes."

"Which is why you pay me the big bucks, Detective. I hope you make some headway today."

"That makes two of us." He then resorted to his usual lack of telephone manners by hanging up without uttering a single ciao, arrivederci, or sayonara.

When I first met Spader, I worried that he wouldn't make it to retirement. Since then, he'd jettisoned two enormous bad habits. He no longer smoked, and he'd dramatically cut back on his drinking. Both had resulted in him shedding considerable excess weight to improve his odds of reaching retirement and enjoying his golden years. Surely, a man capable of such huge lifestyle changes could remember to say *hello* when answering the phone and *goodbye* before disconnecting the call.

Or maybe not. Old dogs, new tricks. Some do occasionally learn, but maybe Spader had used up his allotment when he kicked his nicotine habit and cut back on his drinking. If so, he'd chosen wisely, and I could forgive him his lack of telephone manners.

Before arriving at work, my phone chimed with another call. "Good morning, Mama. You're up early."

"I thought I'd catch you before you started work this morning."

"That was very thoughtful of you." Yet completely out of character for Mama.

"I wanted to let you know I heard from Melissa Dugan late last night. The FBI had interviewed her and Jeremy. They were both shocked to hear what had happened to me. She wanted to make sure the phony Jeremy hadn't conned me."

A red flag sprang up in my cerebral cortex. "How did you hear from her, Mama?"

"She sent me an email."

"Did you respond?"

"Of course, dear. We email chatted back and forth for about half an hour."

I took a deep breath. I knew Zack had changed all of Mama's passwords on her various accounts and frozen her credit, but had Melissa and her son done the same? "Mama, I think you should call Melissa to verify that the emails came from her."

"Of course they came from her. She knew all about what had happened to me."

"So might Brad Jankowitz's accomplices. Someone may have spoofed her email again."

"What accomplices? No one ever said anything about accomplices."

"That's just it, Mama. We don't know if he was working alone. Either he crisscrossed the country, pulling similar scams in various locations, or he was part of a nationwide ring of scammers. He refused to tell the FBI anything before the judge released him on bail."

"Which he never should have done. What was that man thinking? He should be disbarred."

"He was following the law, but that's beside the point. You may have been emailing with another scammer. Please, call Melissa immediately. If she didn't send that email, we may need to change all your passwords again."

"Why? I didn't divulge any information about my accounts in the emails I sent. We were just catching up."

"Catching up on what?"

"Our lives and families, of course."

"Families? As in me, the boys, and Zack?"

"Do I have any other family?"

I wisely ignored her uncharacteristic use of sarcasm. Mama believed that lectures were meant to be directed from parent to child, never the other way around. Instead, I asked, "What exactly did you tell her about us?"

"I mentioned your recent marriage, how that commie thorn in our sides finally moved out, and how Alex was now at Harvard. And talk about coincidence, Melissa's grandson Rowen is also at Harvard. I gave her Alex's phone number to give to Rowen so the boys can get together."

I choked back a string of expletives as I quickly shot off a text to Alex, warning him not to respond to any text sent from someone named Rowen Dugan until he heard back from me.

He immediately texted back a thumbs-up emoji, no questions asked.

Then, in as calm a voice as I could muster, I said, "Mama, I'm not saying you weren't chatting with Melissa, but given what we just went through with Jankowitz, there is the remote possibility that you were emailing with a scammer pretending to be Melissa. If that's the case, you've opened your grandson up to possible identity theft. Not to mention, once again making yourself vulnerable."

"Don't be ridiculous, dear. I didn't give out any of my personal information."

Somehow, I managed to refrain from screaming as I responded, "You gave out your grandson's phone number."

"Yes, I already mentioned that. How else would Rowen contact Alex? I think you're getting upset for no reason, Anastasia."

I had plenty of reason to be upset, but I wasn't getting through to her. "Do me a favor, please?"

"What's that, dear?"

"Call me back as soon as you've spoken with Melissa."

"I promise, but I'm sure you're overreacting."

"If I am, Mama, you'll have the satisfaction of saying 'I told you so.'"

When I arrived at work half an hour later, I still hadn't heard back from Mama. I tamped down the panic threatening to unleash itself within me. Assuming Melissa Dugan still lived in St. Louis, she was an hour behind us. Mama wouldn't have wanted to wake her, especially since I hadn't convinced her of the need to verify the email.

Maybe I did overreact. If Mama hadn't clicked on any links, she wouldn't have launched a virus, malware, or spyware onto her devices. However, with the insidiousness of artificial intelligence in the wrong hands, I'd rather err on the side of caution. For all I knew, someone had recently created a program that could take over your devices without the necessity of the mark clicking on a link. And if not yet, it was only a matter of time.

Cloris was pouring herself a cup of coffee when I entered the break room. She grabbed another mug and poured one for me. "Anything new to report in the world of reluctant amateur sleuthing?"

I added a splash of half and half to the cup she handed me and took a sip. Then I surveyed the morning's baked offerings and helped myself to a slice of chocolate chip banana bread. "Not much. Spader still thinks one of the blackmailers is responsible for the body in the memorial garden. Based on Dory's limited description, he's narrowed his suspects down to two of the younger ones."

"Does your gut agree?"

"Never having met either guy, my gut is neutral, but I suppose it makes the most sense."

"You don't sound convinced."

I chewed on a mouthful of banana bread and swallowed before answering. "I'm having a hard time coming up with a motive for any of the blackmailers. What was there to gain by not only dumping the body in the garden but taking the time to pose it the way he did? How does that get back at Gloria? She's on the other side of the country. I'm not even sure she knows about the murder."

"You haven't told her?"

"I saw no point. Especially since we don't yet know who the victim is, who killed him, or why the killer risked moving the body to the garden. Why upset her?"

"Makes sense, but she'll eventually find out from someone, if she hasn't already seen it on social media, won't she?"

"Given Gloria's history with the blackmailers, I suspect she stays off social media. Anyway, I'll leave that to Spader."

After we headed down the hallway to our cubicles, I settled in for a morning of transforming heart-shaped Valentine's Day chocolates boxes into keepsakes. I'd settled on three different versions, one decorated with embroidered felt hearts, one trimmed with ribbon and buttons, and a third with lace trims.

I was so engrossed in my crafting that nearly four hours had passed before I realized that I still hadn't heard from my mother. I shot her a text: *Did you speak with Melissa?*

No response. I waited, giving her time to finish any personal necessities if she happened to be in the bathroom. After ten minutes had ticked away, and she still hadn't responded to my text, I called her.

She answered immediately. "Hello, dear."

"Mama, didn't you see my text?"

"I did."

"And?"

"And what?"

"Why didn't you respond?"

"Because I have nothing to tell you."

"You haven't spoken with Melissa Dugan?"

"I tried. She didn't answer her phone. I left a voicemail message asking her to call me."

"Let me know when you hear back from her, please."

"I will, but honestly, Anastasia, you're sounding like the Grand Inquisitor. Don't you think you're blowing this way out of proportion?"

"Let us both hope so, Mama. I'll talk to you later. I have to get back to work."

"Well, don't let me stop you, dear. After all, you called me."

I disconnected the call and let loose a low growl.

"What's going on?" called Cloris from across the hall. "Sounds like you've got a grizzly bear in your cubicle."

"My mother is driving me slightly crazy today."

"It's better than your mother-in-law driving you completely crazy."

I snorted. "And Zack thinks I'm the Pollyanna. You've got me beat by a mile."

Cloris stepped into my cubicle and glanced at the progress I'd made on the heart boxes. "Cute." She then turned to me. "What's Flora done to get you in such an uproar?"

I told her about the call I'd received from my mother this morning. "I want proof that she really did receive an email from Melissa Dugan. I don't think that's too much to ask, do you?"

"I don't. Maybe you should try calling Melissa yourself. Do you have her phone number?"

"No. The Dugans moved away when I was in preschool. I'm sure I can find a listing for her somewhere online, though."

"And if not, you do know someone who can help you."

"I'd rather not bother Tino unless it's an emergency. Let's see what I can find on my own first." I settled into the chair in front of my computer and consulted Google.

A link to Melissa Dugan's Facebook page came up first in the search. I clicked on the link and began to scroll through the feed. "She does have a grandson named Rowen, and he is a student at Harvard."

"Information anyone could glean from her Facebook page," said Cloris.

"Exactly."

I exited out of Facebook and returned to the URLs generated by my search. The second link in the queue brought me to a search site for people by state. I typed in Melissa's name and Missouri, then hit Enter. A dozen names popped up, along with each woman's age and city of residence. "Melissa must be around the same age as Mama. Three Melissa Dugans live in St. Louis, but none are anywhere near Mama's age."

Cloris studied the list. "Click on the one from Webster Groves. One of my college roommates used to live there. It's a suburb of St. Louis, and that Melissa Dugan is sixty-seven years old."

When I clicked on the name, it brought me to a page with the personal information for the Webster Groves Melissa Dugan. Not only did the site give her complete address, phone number, and maiden name, but also her city of birth—Newark, New Jersey. "This has to be the right Melissa Dugan."

Beside me, Cloris shuddered. "Scary how easily so much of our personal information is available online."

"We're all vulnerable targets of identity thieves these days. It's a miracle some hacker hasn't swooped in and wiped us all out." I picked up my phone and punched in Melissa's number.

A message clicked on after the third ring. I hit the speaker button for Cloris to hear.

In a decidedly New Jersey accent, the voice on the other end of the line said, "As you can see, I'm not presently available to take your call. Please leave your name, phone number, and a short message at the sound of the tone. However, if you're a salesperson or a scammer, don't bother because I won't return your call, and I will block your number."

"Interesting voicemail prompt," said Cloris. "I see she's maintained her Jersey Girl attitude, even after decades in the Midwest."

"Once a Jersey Girl, always a Jersey Girl. At least I know Mama was being truthful when she said she'd gotten Melissa's voicemail."

I returned to my computer screen and continued scrolling through the URLs. The next several were websites that offered to sell me various information, including arrest records, on all women named Melissa Dugan. Clicking on MelissaDugan.com brought up a landscape artist who lived in California. One with a .net extension belonged to a CPA in Arkansas. I also came across obituaries for two of the Melissa Dugans, one who died in 1998 at the age of eighty-three and another who passed away in 2004 at the age of ninety-one.

The last link on the search page was for the *Webster-Kirkland Times*, a weekly newspaper that serviced several St. Louis suburban towns. "I don't think Mama was emailing with Melissa Dugan," I said after clicking on the link that brought me to a local news article.

Cloris leaned over my shoulder to read the article that had popped up on the screen. "Only if she was emailing with Melissa's ghost."

Melissa Dugan, the Melissa Dugan Mama knew from my childhood, had been struck and killed a week ago by a hit-and-run driver in the parking lot of a local Webster Groves strip mall.

ELEVEN

"Do you think it's coincidence?" asked Cloris.

I stared at my computer screen. "I certainly hope so."

According to the brief article, Melissa was struck as she stepped out between two parked cars, directly into the path of a third vehicle speeding toward the strip mall exit. A witness stated that instead of stopping upon impact, the driver increased his speed, ran the stop sign at the end of the driveway, and headed toward the Interstate.

A day doesn't go by that I don't see pedestrians crossing streets or walking through parking lots with their noses glued to their phones. Then there are the drivers who multitask, doing everything from texting to applying mascara, while driving. When accidents happen, both drivers and pedestrians are often at fault. Maybe Melissa was one of those clueless pedestrians, more concerned with scrolling through her social media feeds than looking both ways. However, most drivers have enough of a moral compass not to leave the scene of an accident after striking a pedestrian.

Sometimes, those who don't stop panic out of fear and bad judgement. But others have something to hide—an outstanding arrest warrant, stolen possessions or contraband in the vehicle, obvious signs of drug or alcohol impairment.

A more sinister possibility also nipped around at the edges of my brain. What if the accident was no accident? What if someone had deliberately targeted Melissa Dugan?

I mulled this thought over after Cloris returned to her cubicle. As I had told Mama earlier, we don't know if Brad Jankowitz was a lone wolf con artist, hopping from state to state, or part of a nationwide ring of hackers who gained the confidence of their victims by spoofing the accounts of friends and relatives. If the latter, what if the other hackers were eliminating anyone Jankowitz had hacked during his grift spree? But if so, why?

Or perhaps, Jankowitz's kidnappers had gained valuable information from him before killing him and dumping his body out in the Atlantic Ocean. Did they now have possession of his computer? Had they gained access to all his passwords and his victims' accounts?

Were they now systematically eliminating everyone he'd impersonated, then quickly draining their accounts before anyone was the wiser? After all, what grieving spouse or offspring would think to check the deceased's financial statements immediately after such a shocking and unexpected death?

That scenario unleashed a shiver of fear coursing up and down my spine. Was my mother now in a killer's crosshairs? She claimed she hadn't provided Jankowitz with any personal information, but she wouldn't have had to. According to Ledbetter, Jankowitz had mad hacking skills, and we had no idea what information was stored on his computer.

I clicked back into the newspaper article and copied the link. Then I composed a long text to Special Agent Aloysius Ledbetter, outlining my theories, along with my worry for my mother's safety. Before hitting Send, I added Zack to the text chain.

Within seconds my phone rang. "How did you find that article?" asked Ledbetter, taking a page from Spader's playbook by dispensing with any salutation.

I quickly explained the email Mama had received last night. "I wanted to make sure my mother was really emailing with Melissa Dugan and not another hacker. A link to the newspaper article popped up in my online search for Melissa's phone number. Did you know she was dead?"

"No. We haven't had any communications with her or her grandson since notifying them that Jankowitz had spoofed their email accounts to contact your mother. At the time, we recommended they both change all their passwords, alert their credit card providers, place fraud alerts with the credit monitoring companies, and file reports with their local police departments. Same advice I gave your mother."

"Which Zack immediately took care of for her. What about Melissa and Jeremy?"

"I have no idea. Have you spoken with your mother?"

"Not yet. I thought I'd better contact you first. She's not going to take this well."

"That's understandable. I'll have a team keep an eye on her while I find out more about that hit-and-run. I'll be in touch as soon as I know something."

After disconnecting with Ledbetter, I first spent several minutes debating whether to call my mother. Every time I reached for my phone, I hesitated. What I had to tell Mama needed to be said in person. I powered down my computer, donned my coat, and grabbed my purse and tote.

Before leaving, I popped my head into Cloris's cubicle. "I'm heading out. I'll see you tomorrow. If anyone asks, I needed to purchase some supplies for the projects I'm working on."

One of her eyebrows rose under her pixie bangs. "What's the real reason?"

"There is absolutely no way I can tell Mama about Melissa Dugan's death over the phone."

"Understandable. I'll cover for you."

Zack had called while I was on the phone with Ledbetter. I returned his call after settling into my car. "I'm leaving work early to tell my mother about Melissa."

"I'm on the train. You want me to meet you at her condo?"

"No, I'm going to bring her back to the house."

"Call me if you change your mind."

I was about to deliver Mama a double whammy by telling her that her friend had been the victim of a hit-and-run driver and she'd once again been emailing with a scammer. How did I do that without causing her both heartache and worry for her own safety?

I wish I could assure her that the hit-and-run was a random accident, but I was having a hard time believing that. Yet, if the hit-and-run was somehow connected to Jankowitz, why would someone wait a week after Melissa's death to contact Mama and pretend to be Melissa? Didn't he run the risk of Mama already knowing Melissa had died?

Then again, what were the odds that this second scammer had no connection to Jankowitz? Maybe if he'd pretended to be another one of Mama's friends. However, by impersonating Melissa Dugan, the odds of having no connecting to Jankowitz were so incredibly astronomical that they defied even the most convoluted stretch of logic.

As I pulled up to a parking space in front of Mama's condo, another thought smacked me in my cerebrum. My breath caught in my throat as I white-knuckled my steering wheel and stared out the windshield at Mama's front door. Was it possible that the person who had emailed Mama today was the same person who had left me that ominous voice message two days ago? Had I jumped to the wrong conclusion by assuming the message referred to the murder victim deposited in the memorial garden? What if instead, the connection was to Brad Jankowitz's scam and subsequent murder?

Once again getting sucked into yet another murder investigation was more than enough for any reluctant amateur sleuth. But two unconnected murders at the same time? How in the world did I juggle that while maintaining my sanity and ensuring the safety of my loved ones?

I sat motionless in my car while questions ricochetted around my brain. When a tap on my driver's side window broke my stupor, I yelped loud enough to be heard in Staten Island and nearly jumped out of my seat. Luckily, I still wore my seatbelt, preventing me from crashing through the roof of my Jetta. Once my heart settled back into my chest cavity, I turned my head to find Mama gaping at me.

After undoing my seatbelt, not the easiest of feats, given my shaking hands, I grabbed my purse and stepped from the car. "Mama, you scared the caca out of me."

"I'm sorry, dear. How long have you been waiting for me, and why didn't you call? I've been out shopping."

To prove her point, she lifted her arm to better display an iconic Bloomingdale's big brown bag. Behind her, I noticed an Uber pulling out of the parking spot next to me.

How long had I spaced out?

With my adrenaline returning to close to normal levels, I tried to compose myself before speaking. After taking a shaky breath, I said, "I only arrived a few minutes ago. I left work early and thought I'd drop by before going home."

She shot me daggers of skepticism. "Is everything all right? You seem extremely jumpy for someone who's just dropping by for a visit, dear."

My mother always knows when I'm fibbing. Instead of answering her, I deflected. "How about offering me a cup of coffee, and we'll chat? I do have a few things to discuss with you."

Mama stood firm. "First, you're going to assure me that my grandchildren and your husband are all safe and sound. Tell me no one's dead, in the hospital, or has been diagnosed with some awful disease."

Had I looked like I'd arrived to impart such horrendous news? Well, I suppose I had, given how I'd responded to a rap on my car window, but I shook my head. "Nothing of the sort, Mama. All family members are alive and healthy."

She studied my face for several long seconds before finally nodding. Then she spun on her trademark Ferragamos and marched toward her front door.

Once we entered her condo and she started a pot of coffee, she channeled Torquemada, minus any physical torture. "Well?"

"I do have some disturbing news, Mama."

She crossed her arms. "I knew it. Out with it, Anastasia."

"Melissa Dugan died suddenly."

Mama gasped as she gripped the back of the kitchen chair. "How? She never said anything about an illness or not feeling well."

"She was killed by a hit-and-run driver in a strip mall parking lot."

Mama cringed. "How awful! And to think we were chatting over email just last night."

"The accident occurred a week ago, Mama."

My mother pulled the chair away from the table and slowly sank into it. Catherine the Great leaped onto her lap. Mama hugged the cat to her breast. Her hands twisted into a knot of fingers, and she buried her face in the cat's fur as my words sank in. "This is somehow connected to that horrible man who impersonated her son and tried to scam me, isn't it?"

"Possibly."

She raised her head and stared at me from across the table. "But how? He's dead."

I reached across the small table and placed a comforting hand over hers. "I don't know, but I have a couple of theories."

The coffee had finished brewing. Before continuing, I rose to pour two cups, grabbed the half and half from the fridge and returned to the table. She sat silently as I speculated about the possible identity of the emailer.

Her eyes grew wide. "Are you saying the hit-and-run was deliberate?"

"We won't know the answer to that until the driver is caught."

"I've watched enough crime shows to know that someone could be cleaning up the fake Jeremy's mess."

I nodded. "That's one theory."

Mama's voice trembled. "Which means, I could be next."

"Which is why you're going to pack a bag after we have our coffee and come home with me until Special Agent Ledbetter has answers for us. Until then, the FBI will keep an eye on you."

"Did you find out about Melissa's death from Agent Ledbetter?"

"He hadn't heard about it."

Her jaw dropped, and her voice rose several decibels. "How could he not know?"

"Local law enforcement wouldn't have notified the FBI unless they knew Melissa had recently been a victim of identity theft in a case the FBI was investigating."

"But wouldn't she have filed a police report? That's one of the things Agent Ledbetter told me to do."

"Melissa may not have bothered. We don't know if she took any steps to protect her identity after the FBI contacted her."

"Then how did you find out she'd died?"

"I was worried that someone else had gotten hold of your information and was targeting you."

"How?"

"Spammers buy and sell hacked information on the Dark Web all the time." I then explained my Google search and how I'd stumbled upon the news article.

"Then whoever emailed me last night may not have had any connection to the fake Jeremy. It could be another hacker who bought my information."

"It doesn't mean the new emailer is any less dangerous than Jankowitz was, Mama."

"Which also means I need to change my passwords again."

"I'm afraid so. Zack and I will help you with that."

She exhaled a huge sigh. "Life was a lot simpler before we relied so much on the Internet and our smart phones."

In some ways Mama had brought these problems on herself with her easy-to-replicate passwords and her constant social media postings, but I wasn't about to rub salt and vinegar in her wounds. Instead, I said, "Which is why it's so important to stay vigilant."

She scowled. "A lesson I'm learning the hard way."

After we finished our coffee, in typical Flora fashion, my mother packed enough clothes, accessories, and toiletries for a round-the-world cruise. I made three trips to the car, lugging multiple suitcases for her and assorted Catherine the Great paraphernalia, including an enormous amount of litter, her high-tech litter box, two weeks' worth of gourmet cat food, a box of kitty toys, and the empress herself, reluctantly ensconced in her kitty transport case.

Both Nick and Zack had arrived home before us. I allowed them the pleasure of hauling Mama's possessions from my car into the house.

After Mama headed to the bedroom to unpack, Zack said, "Detective Spader is bringing dinner."

"In exchange for an evening of picking our brains?"

"Maybe he's just in need of some sympathetic company. He sounded exhausted."

"When hasn't he lately? Did he mention anything new in the investigation?"

"Not a word."

Just then, Zack's phone dinged an incoming text. He fished the phone from his pocket and glanced at the screen. "Seems our friendly neighborhood Special Agent also wants to stop by this evening."

"I hope he's arriving with the news that they've caught the guy who mowed down Melissa Dugan."

"I'll invite him to join us for dinner. Spader always brings more than enough food."

"Sure, I could use some entertainment this evening." When Zack raised an eyebrow, I added, "We haven't had a good law enforcement inter-agency smackdown in a while."

He chuckled. "I think Spader and Ledbetter have developed a grudging respect for each other."

"Let's hope so. New Jersey outlawed duels more than two centuries ago."

His raised eyebrow returned for an encore. "Do I want to know how you have such arcane knowledge floating around in your head?"

"I probably read it somewhere."

"Don't you think Mom should try out for *Jeopardy*?" asked Nick.

I jumped in before Zack could answer. "Thanks, but no thanks. I've already had more than enough unwanted national exposure the last few months."

Nick turned beet red, hung his head, and mumbled, "We only wanted to help, Mom."

No parent is perfect. We all have those moments we wish we could take back. This was one of them. I reached for my son and drew him into my arms. "I know, Nick. I'm sorry. I shouldn't have said that. The three of you had the best of intentions."

I placed my hands on his shoulders and held him at arm's length as I studied his face. "Forgive me?"

"Sure. Heck, you're the coolest mom in Westfield."

Who knew? "I am?"

"You kick butt, Mom. All my friends wish they had a mom like you."

This coming from the son who until recently constantly berated me for breaking my promise about not getting involved in anymore murder investigations. I turned to Zack. "Is it too late to dampen his recent obsession with criminology and steer him toward a safer career?"

"Have anything in mind?"

I turned to Nick. "Ever think of becoming a fortune cookie writer or a professional sleeper?"

He rolled his eyes. "Very funny, Mom. Ever think of doing standup comedy?" When I answered with an eyeroll of my own, he changed the subject. "I'm taking Leonard for a walk before dinner."

Spader and Ledbetter arrived within seconds of each other. Both stood at the front door when Zack swung it open. Spader held a large reusable canvas bag emblazoned with the logo of a local gourmet shop specializing in seafood and assorted salads. Two baguettes poked out from the top of the bag.

Ledbetter juggled three bottles of assorted white wines. Seeing my gaze shift between the bag of food and the wine, he said, "We bumped into each other at the gourmet shop."

"Convenient," said Zack ushering both men inside.

Spader and Ledbetter made their way into the kitchen and deposited their offerings on the island. While they returned to the foyer to hang up their coats, I unloaded the contents of the bag.

Spader had arrived with a feast. Three different seafood salads, plus an assortment of veggie and pasta salads and a Black Forest cake for dessert—not in the shape of a taser this time.

Nick and Leonard returned home as Zack sliced the baguettes and I removed lids from the various salad containers. "Both of you?" he asked, his head bobbing between Spader and Ledbetter. "What's up?"

"Does something have to be up?" asked Spader.

"I was hoping you had a breakthrough in identifying the dead guy."

"What dead guy?" asked Ledbetter, turning to Spader.

"Someone dumped a John Doe in the park across the street late Sunday night or very early Monday morning."

"Not just dumped," said Nick. "He was posed on the bench with a huge dictionary on his lap and his finger pointing to the word *joker*."

"Which may or may not be deliberate," said Spader. "The dictionary was used as a weight to prop up the body, but young Sherlock here thinks it refers to Batman's nemesis, and the killer is taunting either the police or Mrs. Barnes."

Ledbetter turned to me. "Why you?"

I told him about the anonymous call I'd received Tuesday.

He turned back to Spader. "You have no leads?"

"None that have panned out so far. We thought the killing was tied to the one that occurred across the street last month, but it's looking less likely the more we dig."

"Let me know if I can help in any way."

"Appreciate that."

"Good evening, gentlemen," said Mama making her grand entrance. She ignored Detective Spader and zeroed in on

Ledbetter. "I hope you have some good news for me, Special Agent Ledbetter."

"Yes and no, ma'am. The St. Louis police found the pickup involved in the hit-and-run. It was abandoned behind a burned-out warehouse about five miles from the scene."

"And the driver?"

"No sign of him so far."

Mama skewered him with a reprimanding look. "That's hardly what I'd call good news."

"What's this about?" asked Spader.

Mama kept her eyes fixed on Ledbetter. "About a killer on the loose, and I might be his next victim."

"We don't know that, Mama. Melissa's death may have nothing to do with Jankowitz."

"But it could." Her voice began to tremble with rage. "What do you suggest, dear? That I worry only half of each day? Which half? Or perhaps, I should alternate, worrying one hour, not worrying the next, and on and on until I fall asleep from sheer exhaustion each night. Assuming I can fall asleep at all."

She next turned to Zack. "I'm going to need something stronger than white wine this evening, Zachary, dear."

"What would you like, Flora?"

"Bourbon. Straight up. And make it a double."

Zack and I both executed a simultaneous double-take. Mama rarely drank hard liquor. When she did, it was always diluted with a generous amount of fruit juice as part of an umbrella drink.

Zack nodded toward Nick. "There's a bottle of Maker's Mark in the upper cabinet to the left of the sink in the apartment. Would you mind getting it?"

After Nick darted out the back door, Spader asked, "How is a hit-and-run in St. Louis connected to Mrs. Tuttenauer?"

"O'Keefe," said Mama. "I refuse to use that man's name after what he did. Kindly remember that, Detective."

"Yes, ma'am. My apologies."

As I escorted my mother to a seat in the dining room, Ledbetter filled Spader in on the death of the woman Jankowitz had hacked to glean Mama's information.

"What makes you think there's a connection to your case?" asked Spader.

Ledbetter nodded toward me. "It's one of Anastasia's theories. I can't rule anything out at this point. We think Jankowitz was responsible for running similar cons throughout the country."

"But isn't he dead?"

"Swimming with the fishes."

"Then where's the connection?" asked Spader. "Sometimes a cigar is just a cigar, and a hit-and-run is just a hit-and-run."

Ledbetter offered him both of my theories. "I've learned to trust Anastasia's intuition."

Spader glanced toward me. With his mouth set in a tight line, he nodded. "That makes two of us."

~*~

After a leisurely dinner filled with lively conversation, we were cleaning up when there was a loud pounding on the front door. Zack checked his phone. "Brent Fredericks." He pushed back his chair and rose. "He looks extremely upset."

Zack rushed to the front door. We all followed. As soon as Zack swung open the door, Brent Fredericks said, "That's your cop friend's car parked on the street, isn't it? Is he here?"

"I am," said Spader, stepping into the foyer. "What's going on, Mr. Fredericks?"

"There's another dead body across the street."

TWELVE

"Where?" asked Spader.

Mr. Fredericks pointed a shaky finger toward the memorial garden. "In the fountain."

"Stay here," Detective Spader told him.

"Don't worry," said Fredericks. "You don't have to tell me that twice. Not after what I saw."

Spader and Special Agent Ledbetter reached for their weapons, then raced across the street. Zack followed.

At the mention of another dead body, Mama chose flight over fight. She scooped up Catherine the Great and rushed down the hall to her bedroom. A moment later, I heard the bedroom door slam, followed by the distinctive sound of the dresser being dragged across the hardwood floor to barricade the door.

I could tell Nick was itching to follow the men. I placed my hand on his arm to hold him back. "The fewer people over there, the better. We don't want to contaminate the crime scene."

Nick cocked his head toward Brent Fredericks. "But hasn't Mr. Fredericks already contaminated the site?"

"I hope not." I turned to Fredericks. "Did you touch anything in the garden?"

"Heck, no. I want no part of what's going on over there. That property is cursed. First Batty Bentworth. Then that crazy guy who spent hours mowing his dirt and weeds. Now two more dead bodies in three days. I won't step foot inside that garden. Saw the whole thing from my kitchen window."

I continued probing. "What exactly did you see, Mr. Fredericks?"

"Someone hauling what looked like a rolled-up carpet fireman-style coming from the back of the property. When he got to the fountain, he set the bundle on the edge, unfurled it, and dumped the contents into the water."

"What did he do after that?" I asked.

"Rolled up the carpet, swung it over one shoulder, then high tailed it out the way he came. Once he'd moved away from the fountain, I saw the body. I waited until he cut through to the property in the back before I left the house and came across the street to you."

"Why didn't you call 9-1-1?" asked Nick.

A logical question, to which Fredericks shrugged. "Saw that detective's car in front of your house earlier and figured it would be faster to knock on your door."

Except seconds matter in murder investigations. With his advanced age and suffering from rheumatoid arthritis, Brent Fredericks lumbered like a sloth. If he'd called the police as soon as he saw the body, there was a decent chance that a patrol car in the vicinity might spot the killer before he made it back to his vehicle and fled. I heaved a sigh but saw no point in berating the man.

Nick and I remained at the front door, but Brent Fredericks turned to leave. "Where are you going, Mr. Fredericks?"

"Home."

"Detective Spader asked you to wait here. He's going to want to question you."

"He knows where to find me. Besides, I already told you everything. You can tell him for me. I've had enough excitement for one evening."

He patted his chest. "Not good for my ticker. Besides, I don't want Joanna worrying that I'll catch my death of cold standing out here."

"I understand, but before you leave, were you able to get a good look at the man?"

He shook his head. "Tall and obviously strong enough to heave a body rolled in a carpet over his shoulders. Beyond that, I can't say. I don't see all that well in the dark."

"Even with the lights from the fountain?" I asked.

"I've got cataracts."

"Then how did you notice the guy walking through the garden?" asked Nick.

Fredericks turned on him. "I'm not blind, sonny. I just can't see clearly in the dark." He then muttered something under his breath about insolence and today's youth before turning his back on us and slowly making his way toward the sidewalk.

Once Fredericks was halfway down the front path, Nick said, "I wasn't being insolent, Mom. It was a legitimate question."

"I know."

"Then why'd he snap at me?"

"Because what you said reminded him of the limitations that affect people as they age." I pulled my son into a side hug. "Don't let it get to you, Nick."

We watched as Brent Fredericks slowly plodded across the street and made his way up the steps to his front door. Once he'd entered his house, I turned my attention back to the fountain, fixating on the illuminated statue of a half-naked Barry Sumner forever pushing his lawn mower.

I puzzled over why anyone would risk dumping not one, but two dead bodies in a place where they'd easily be discovered. The killer had posed the first body in the middle of the night with little chance of getting caught in the act.

However, this time, although darkness had descended, it wasn't quite nine o'clock. People were still out and about, either walking their dogs or returning home after working late, dining out, or running errands.

For the second murder, the killer also hadn't taken pains to pose the body. He'd unceremoniously dumped his victim in the fountain, then took off. Was this even the same killer, or was it possible that this was the work of a copycat?

According to Mr. Fredericks, the killer had entered through the property that abutted the back of the garden. He would have had to park his car on the street parallel to ours, then carry his victim down the driveway and through the backyard of the other home, increasing the chance of someone noticing him.

Then again, that street had undergone a huge transformation the last few years. A builder had bought up all the Cape Cods and small ranchers, offering top dollar, then combined two lots to erect each multi-million-dollar McMansion. Some of the homes had winding driveways leading to three-car attached garages at the back of the houses. Was the house that backed up on the garden one of them?

Their landscaping included plantings that blocked a view of their yard. If the killer knew the residents weren't home, he could have driven around to the back of the house, and no one would have seen him remove the body from his vehicle.

I wondered if our security cameras had caught the killer in the act this time, or if he'd once again shot paintballs at the lenses. After pulling my phone from my pocket, I accessed the app.

Nick leaned over and watched as I played through the video. "I'm not seeing anyone walking around the garden."

"Neither am I."

"Then how did Mr. Fredericks see the killer dump the body?"

I studied the angle of the recording. "If he entered the garden midway between the side property lines, he could have walked directly toward the back of the fountain. The massive pedestal and water spray would have blocked the camera's view."

"Wow, this guy's a criminal mastermind. He thinks of everything."

The only way any of this made sense, though, was if the killer was sending a message. But what message? And to whom? Was he delusional? Convinced of his own superior abilities to outwit the police? Was this all a game to him? A deadly version of catch-me-if-you-can? And if so, directed toward whom? The police? Or me?

The sound of approaching sirens interrupted my speculation. Shortly after, our street was crowded with various law enforcement vehicles, including the crime scene unit and the medical examiner. Porch lights flickered on up and down the street with neighbors poking their heads out their front doors. Some of the braver ones stepped from their homes and congregated in clusters on the sidewalk on either side of the garden as well as on our side of the street.

Expecting the press to arrive at any moment, I pulled Nick into the house and shut the door. Then, I made my way to the bedroom where Mama had barricaded herself and knocked on the door. "It's safe to come out, Mama."

Her voice trembled as she spoke. "You don't know that. I could be next on the killer's hit list."

"Shoving a dresser in front of the door isn't going to protect you, Mama."

She gasped. "This is how you comfort me?"

I didn't press. Mama was a woman of a certain age, with a bladder to match. Eventually, nature would force the issue.

Before returning to the kitchen, I pulled the blinds in the living room and dining room. I wouldn't put it past Darlene Jamison to order her cameraman to stick his lens up against one of my windows. The woman was relentless in her pursuit of me. Once her network invaded my privacy, the other networks would follow, no matter how many times Spader had warned them about trespassing on my property.

By the time I entered the kitchen, Nick had nearly finished with dinner cleanup. "Cut through Mrs. Schneider's backyard when you take Leonard out later. I'll alert her. The press will camp out front until after the eleven o'clock news."

Zack and Ledbetter returned to the house an hour and a half later while Nick was walking Leonard. "It's a Fourth Estate feeding frenzy out there," said Zack. "We had to fight our way through a scrum of reporters and cameramen to get to the front door."

"They're supposed to stay on the sidewalk."

"I reminded them of that. It took Al flashing his badge to get them to comply."

Zack ducked into the kitchen. When he returned with the bottle of Maker's Mark and three glasses, I asked, "Does Spader think it's the same killer?"

"Definitely." Zack poured the bourbon and passed around the glasses. "Same M.O. Victim is male, in his twenties or early thirties. Average height and build. Van Dyke beard. Dressed in black jeans, long-sleeved T-shirt, and running shoes."

"How was he killed?"

"Same as the first victim. Execution-style. Bullet to the back of the head at close range."

"But no dictionary this time?" I asked.

"No dictionary," said Ledbetter.

"Any other obvious clues?"

"Nothing," said Zack. "The dictionary might have simply been a way to keep the first victim anchored on the bench."

"If so, he went to a lot of trouble to get it," I said. "And why go to those lengths with his first victim but just dump the second one in the fountain? That's where he veers from the M.O. of the first killing."

I mentioned the possibility of a copycat, then remembered something else. "What about tattoos? Didn't Spader say the first victim had several?"

"Nothing visible," said Zack. "Only his hands and face were exposed. Spader will learn more once the M.E. has the body back at the morgue."

"Maybe the perp's getting cocky," said Ledbetter. "Or careless. It wouldn't be the first time arrogance and hubris brought down a killer. Or he could be deliberately switching up his routine to avoid a pattern."

"Yet he dumped both bodies on the same property," I said. "That doesn't sound like much of a change in routine."

"Valid point," said Ledbetter, "but most murders are solved because the killers make dumb mistakes."

"How many killings does it take to make a serial killer?" I asked.

"Three or more," said Ledbetter, "but Detective Spader is determined there won't be a third."

"I hope he's right."

"I do have some good news," said Ledbetter. "Is your mother still awake? She'll want to hear this."

"I'll check."

Several minutes later, I returned with Mama, still clutching Catherine the Great to her chest. She dropped onto the corner of the sofa, focused in on Special Agent Ledbetter, and demanded, "You have news for me?"

"Yes, ma'am. I received a text from the Webster Groves police chief. They've identified the hit-and-run driver who killed Melissa Dugan. He's a St. Louis meth head with a long list of priors. He's been in and out of prison for most of his life."

Ralph chose that moment to squawk his two cents from atop the china cabinet. "*Braack! I say he shall go to prison. Taming of the Shrew.* Act Five, Scene Two."

Mama shot Ralph a dirty look, before asking, "Why do they keep releasing him?"

"Only the most heinous offenders receive sentences of life without parole, Mrs. O'Keefe. This guy serves his time, gets released, and within days usually commits another crime. He stole the vehicle used in the hit-and-run."

"Is he now in custody?"

"Not yet, but the chief assured me it's only a matter of time. The St. Louis police are familiar with his usual haunts. They've got a BOLO out on him."

"Be on the lookout," I explained to Mama.

"I know what a BOLO is, dear. I've watched enough crime shows."

I turned back to Ledbetter. "Then there's no connection to Jankowitz?"

"Highly improbable. From what the chief told me, this guy's brain is so fried that half the time he doesn't remember his own name. There's no way he was part of any sophisticated ring of scammers."

Ledbetter turned back to Mama. "You don't have to worry, ma'am. Melissa Dugan's death had nothing to do with Brad Jankowitz and his attempted scam of you."

Mama didn't look convinced, but she chose not to question Ledbetter's pronouncement. Instead, she rose, thanked him for keeping her informed, and announced the excitement of the evening had exhausted her. "If you'll all excuse me, I need my beauty rest."

~*~

Since the body in the fountain had no connection to any of Special Agent Ledbetter's open cases, he decided to call it a night shortly after Mama headed to bed. A few minutes later, Detective Spader texted to say he'd be wrapping up across the street shortly and asked if we'd wait up for him.

Shortly wound up stretching on for another hour. Zack, Nick, and I settled in to watch the eleven o'clock news. It aired with only the briefest announcement about the latest body in the memorial garden, including Spader tossing the press the tiniest crumb of information. "For now, the victim is another John Doe. Hopefully, we'll have more information for you tomorrow after the M.E. concludes his examination."

The press persisted with rapid-fire questions that Spader ignored. As he shouldered his way through the gaggle, Darlene Jamison shoved her microphone in his face. "Was this latest victim murdered in the same fashion as the body discovered Monday?"

Spader's lips tightened into a thin line. He then sidestepped her and lumbered toward a group of officers huddled near the Crime Scene van.

Darlene was fishing. "Law enforcement hasn't released the manner of death for John Doe Number One, have they?" I asked Zack.

"Not to my knowledge."

Darlene positioned herself in front of her cameraman. Her facial expression and on-air muttered grumble spoke volumes as to what she thought of Spader, but I doubted she was alone. The press had spent several hours cooling their stilettos and wingtips in plummeting October temperatures with a breeze that had grown to a whipping wind while waiting for a multi-network scoop that never materialized.

Once the eleven o'clock news ended, I ordered Nick to bed. "You have school tomorrow."

"*Tomorrow, and tomorrow, and tomorrow, creeps in this petty pace from day to day,*" squawked Ralph where he sat perched on his favorite human's shoulder. "*Macbeth.* Act Five, Scene Five."

"An oldie but goodie," I said, watching Ralph shift from talon to talon as he impatiently awaited his sunflower seed reward.

Nick pressed. "I want to hear what Detective Spader has to say."

"If we learn anything important, I'll tell you in the morning."

He scowled. "Fine, but you've just lost some Cool Mom points."

"If you don't tell your friends, they'll never know."

Before he exited the den, he gave me a goodnight hug, anyway.

"I guess I didn't lose too many Cool Mom Points."

Ralph squawked once more but apparently The Bard of Avon had never written a play or sonnet that included Cool Mom Points.

Spader finally knocked on the door at eleven-forty. "Thanks," he said as he stepped into the foyer. "I won't keep you up long. My bladder is about to burst." He then made a beeline down the hall to the bathroom.

Zack and I waited in the foyer. Eventually, Spader returned, a sheepish grin plastered across his face. "Thanks again for waiting up. I should've listened to my mother. She always said to go before leaving the house."

"Number Two in Every Mother's Top Ten List of Advice," I said.

The sheepish grin grew wider. "In my defense, I was racing across the street to a dead body."

"A legitimate excuse," said Zack. "Care to share any non-bodily function insights while you're here?"

"Not much to tell at this point."

"And still no word on the identity of the first John Doe?" I asked.

"We're still waiting on DNA. He wasn't in the system. Facial recognition and fingerprinting turned up nothing. All we know so far is that he had no priors and didn't work at any job that required fingerprinting of employees."

When Spader tried but failed to stifle a yawn, I said, "Go home, Detective. Get a good night's sleep. Maybe you'll have better luck tomorrow."

"Is that also in Every Mother's Top Ten List of Advice?"

"Number Three."

~*~

Detective Spader called the next morning as I was catching Cloris up on all that had transpired over the last twenty-four hours. At least all I could mention without jeopardizing the investigation. I trusted Cloris with my life. After all, she'd once saved my life. But anything Detective Spader discussed in confidence with Zack and me needed to remain within the cone of silence.

"We have a break in the case," said Spader. "A connection between the two bodies in the garden."

"Hold on a second." I race-walked to my supply closet, locking the door behind me once I entered. "Okay. What kind of connection? Was the same gun used to kill both victims?"

"Same caliber bullet, different guns."

That made no sense to me. "Why would the killer execute both victims in the same manner, with the same ammunition, and deposit them in the same location, but use different guns? Is it possible we're dealing with two killers working in consort? Or the beginnings of a gangland war?"

"Anything is possible. Someone may have ordered a hit on these guys. Possibly drug related, although the street crimes unit hasn't heard any rumblings about a new turf war breaking out between gangs. That's not why I called you, though. Both victims had the same small tattoo on their inner right thigh in the groin region."

"That age group is ruled by whatever is trending on social media. It's a hive mentality. What was it? A spider web? Skull? Dagger?"

"He had several of those, as well as a few crosses, barbed wire circling both biceps, and a giant eagle on his chest, but the one that matched the first victim was an icon of some sort. I'm texting you a photo."

I opened the text to find a symbol consisting of a thick black V with a series of thinner horizontal bars connecting the two sides of the letter. Superimposed in the center of the horizontal bars was a stylized B within a circle. "It looks like a garment neckline with a fabric insert and monogram, but I'm guessing it must have some other meaning than a logo for a new fashion house."

"Yeah, I don't think these guys worked as clothing designers."

"You never know. The couture world is cutthroat. If not for the monogram, I'd say it's an ancient symbol. Maybe Egyptian, Mayan, or Native American. Did you do a search?"

"Nothing's popped so far. I know it's a stretch, but with your art background, I thought you might recognize it. We're up to our eyeballs here. I need all the help I can get."

"Are you asking me to do a deep dive down the research rabbit hole, Detective?"

"I thought you'd never ask. Come up with an answer, and dinner's on me tonight." Then in typical Spader fashion, he disconnected the call.

I returned to my cubicle and fired up my computer. Fifteen minutes later, I'd found a credible possibility.

THIRTEEN

What were the odds that knowledge gleaned from mandatory art history classes in college would aid in a murder investigation more than twenty years later? I hurried back to my supply closet and once again locked the door after entering. Then I called Detective Spader.

"Find something already?"

"I think it's a mashup of two symbols. The V with the horizontal bars is an ancient Native American symbol found on rocks as both pictographs and petroglyphs, mostly in the Southwest and Utah."

"I'm guessing you know the difference between the two, but I don't."

"Pictographs are rock paintings; petroglyphs are rock carvings."

"Were you able to find anything about a meaning?"

"Abundant wealth, both spiritual and external, but I think the killer's victims were more interested in the latter."

"What about the B in the circle?"

"Possibly a cryptocurrency symbol. Did you know there are already thousands of crypto companies?"

Spader grunted. "Yeah. And more cropping up every day. It's like the wild west out there. Makes me glad I work in homicide and not the fraud division."

"You might be dealing with both on this case."

"How so?"

"That tattoo could be related to a crypto company, maybe a new startup. If your victims were involved in crypto fraud, that could be what got them both killed."

"I'll send the image over to the fraud division. Maybe they know something about it."

"Meanwhile, Detective, I think it's time to give up on the blackmailer theory."

Spader heaved a heavy sigh. "Already have. But that leaves us back at Square One with no viable suspects."

I wracked my brain. "There has to be some connection to Gloria Forester and Barry Sumner. Why else would the killer go to the lengths he has to dump both bodies in the memorial garden? Not to mention the risk of getting caught. Why not leave the bodies where he killed them? Or dispose of them in a way where no one would ever find them?"

"I think we can assume at this point that he wanted the bodies discovered. Beyond that, maybe you can come up with a connection. I'm hitting a brick wall. We've eliminated all the blackmailers and everyone else who had a connection to Sumner and Forester. Everyone with a beef against one or both of them is either dead, in prison, or has an ironclad alibi."

"All but one, Detective."

"Who?"

"Yours truly."

Spader roared with laughter. "Are you confessing, Mrs. Barnes? If so, let me remind you that I was in your dining room with you last night when the killer dumped the second victim in the fountain. Did some diabolical mad scientist clone you to create an evil murderous twin?"

"Let me remind you, Detective, of a classic Holmesian aphorism. 'When you have eliminated the impossible, whatever remains, *however improbable*, must be the truth.' Although I'm not suggesting that I have a clone, but let's face it. I've become a murder magnet."

"Are we talking about your true crime podcaster theory?"

"We are."

Spader grew silent long enough that I thought the phone connection had dropped. Finally, he said, "I wonder how many of those true crime podcasters live in New Jersey."

"If you're asking me to do more research, it will have to wait until this evening. In case you've forgotten, I do have a paying job. Right now, unless, you want to put me on salary, I need to get back to it."

Before ending the call, I added, "I'll let Zack know he's off the hook for dinner tonight."

Cloris waylaid me as I stepped from the supply closet. "What's going on?"

"My side hustle boss needed to brainstorm."

"And?"

"I told him he'd have to wait until this evening."

~*~

Cloris, Jeanie, and I had a working lunch scheduled at noon with Creativity Books editor Danica Magee. The first book in our *American Woman Through the Decades* series was moving along smoothly enough that we could now step out of the sixties and start brainstorming about the seventies.

"We need an overall theme," said Danica. "Any suggestions?"

"Ecology," I offered. "I did some research. Did you know the first Earth Day was held April 20, 1970?"

"Before my time," said Danica.

"Hey," said Cloris, "We weren't around back then, either."

"Doesn't matter," said Jeanie, our designated Earth Mother and expert on all things ecological. "It's a great idea. If it weren't for Earth Day, we'd all probably be walking around wearing gas masks by now."

Danica's eyes grew wide as she shuddered. "Gas masks?"

"Look it up," said Jeanie. "It's eye-opening. You know how we sometimes have air quality alerts that warn the elderly and people with health issues to stay indoors?"

Danica nodded. "But that's only when there's a terrible forest fire somewhere, and the smoke blows our way."

"Not back then," said Jeanie. "The sky in Los Angeles was often green each morning until the smog burned off later in the day. Earth Day changed people's minds about how we treat our planet. It heralded in a planet-wide movement to clean up all the human-created damage that began with the Industrial Revolution."

Cloris and I exchanged a quick look. When Jeanie jumped onto her soapbox, it was nearly impossible to drag her off it. Before she launched into a history lesson, I interrupted her by pulling out my recycled Valentine's Day candy box and passing it across the table to Danica.

"This project will appear in the February issue of *American Woman*. "It's one of the crafts I also have in mind for the book featuring crafts of the seventies. While going through magazine issues from that decade, I found several examples that featured various crafting techniques used to decorate and repurpose a wide variety of containers."

"What kind of items did you have in mind?" asked Danica.

"Round cardboard oatmeal boxes, coffee cans, shoe boxes, milk cartons. Just about anything can be given a makeover and transformed into a new use."

"And kept out of landfills," added Jeanie. "Trash to treasures. I can do the same with discarded furniture and household items."

Danica turned to Cloris. "Please tell me you're not planning to repurpose moldy bread and rotten tomatoes."

Cloris laughed. "I give those to Jeanie for her mulch pile."

Jeanie nodded. "The worms love them."

"Worms?" Danica made a face. "Eww! They make my skin crawl."

"They're a crucial part of the ecosystem," said Jeanie, jumping back on her soap box. "Not to mention a friend of every backyard gardener."

Danica didn't look convinced. She turned her attention back to Cloris. "Have you researched the most popular foods from the seventies?"

Cloris nodded. "Quiche and fondue were big. According to my mother, every bride-to-be received at least one fondue pot as an engagement or bridal shower gift back then. My mother still has hers, although it's been gathering cobwebs in the attic for decades."

"We need more than quiche and fondue recipes," said Danica.

Cloris continued, "Not to worry. I have a long list. Hamburger Helper was a staple in every kitchen. Church potlucks and cocktail parties always included ambrosia salad, deviled eggs, cheese balls, and Hawaiian meatballs. Carrot cake and Black Forest cake were favorite desserts. I'll have plenty of recipes to draw on from past issues and give them a modern spin."

~*~

The traffic gods smiled on me once again during my trip home that evening, and I arrived before either Zack or Nick. With no lights on in the house, I assumed Mama was out shopping somewhere because Mama was always out shopping somewhere.

In the waning light, I stared across the street at the hideous fountain. As I did, the lights turned on, illuminating bronze Barry and his bronze lawnmower.

I glanced up and down the street, finding myself alone except for the chatter of a few squirrels, the rustle of falling leaves, and the splashing of water cycling through the fountain. No crime scene tape barred entry into the garden. I strode down my driveway, crossed the street, and stepped through the wrought iron arch into the Barry Sumner Memorial Garden.

I didn't expect to find anything. The crime scene unit had spent several hours last night combing the property. Maybe, though, walking the grounds might trigger whatever insights currently eluded me. It certainly couldn't hurt.

I first strode to the rear of the property, curious to see if the killer could slip into the garden from the property behind it. The owners of the McMansion had planted a row of arborvitae trees along their property line, but the house was new enough that the trees hadn't yet matured to create total privacy. The killer could easily slip between trees to enter the garden.

I peered through a break between two of the trees and confirmed that the driveway wound around to an attached three-car garage at the rear of the house. Turning my attention back to the garden, I accessed the security app on my phone and watched in real time as I traced a straight path to the fountain. The camera never captured me.

The Fredericks' kitchen was situated at the back of their house with the window over the sink looking out onto the garden. Not that I doubted him, but I'd just confirmed that even though our state-of-the-art security cameras had failed to capture anything last night, Mr. Fredericks's cataract-impaired eyes would have seen the killer dumping the body into the fountain.

My phone dinged an incoming text as I exited the garden. A one-sentence message appeared on my home screen: *Enjoy your stroll through the body garden?*

I quickly scanned the street but saw no one. I refused to believe the disturbing text had come from one of my neighbors spying on me from their homes, but I glanced at each house anyway. I saw no one standing on a porch, no silhouettes in any lit windows, nor any lurking shadows in darkened ones.

Turning my attention to the street, I noted several cars parked at the curb. As I stood on the sidewalk, one of them at the end of the block roared to life, executed a swift U-turn, and pulled onto Central Avenue—all at breakneck speed and without benefit of headlights.

Coincidence? Doubtful. How long had he sat watching me from the opaque interior of his car? Had he followed me home from work?

I was still standing frozen on the sidewalk when Zack pulled into our driveway a minute later. Snapping out of my stupor, I forced one trembling foot in front of the other and crossed the street to meet him.

Even though Zack has massive mindreading skills, most likely learned at the spy school he claims he never attended, I'm guessing he didn't need to rely on them. Likewise, I didn't need to look in a mirror to see the fear plastered on my face. It vibrated through every nerve of my body.

He immediately jumped to the most logical, albeit wrong conclusion. "Is there another dead body in the garden?"

I opened my mouth, but the words refused to come. Instead, I shook my head.

He reached for my hand. "Let's get you inside."

Zack unlocked the door, flipped on the lights, and led me into the living room. After seating me on the sofa, he hustled into the kitchen, returning a moment later with a glass of water. I dropped my phone onto my lap and clutched the glass with both hands, sipping slowly through my still slightly trembling lips.

When I'd drained the last drop of water, he asked, "Want something stronger?"

Now that I sat in the safety of my home with Zack by my side, I felt more in control. The trembling ceased, and my voice returned. "Not right now."

"What's got you so spooked?"

I picked up my phone and showed him the text. "I had just exited the garden when this came in."

"What were you doing in the garden?"

I explained how I wanted to satisfy my curiosity about how the killer could have entered with the body without being detected by anyone on the street adjacent to us or captured on our surveillance cameras. "But that's not all."

"Go on."

I told him about the car that drove away right after I'd received the text. "I think the killer is stalking me."

Zack's expression left no doubt that he agreed with me. He drew me into his arms. We sat entwined in silence, until we heard Nick enter the house through the kitchen door.

Five minutes after Nick left to take Leonard on his evening walk, Detective Spader rang the front doorbell. Zack went to answer the door while I headed into the kitchen to grab dinnerware for the table. I could hear the two men speaking in hushed tones and knew beyond any doubt that I was the topic of conversation.

Sure enough, a moment later, Spader strode into the kitchen, placed three boxes of pizza and a large shopping bag on the island, then held out his hand. "Let me see that text."

I handed over my phone. Spader scowled at the screen, then sent off a text on his own phone before returning to my phone and forwarding the text I'd received. "My guess is that it came from the same burner phone that called you the other day."

"I'm not sure how comforting that is, Detective."

I turned to Zack. "Did you tell him everything?"

Zack nodded.

"I don't suppose you got a license plate number?" asked Spader.

"No, he was too far away and drove off without turning his lights on. I can't even tell you the make, model, or color of the car, other than it was a sedan."

"And probably stolen," said Spader, "if we're dealing with the killer."

When Nick returned with Leonard, he took one look at the pizza boxes and nearly drooled his approval. We were still missing one member of the family, though. I picked up my phone from where Spader had placed it on the island and called my mother.

"Yes, dear?"

"Mama, are you joining us for dinner?"

"Not tonight, dear. I'm on a date."

"With whom?" To my knowledge, Mama hadn't yet set her sights on my sixth stepfather.

"Really, Anastasia, don't you think you're being a bit nosey?"

"No, I don't, Mama. Not with what's been going on lately. Who is he? Where did you meet him? And how long have you known him?"

She responded by hanging up on me.

The logical side of my brain reminded me that my mother was a grown woman who lived alone and led an active social life. The illogical side of my brain wanted to round up a posse and hunt her down.

Zack restrained me. "She'll be fine."

I wish I could believe him. "You haven't by any chance hidden an air tag in her purse, have you?"

Zack was already tapping away on his phone. "What do you think?" He showed me the screen. Mama was less than a mile away at one of her favorite Westfield restaurants. "We'll keep tabs on her throughout the evening."

Meanwhile, I noticed Nick staring at me. "Everything okay, Mom?"

My younger son was no longer a clueless kid obsessed with sports and video games to the exclusion of everything and everyone else. He'd matured into a discerning young man now aware of emotional undercurrents. He sensed when something was off kilter in the yin/yang of the family dynamic.

At least he hadn't been home to witness my aberrant reaction. "Finish setting the table before the pizzas get cold. We'll fill you in over dinner."

Along with the pizzas, Detective Spader had brought Cesar salad, gelato, a bakery box filled with an assortment of Italian cookies, a half-gallon jug of apple cider for Nick, and several bottles of wine for the adults. As we feasted, I told Nick about the car that had driven off immediately after I'd received the anonymous text. I omitted any mention of his kick-butt mom's meltdown.

Instead of saying anything to me, he pounced on Zack and Spader in a tone that sounded half furious and half scared to death. "What are you guys doing about this?"

"We're working on it," said Spader.

"How?"

"Nick, it happened minutes before you came home," said Zack. "Detective Spader already has people trying to trace the phone."

As if on cue, Spader's phone chimed an incoming text. He glanced at the screen, then set the phone back on the table. "Another burner. Not the same one used the other day."

Nick scowled. "Not helpful." One by one, his gaze speared each of us. "Now what?"

The million-dollar question and one for which none of us had an answer. "We continue trying to figure out who he is," I said.

"And if you don't?"

"We will," said Spader. "And I promise, we'll keep your mom safe."

Short of taking me into protective custody, I didn't see how Detective Spader would keep that promise, but I wasn't about to worry Nick even further.

Zack offered him more assurance. "First thing we do is contact Gloria for permission to hide cameras with silent alarms in the garden. The next time the creep sets foot on the property, we'll catch him red-handed."

Spader shook his head. "Best not to alert her. Given the situation, I won't have any trouble getting a judge to sign off on a surveillance request."

"Won't the alarm go off each time anyone enters the garden?" I asked. "We can't have the police rushing over here every ten minutes."

"We'll set it up so that it only notifies Detective Spader," said Zack. "Once he checks the app, he'll determine if action needs to be taken."

I glanced at Spader. He concurred with a dip of his head.

"You think there's going to be another murder?" Nick asked Zack.

"I think it's a strong possibility."

Nick turned to me, then Spader. We both nodded in agreement, with Spader adding a grimace. "Looks like we might have a serial killer on our hands, after all."

Which meant, we wouldn't have long to wait before the next body appeared in the garden.

FOURTEEN

New Jersey has seen its share of serial killers over the years. Mama had a classmate killed by one of the most notorious of the lot.

Robert Zarinsky had targeted young girls in a killing spree beginning in the late sixties and lasting for several years, but it took more than fifty years before forensics advanced enough to convict him. He died in prison, having been found guilty of one murder, indicted for another, and suspected in the deaths of at least two more young girls. There may have been many more.

Part of me was relieved Mama wasn't here for this discussion. My mother likes to project an aura of someone in control of her life, even if, like Blanche Dubois, she relies on the kindness of others. Especially, one specific *other* with a guilty conscience over introducing her to Lawrence Tuttenauer.

I know for a fact, though, that Mama has never gotten over her friend's horrible death. I worried that any mention of serial killers might dredge up that awful time in her life.

However, the other part of me still worried about the mystery man currently wining and dining her. "Is Mama still at the restaurant?" I asked Zack.

"Last time I checked." He glanced at his phone. "Which was less than ten minutes ago."

"Check again." When Zack cocked his head and raised an eyebrow, I added, "Humor me."

He tapped his phone. "She's still there."

I breathed a sigh of semi-relief. Full relief would occur only after Mama crossed the threshold into my house.

The What If Gremlins in my brain weren't buying the reassurance. *What if the mystery date had already killed Mama and dumped her body behind the restaurant?*

Zack broke into my thoughts. "You need to stop before you drive yourself and everyone else crazy."

I gaped at him. Had I spoken those thoughts aloud? I glanced at Nick and Spader. All three stared at me. I guess that answered my question. "But—"

Zack took both of my hands in his. "Take a deep breath."

Easy for him to say. But I complied with a long-drawn inhale and a slowly released exhale. Not that it worked. Much like the way meditation and yoga never work for me.

Instead, I tried banishing the brain gremlins by forcing my thoughts back to the prior topic of installing spy cameras in the garden. "Where would you hide cameras?"

"In the lights on the fountain," said Zack. "That will give us a three-hundred-sixty-degree view of the garden."

"But what if the killer is lurking in the area?" asked Nick. "Won't he see you installing the cameras?"

"I won't do the installation."

"Then who will?" I asked.

"I'm calling in a few favors."

"Ledbetter?"

"Ledbetter. He'll set it up as routine fountain maintenance."

Said the guy who claims he's not a spy. But I kept my mouth firmly shut. We needed to catch a killer before he struck again. I'd take all the help we could get.

Mama finally sashayed into the house as Detective Spader was about to leave. At least I knew her date had dropped her off directly from the restaurant. We'd watched the app map as they made their way down Central Avenue and turned onto our street.

If the gentleman had been a gentleman and escorted Mama to the door, she hadn't invited him in to meet us. No matter. Our security cameras would have captured his license plate, and Zack wasn't the only person in the family with connections in high tech spy places.

As reluctant as I was to call on his services, Tino Martinelli would do anything for me. If Zack or Spader didn't tap into their contacts to find out about this mystery man, I'd call Tino.

"Have a nice dinner?" I asked as Mama hung up her coat.

"It was lovely, dear. Thank you for asking." She then turned to Spader. "Good evening, Detective."

"Mrs. O'Keefe."

Catherine the Great had entered the foyer and began rubbing her luxurious white fur against Mama's legs. Mama stooped to pick her up, then announced, "If you'll all excuse us, I'll say goodnight. We both need our beauty rest."

Once Mama was out of earshot, Nick rolled his eyes and whispered, "Doesn't that cat sleep at least seventeen hours a day?"

"I doubt your grandmother's aware of that," I said. "She's always either out shopping or husband hunting."

But at least she'd made it back to the house this evening. Mama may be able to get her beauty rest tonight, but I suspected I wouldn't get another good night's sleep until this elusive killer was caught.

~*~

The next morning, I noticed an aqua blue truck parked across the street as I made my way through the living room toward the kitchen. The signage on the truck read:

Tueur

Custom Fountains and Irrigation

"Tueur?" I asked as I entered the kitchen. "Who came up with that name?"

"Beats me," said Zack as the toaster dinged and the slices popped up. He placed the toast on two plates, added two over-easy eggs to each, and handed me both plates. "Does it matter?"

I placed the plates on the island. "How rusty is your French?"

Zack thought for a moment before the lightbulb in his brain flashed on. "Tueur translates to killer in French."

"Quite the double entendre. Let's hope our killer isn't fluent in French. Someone's idea of a joke could tip our hand."

He shrugged. "Too late now. Hopefully our killer is sleeping in this morning. Those tech guys should be gone shortly."

I poured myself a cup of coffee and topped off Zack's cup before taking a seat. With Mama and Nick still in the middle of forty winks, we had the kitchen to ourselves.

Zack grabbed a bowl of fruit salad from the fridge and joined me. After taking a sip of coffee, I asked, "How did Ledbetter pull this off so quickly? Did someone spend all night painting graphics on a truck, or is that one of their standard spy vehicles?"

He winked. "I'm guessing the latter, but the graphics are probably the shrink wrap type. You'd be surprised what those guys have in their James Bond arsenal."

"Maybe I should ask Ledbetter for a private tour. I'm assuming you've already had one?"

"Part of Bring Your Ex-Cousin-in-Law to Work Day."

"Cute."

Before we'd finished breakfast, both Zack and I received a text from Detective Spader: *Installed and tested. We're good to go.*

Sure enough, as Zack and I crossed the living room on our way to shower and dress, we noticed the Tueur truck had departed. If the killer returned to dump another body, the Union County Homicide division would catch him in the act.

~*~

Spader had arranged for stakeouts on both our street and the street where the killer had parked in the driveway of the McMansion to access the garden through the arborvitae trees. As soon as he entered the garden and triggered the silent alarm, Spader would give the go-ahead for the SWAT team to move in.

Patience has never been one of my virtues. When the gods were handing out patience, I was too impatient to wait in line. Knowing this about me, Zack suggested we take Nick and Mama out to dinner Saturday night, rather than have me sit around chomping my nails down to my knuckles.

The sun had set by the time we left the house for our six-thirty dinner reservation in downtown Westfield. Summer was behind us, and Indian Summer had never made an appearance this year. October was nearly half gone with each day shorter than the previous one. In less than three weeks we'd turn back the clocks.

The temperature had dipped, and the wind had picked up enough to require winter coats. No moon and full cloud cover blocked the few stars normally visible in the suburban night sky. An inky blackness had already settled over the street, interrupted only by the lit fountain, a few porch lights, and several strings of flickering purple, green, and orange Halloween lights strung across several door frames and porch railings.

Silence accompanied the blackness of the street, broken only by the rhythmic splashing of water from the Barry Sumner Memorial Fountain. Even my mother was uncharacteristically quiet. Her only comment after stepping outside was, "Brr." She then hugged her arms to her chest and added, "Feels like we're in for an early winter."

As I made my way to the car, I glanced up and down the street. I saw no one, not even a lone dogwalker. Although I knew we were under the watchful eye of Union County's finest, strategically placed at either end of the block, a shiver still coursed up my spine.

I'll admit, I'm no fan of Halloween, not since, as a kid, I was pelted with raw eggs while out Trick or Treating one year. I'd successfully buried that traumatic memory for decades, assigning it to the deepest recesses of my cerebral cortex. It had lain dormant until the first murder on our street occurred this time last year, when suddenly, frightening ghouls moved from the stuff of fairy tales into reality.

Other neighborhood murders had since followed. Not all have occurred at the end of October, though. Only four of those so far, with a possible fifth if our killer dumped another body tonight. But who's counting?

By mutual agreement, we'd decided not to tell Mama about Operation Catch a Killer. With any luck, by the time we finished dinner and returned home, the perpetrator would be a guest of the county, cooling his heels in a jail cell while awaiting arraignment for what we anticipated would be at least three murders.

Were there more? Had the killer gone on a killing spree prior to the bodies in the garden? Knowing next to nothing about the man, we couldn't assume these murders were his first. What if he'd previously killed elsewhere, dumping bodies in another garden somewhere in the state. Was this his M.O.? Would he gain the moniker of The Garden Killer, a monster who planted bodies throughout the state? Or in multiple states?

As we drove down Central Avenue toward the restaurant, I pulled out my phone and shot Detective Spader a quick text: *Have you ever investigated whether there've been other bodies dumped in public gardens around the state? Or in other states?*

He immediately responded with a thumbs-up emoji. However, that didn't mean our killer hadn't killed prior to this recent spate of murders. I'd learned enough about serial killers to know that they're creatures of habit. They have patterns. Although sometimes those patterns change. Or the true pattern doesn't emerge until substantially more murders occur.

I wasn't the only passenger lost in thought. Or screens. The only sounds coming from the back seat were digitally generated. I twisted around to find both Nick and Mama buried in their phones. Given the cacophony of sounds, Mama appeared to be texting with someone, while Nick's phone emitted the telltale sounds of a battle to save the planet from some alien invasion. Neither noticed me staring at them.

I turned forward as Zack slowed for a red light. After coming to a stop, he reached over, placed his hand on my thigh, and turned toward me. With the interior of the car lit only by the dashboard and the streetlights, I noticed his brow had creased with concern. He silently mouthed, "Everything okay?"

I forced a smile and whispered, "One can only hope."

His brow crease grew deeper, but the light had changed from red to green. Zack took one more long look at me before facing forward and stepping on the gas. A minute later he nosed into a parking space on Broad Street, a few doors down from the restaurant.

We were entering the restaurant when a patrol car, with its lights flashing and siren blaring, sped down the street. By the time the maître d had seated us, several other law enforcement vehicles, both town and county, had followed. Sirens wailed from all directions, at first growing louder, then tapering off as they continued toward their destination.

My first thought was the killer had returned to the garden, but then I realized that all the vehicles had rocketed down the street heading east. Whatever had happened wasn't related to Operation Catch a Killer.

As we perused the menu, alerts began sounding, both on our phones, and those of the diners seated around us. A hush came over the room as everyone grabbed their cell phones and stared at their screens.

Several armed men had opened fire in a movie theater in Roselle Park. Initial reports indicated that there were an unknown number of dead and wounded. Authorities suspected terrorism.

"Is this ever going to stop?" asked Mama. Tears glistened in her eyes. I reached over and placed my hand over hers. Like most of us in the New York Metro area who had lived through 9/11, Mama had lost several friends and neighbors. She didn't need those memories resurfacing, especially while we dealt with a possible serial killer on the loose.

Even though a pall had settled over the room, an undercurrent of buzzing conversations eventually broke through the stupor and began to fill the air, most in hushed tones but occasionally peppered with a forceful political statement from some loudmouthed guy espousing a crazy conspiracy theory.

However, after decades, we'd all become so inured to such news, that even when it occurred in a neighboring community, people held the victims in their hearts but quickly went on with their lives.

Eventually, the sounds of silverware clattering on plates replaced the worrying conjectures whispered around us as people returned to their meals and their earlier conversations.

When our waiter appeared, Mama ordered a double bourbon instead of a glass of wine or an umbrella drink, a sure sign of her frayed nerves. Hopefully, we wouldn't have to carry her out of the restaurant.

Zack chose a bottle of Sauvignon Blanc for the two of us, and Nick settled on a glass of cold-pressed apple cider. After the waiter returned with our beverages, we placed our dinner orders, house salads and lobster tacos all around.

We were finishing our meal when everyone's phones once again began blowing up with alerts.

"A hoax!?!" Mama's eyes bugged out as she stared at her screen, and her voice squeaked into coloratura soprano range. Around us, others were experiencing similar reactions. "What kind of sick malcontent would do such a heinous thing?"

I scowled. "Given the world we live in? There aren't enough prisons to hold them all. We should be grateful it was only a hoax and not a mass casualty event."

"Well, of course, dear. I'm certainly glad no one was harmed. Or worse. But still...If this is someone's idea of a joke, it's not funny. The police should lock him up and throw away the key."

"They'd have to catch him first," said Zack.

Mama stared at him. "What do you mean?"

"It's possible this was a large-scale swatting incident that may have originated from some overseas hacker."

Swatting. Something else that had happened to me and my family a year ago. Adding yet another reason why I'm not fond of Halloween.

Days before the annual evening of candy extortion, someone had phoned in an anonymous tip to the police, regarding a hostage situation occurring in my home. The cops broke in with guns drawn. Mama had passed out.

At the time, Detective Spader had suggested the perpetrator was an online gamer, but as much as Nick enjoyed saving the universe from malicious space aliens, neither he nor Alex participated in online gaming. The true culprit had come as quite a shock to all of us—especially to my mother.

~*~

With all the excitement during dinner, we didn't arrive home until after nine o'clock. As we turned onto our street, I saw no unmarked car on the corner and no vehicles parked in front of either home at the end of the street.

I didn't mention anything to Zack until we'd entered the house, and Mama's bladder sent her running to the bathroom. At the same time, Nick grabbed Leonard's leash and headed out for the dog's final walk of the day.

"I didn't notice any unmarked cars parked on the street," I said. "Did you?"

"None."

"Do you think Spader caught the killer?"

"One way to find out." He shot Spader a text.

A minute later, his phone dinged a response: *"Had to abort. All units called to Roselle Park. Mass shooting at movie theater. Wound up a hoax. Probably overseas hacker. Still had to lock down scene and interview everyone to rule out homegrown prank. Long night ahead."* He signed off with a grimacing red-faced emoji, the one that's euphemistically spewing a slew of four-letter words.

After my first husband dropped dead in a Las Vegas casino nearly two years ago, I lost a lot more than financial security and gained far more than massive debt. Since learning of his duplicitous double life, I now view everyone and everything with an eye toward suspicious behavior and ulterior motives.

Rather than considering this a negative personality trait, I see it as my superpower, enabling me to deal with all the dead bodies that have piled up at my feet since Karl's demise.

That superpower never believed in coincidence when it came to murder. "I'm wondering if there's a connection between the swatting incident and the stakeout," I told Zack. "How likely is it a foreign hacker would target a movie theater in Roselle Park, New Jersey?"

"You think someone deliberately created a situation that would draw maximum police presence?"

"Don't you? What better way to drop another body in the garden without anyone noticing?"

"He'd still be captured on camera."

"He may not care, especially if he's disguised himself."

Zack pulled up our security app. "Nothing on our system, but we have a few blind spots."

"We don't have access to the cameras installed on the fountain?"

Zack shook his head. "Only Spader, as far as I know." He reached for my hand. "Time for a quick field trip."

Less than a minute after leaving the house, Zack and I stood over another dead body.

FIFTEEN

Once again, the victim was a man in his twenties or early thirties. Zack enabled the flashlight on his phone, giving us a better look at the body. We saw no discernable tattoos or piercings, emphasis on discernable. His entire body was covered, including half his face, which sported a hay-colored full beard and a cartoonish handlebar mustache with twirled waxed ends. A pair of aviator sunglasses perched on the bridge of his nose.

He wore black jeans and a black knit cap pulled low over his forehead and ears. Even though we couldn't see a point of entry or exit, I had little doubt that the removal of the cap would reveal the cause of death as a bullet to the back of his head.

Scowling white ghosts with flashing green LED eyes cavorted across a purple long-sleeved knit sweater trimmed in orange ribbing. Black leather gloves and a pair of black cowboy boots completed the ensemble.

He sat with his legs spread-eagle on the ground and his back propped against the post supporting the Little Free Library. A closer look revealed that he was secured to the wooden post by a belt, probably his own. The sweater covered his waist.

An orange plastic jack o' lantern nestled between his legs against his groin. A rolled piece of paper partially stuck out of the top of the jack o' lantern.

As curious as I was, I knew we'd have to wait until Spader arrived to view whatever message the killer had left this time. One thing was clear, though. With this third murder, New Jersey now officially had a new serial killer.

Zack snapped a photo of this latest victim and shot it off to Spader, adding a message: *Sorry to add to your evening's workload.*

A reply arrived within seconds: *On my way.* Followed by a second appearance of the red-faced, foul-mouthed emoji.

I had a feeling Spader wouldn't be the only one dealing with a long night. Having discovered the body, Zack and I would need to give statements.

At least I didn't have to get up early to go to work tomorrow. I could sleep in. Assuming I'd ever get to sleep tonight.

In the distance, I heard the rapidly approaching sirens of various law enforcement personnel. I knew the press would follow close behind, hoping for a breaking news scoop to lead off their eleven o'clock network broadcasts.

Luckily, Nick had returned with Leonard prior to the arrival of the descending hordes. When Zack and I told him about the third body, he took the news as if it were an everyday occurrence, which I suppose it had become.

"Can I run across the street to take a look?" he asked.

"Absolutely not!"

His growing acceptance of murder and his newly developed fascination with investigative techniques continued to bother me.

Nick was my baby, even if he was swiftly closing in on young adulthood.

By the time Zack and I had returned from across the street, Mama had fallen fast asleep, thanks to the double bourbon she'd ordered at dinner. At least, I assumed the snoring emanating from behind the bedroom door came from her and not Catherine the Great.

Mama had been known to sleep through the occasional New Jersey earthquake. With any luck, she wouldn't wake until mid-morning. By then, the street should have cleared of all press and law enforcement, but I'd still have to tell her that the killer had deposited another dead body in the garden across the street. I wasn't looking forward to that conversation.

Within minutes our street was a hive of activity as the police cordoned off the area and the press positioned themselves and their camera crews. Reporters shouted questions at plainclothes personnel as well as anyone in uniform or hazmat coveralls. The more law enforcement ignored them, the louder they shouted.

I stood at the living room windows, surreptitiously squinting through a slit between the blinds as the vibrating hum of equipment and voices penetrated the walls of my home. Both my son and my husband joined me until one aggressive reporter, annoyed with being ignored, turned her attention toward our house.

"She's spotted us," said Zack.

Sure enough, Darlene Jamison had spied us spying on the activity on the street. She and her cameraman now broke from the scrum and strode up the path to my front door.

Zack quickly doused the living room, foyer, and outside lights. He then opened the security app on his phone, and we watched as the cameraman switched on his lights and Darlene rang the doorbell. When no one answered, she resorted to several loud knocks.

In a voice that brooked no argument, Zack announced, "You're in violation of a trespassing order. Leave immediately."

"But I—"

"No comment. Now or ever."

We watched as Darlene glared at the front door and stewed for a few seconds. She finally gave up, turning on her heels and stamping back toward the other reporters. Her cameraman switched off his lights and followed her.

A moment later Zack's phone chimed an incoming text. "Spader. He asked that we wait up for him. Says he should wrap across the street within the next hour."

I shrugged. "Hardly matters how long he takes. I have a feeling Mr. Sandman already decided to bypass our house this evening."

Zack flipped on the outside light before we headed into the den. "Aren't you afraid other reporters will ring our doorbell?"

"I'm more concerned with Spader tripping in the dark and injuring himself."

I nodded. "Valid point."

We found Nick watching the Mets trounce the Giants in the third game of the League Championship Series. Zack and I joined him on the sofa. "At least someone is having a good night."

Leonard, ensconced under the coffee table, concurred with a loud doggie snort. Ralph flew into the room and took up position on Zack's shoulder. He proceeded to dip his beak into Zack's shirt pocket in search of a sunflower seed, too impatient to wait for his favorite human to offer one.

Zack kept one eye on the game, another on the live feed from the security app, offering a competing play-by-play of the events on the street.

Spader's optimistic timeframe came and went. As did the scheduled eleven o'clock news, but some of the more stalwart reporters hung around in hopes of a press conference.

When Detective Spader dashed their hopes by stating there'd be no official statement until sometime tomorrow morning, they hurled questions at him anyway. He ignored all of them and strode toward our front door. Zack rose and left the den.

Seconds later, as the game ended, he returned with the detective in tow. Spader stifled a yawn as he offered a nod of greeting, then glanced toward the television in time to see the broadcast cut to a commercial. "I could use a win tonight. Any chance they gave us one?"

Nick grinned. "Nine to two. We're now up two games to one."

"Best news I've heard all day."

I grabbed the remote and switched off the TV, then stood. "What can we offer you, Detective? Have you eaten this evening?"

He scrubbed his jaw where his five o'clock shadow had grown into a poorly manscaped stubble beard. The dark bags under his eyes now included carry-ons, and his suit contained enough wrinkles that if it were cotton instead of worsted wool, it would have qualified as seersucker. He sighed. "I think I had a cup of standard issue cop sludge around four o'clock."

"How about a sandwich?" I asked. "Or some scrambled eggs and toast?"

Spader placed his hand over his heart. "Mrs. Barnes, once again, I'm in your debt."

Zack chuckled. "It's completely self-serving, Sam."

Sam? Were Spader and Zack now on a first-name basis due to professional courtesy?

I chalked up another checkmark in the ever-growing column of reasons why I believed my husband really was a spy, no matter how many times he denied it. But I bit my tongue. This was neither the time nor the place.

Although, I had long-since concluded there may never be the right time and place for such an admission from him. Zack would say that's because my imagination had once again run amok. Still...I couldn't help but wonder...

Meanwhile, Spader glanced from Zack to me. "How so?"

"I don't want you keeling over from starvation," I said. "I've reached my dead body quota for the evening."

"Make that for a lifetime," added Zack.

"That, too," I agreed. Although, I hoped I hadn't tempted fate by saying so.

Once the four of us had entered the kitchen, Zack grabbed the makings of an omelet from the fridge while Nick popped two slices of bread into the toaster, and I started a pot of coffee.

"Hi-test or decaf?" I asked Spader, after he collapsed onto a stool at the island.

He let loose a huge yawn. "Better make it hi-test. Otherwise, I might fall asleep at the wheel on my way home."

While we waited for everything to cook and brew, I asked Spader, "What can you tell us?"

"Not much about our latest victim yet. We'll have to wait for the M.E. to examine the body. But the good news is that we've had a major breakthrough connecting Brad Jankowitz to our first two victims."

I handed Spader his coffee. "How?"

He first gulped down half the cup. "It was something you mentioned, Mrs. Barnes. About those tattoos possibly being connected to a cryptocurrency company."

"Were they?"

"Not exactly. But it got me thinking. Jankowitz had a background in computer tech. What if the guys who grabbed him weren't seeking revenge over one of his cons but for another reason.

"Like what?" asked Nick, settling onto the stool next to Spader.

"Suppose he'd double-crossed them in some way? Maybe they were originally partners and designed Jurnee as a legitimate travel app. Or he stole the idea from them?"

"Interesting." Zack set a plate of food in front of Spader. Then the two of us positioned ourselves across the island from him while he ate.

"Are you suggesting the dead guys are the guys who kidnapped Jankowitz?" I asked.

Spader nodded. "It's possible."

"But who killed them?" asked Nick. "Jankowitz is dead."

"A triple-cross," suggested Zack. "What if Jankowitz had a partner, and he's killing the guys who kidnapped Jankowitz and dumped his body in the Atlantic?"

"Wow," said Nick. "A tech-bro turf war among competing computer gangs?"

"Sounds like something tailormade for Hollywood," I said.

"But not beyond the realm of possibilities," said Zack.

"And a direction I'm now leaning," said Spader.

"You mentioned a major breakthrough," I reminded him. "This is all conjecture."

"Agreed," said Spader. "Our initial facial recognition searches turned up nothing. Neither victim was in the FBI's NGI system because they had no prior criminal records. We also struck out with a search of the NCIC missing persons database. No one has reported either man missing. At least not yet."

"Then how have you connected both men to Jankowitz?" I asked.

"Sometimes you get lucky, Mrs. Barnes. Today was one of those days. DeFrancisco, our tech guru, had a brainstorm this afternoon. Since we know Jankowitz graduated from UC Berkeley and all students have photo IDs, she started by contacting the university for permission to access their database."

"Without a subpoena?" asked Zack.

Spader shrugged. "It was a longshot but worth a try. The university balked, citing privacy issues. Instead, she began scouring the university website and various social media, concentrating on anything connected to the computer science department or Brad Jankowitz. She hit paydirt while we were dealing with the hoax in Roselle Park.

"Turns out, our first two victims are Jase Everett and Bryson McGraw. They both graduated the same year and with the same computer science major as Jankowitz. I'm betting we'll find our third victim was also a member of that graduating class."

"So we now have a connection between Jankowitz and at least two of the victims," said Zack. "Where do you go from there?"

"And how do the victims connect to the garden across the street?" I asked. "It still makes no sense that the killer is using the garden as his dumping ground. Why haven't the owners of the house that backs onto the garden or any of their neighbors noticed the killer lurking around?"

Spader shook his head. "We checked all available security systems on the street but found nothing suspicious. The owners of the house that backs onto the garden are on vacation."

"Wouldn't one of the neighbors' cameras catch someone pulling into their driveway?" asked Zack.

"You'd think. Except none of them show any activity at all at the property."

"Not even the mailman?" asked Nick.

"They probably have the post office holding their mail," I said, but a bigger question nagged at me. "Unless he's conjured up an invisibility cloak, how on earth did he manage to carry three dead men into the backyard without anyone seeing him or any neighbors' security cameras capturing him?"

Spader scowled. "That's the million-dollar question, Mrs. Barnes."

"You haven't mentioned the note in the jack o' lantern," I said. "What did it say?"

Spader grabbed his phone, tapped the screen a few times, then skimmed the phone across the island. Zack picked it up, and we both stared at the message written on the paper that had been stuck inside the jack o' lantern: *No treats. Only tricks.*

"What's it say?" asked Nick.

Zack turned the screen to show him. Nick furrowed his brow. "What does that even mean?"

An *uh-oh* feeling skittered up my spine. "It means he knew about the cameras installed on the fountain."

Spader nodded. "Appears so."

"Anastasia thinks the killer phoned in the mass shooting hoax to pull the stakeout away from the garden," said Zack.

"What if he's either got his own surveillance set up or remotely tapped into the security cameras on both streets?" I asked. "He knew when the coast was clear to dump the latest body."

"I came to the same conclusion," said Spader. "But tech isn't in my wheelhouse. I called in help to take a closer look at all the video you and the other neighbors shared with us."

"I suspect they'll find gaps in the recordings," said Zack. "Or he could have hacked into the various security companies rather than the individual systems."

"Already working on subpoenas," said Spader.

"You think he deleted himself from all the footage?" Nick whistled under his breath. "This guy sure has scary mad tech skills."

"Which might tie him to Jankowitz and give credence to Detective Spader's theory that the killer was his partner." I turned to Spader. "What now?"

He shoveled the remainder of his omelet into his mouth, then washed it down with a final swig of coffee. "We employ good old-fashioned detective work, Mrs. Barnes. We track down relatives and known associates of our victims. Now that we know who they are, we'll see what connections we unearth."

He yawned again as he awkwardly lumbered off the island stool. "Beginning tomorrow. Right now, I need to catch a few hours' sleep."

I hope he'd have more success grabbing forty winks than I anticipated getting tonight. Between worry over my mother's new relationship and a psycho serial killer dumping bodies across the street, my mind was stuffed to capacity. No matter how exhausted I was, I knew I'd have no success powering down my brain tonight.

SIXTEEN

After an anticipated sleepless night, I entered Sunday not only groggy but with no new insights about what had kept me tossing and turning all night. Mama, on the other hand, slept until mid-morning and woke refreshed from her extended beauty sleep.

I cornered her in her bedroom while she dressed. I didn't want to worry her further, but for her own protection, I needed to impress upon her the seriousness of the situation. Especially when it came to strangers. After mentioning the discovery of the third victim, I said, "Detective Spader uncovered a connection between all three victims and Brad Jankowitz."

She stared wide-eyed and slack-jawed for what seemed like a full minute before she finally spoke. "But this makes no sense on so many levels, Anastasia. I find it hard to wrap my head around it."

"You're not alone, Mama. Hopefully, now that Detective Spader has uncovered the identities of two of the victims, he'll make some headway into unmasking the killer."

"Well, he'd better." She sniffed her distain for any private investigator or member of law enforcement who couldn't wrap up a case within the forty-two to forty-four minutes allotted their primetime network brethren.

"What's taking him so long? It's obvious there's a serial killer on the loose, and whoever dumped that scammer's body in the ocean is also responsible for killing those three young men. Why hasn't that detective of yours set a trap to catch the culprit? What's he waiting for? An invitation? Another murder?"

I decided not to mention the trap that had gone awry last night. No sense adding fuel to her fire of scorn for crime fighters who didn't live up to her television fantasy of how law enforcement works. "Of course not, Mama."

"I should hope not."

Because I didn't want to get into a protracted debate on the competency of Detective Spader and the other members of the Union County Homicide Squad, I changed the subject. Mama was in the process of donning one of her classic Chanel tweed suits, this one in autumnal shades, the jacket edged in burnt umber suede piping with gold clasp closures. Hardly typical attire for relaxing around the house on a lazy Sunday. "Do you have plans for today?"

She offered me a catbird smile as she slipped into a pair of matching brown suede Ferragamo pumps. "As a matter of fact, I'm having lunch in the city, then attending a matinee."

"By yourself?"

"Of course not, dear. I'm going with a friend."

"Anyone I know?"

"No."

My Spidey senses began to tingle. "Male or female?"

Mama threw her hands onto her hips. "Really, Anastasia, I don't appreciate being interrogated."

"Then why are you being so secretive? Is this the mystery man you went to dinner with Thursday evening?"

"He's no mystery man. I know him quite well."

"Then why haven't you introduced me to him?"

"Because we're still getting to know each other."

It was now my turn to stare wide-eyed and slack-jawed at her. "Mama, you just told me you know him quite well. Which is it?"

"When I'm ready for you to meet him, I'll introduce him to you. For now, if you don't mind, I'd appreciate it if you'd stop treating me like you're my mother, and I'm a teenager caught sneaking out to meet the town bad boy. I'm a grown woman capable of carrying on a relationship with a member of the opposite sex without your permission."

"May I remind you, there's a killer on the loose?"

"And may I remind you, he's targeting young men. Last time I looked in the mirror, I was neither young nor male. You have nothing to worry about, dear."

"Mama, I'm not being nosey for the sake of being nosey, and under the circumstances, I can't help worrying. Would you at least tell me where you met this man?"

"Well, if you must know, you're responsible."

"I'm responsible for you meeting someone I don't know?"

"That's what I said, dear."

"I need more of an explanation than that."

Mama exhaled a huge huff of annoyance. "I suppose you're not going to stop bugging me until I tell you something."

"That's the plan."

"Really, Anastasia, you know how I feel about sarcasm. It's so unbecoming."

"And you know how I feel about stonewalling, Mama. So, spill."

She let loose another huff. "Fine. After nearly getting scammed by that awful miscreant who posed as Jeremy Dugan, I felt I'd better learn more about all these scams. As it turns out, the Scotch Plains Library offered a talk two weeks ago on how scam artists prey on the elderly. I attended.

"The presenter began by asking how many of us had either been scammed or knew of someone who was the victim of a scammer. I raised my hand and explained how I was recently targeted. When the talk ended, the presenter said he'd be interested in learning the details of what had happened to me. He invited me to join him at Starbucks for a cup of coffee."

"And?"

"And that's all you need to know."

I threw my arms up in defeat. "Fine, Mama. I hope you have an enjoyable afternoon with this man you know quite well that you're first getting to know. What show are you're attending?"

"I can't tell you that."

"Can't or won't?"

"Can't."

"You don't know what you're going to see?"

"It's supposed to be a surprise. Now if you don't mind, dear, I'd like to use the restroom, and I don't need an audience." She pushed me aside and sashayed from the bedroom toward the bathroom. Because Mama rarely just walks from Place A to Place B.

I stepped into the hall and stared at her departing back before storming through the house into the kitchen.

"What's going on with you and your mother?" asked Zack.

"You heard us?"

"Kind of hard not to, given the decibel levels."

He rose from the table where he was working the *New York Times* crossword puzzle and poured me a cup of coffee—my third and probably far from my last of the day. I'd need all the caffeine I could get to make it to bedtime without melting into a puddle of exhaustion. "Want to talk about it?"

I splashed some half and half into the cup and took a sip before giving him the details. When I finished, I asked, "I don't suppose anyone ever searched the license plate of the car that picked Mama up Thursday evening."

"She took an Uber to and from the restaurant."

I stared at my husband. "What favors did you call in to obtain that information?"

"None. I checked her phone after she returned while she was in the bathroom."

"You have her password?" Even I didn't have my mother's phone password.

"I reset all her passwords, remember?"

"Yes, but I didn't realize you'd kept copies. Clever. Maybe I haven't given Mama enough credit for being cautious when it comes to new relationships."

However, it wasn't only her relationships with the opposite sex that worried me. Mama had also experienced her own brushes with death due to my confrontations with the seamier side of humanity. Part of my worry stemmed from guilt and the fear that history might repeat itself. Because it often did.

"Given her recent past experiences," continued Zack, "Flora should be commended."

"And not castigated?" I sighed while frowning into my mug. "You're right. Looks like I owe her an apology."

He cocked his head and quirked his mouth, his expression once again reminding me of his uncanny resemblance to an amalgam of George Clooney, Pierce Brosnan, and Patrick Dempsey. "Couldn't hurt."

Still, I was glad Zack had hidden that tracker in her purse. I knew my brain wouldn't stop conjuring up all sorts of frightful scenarios until my mother returned from the city and stepped across the threshold into my home.

After Mama departed for her date in the city, I pulled out my phone and logged onto the Scotch Plains Library website. According to the monthly events schedule, the talk had been delivered by Franklin Bond.

His bio claimed he was a retired professor of economics at Rutgers University and the author of several bestselling books on finance and money matters. In addition, he was a regular on the lecture circuit and had appeared on various morning shows and cable news networks.

I could see why Mama had set her sights on him. The guy looked like a cross between Paul Newman and Harrison Ford.

However, in the age of A.I. and with the proliferation of hackers and scammers, how did I know all the information about him wasn't fake? I embarked on a headfirst dive down the Internet rabbit hole to cross-check every cited source.

I was on YouTube, watching an MSNBC clip of Bond appearing on *Morning Joe*, when Zack leaned over my shoulder and whispered in my ear. "I think you can stop worrying."

Could I, though? Although I hadn't found any obvious red flags, and the guy came across as completely legit, the knot in my stomach refused to loosen even a smidgen.

~*~

After completing various household chores, then breaking for lunch, Zack and I retreated to the apartment above the detached garage that now served as our joint workspace. With Nick working the afternoon shift at Trader Joe's, Leonard accompanied us, settling into one corner of the sofa and immediately falling asleep.

Zack released Ralph, who circled the room once before alighting on his perch near his favorite human's desk. I sank into the opposite end of the sofa, my laptop balanced on my thighs, while Zack took the seat in front of the giant monitor at his workstation.

Even though it was Sunday, deadlines loomed for both of us. Besides, outside foreboding slate-gray clouds filled the sky, and a cold wind whipped the fallen leaves into swirling gold and brown miniature tornadoes. Not exactly conducive weather for raking leaves, strolling around an October town fair, or even taking a brisk walk beyond satisfying Leonard's potty needs.

Technically, I was supposed to be working on the next book in the *American Woman Through the Decades* series, which didn't include anything crime related. However, I found it difficult to focus on crafts while my brain cells ping-ponged between worrying about my mother and a killer on the loose. Since I couldn't do anything about my mother, I stared at a blank page as I mulled over the additional information we'd learned from Detective Spader last night.

If I created a suspect board, complete with red yarn, could I convince Zack it was a crafts project for an upcoming *American Woman* issue? I glanced across the room to where my husband was working on sorting through photographs for a *National Geographic* feature.

No, I quickly dismissed the idea. Whether Zack worked for one of the alphabet agencies or not, the man would see right through me.

Instead, I created a timeline of the events that had transpired since the day Brad Jankowitz stepped foot into our home. Under each day, I made a bullet-point list of the significant events that had occurred that day. When I finished, I stared at the results.

Only a little more than three weeks had gone by, setting off a chain of events and a trail of dead bodies. Would there be more victims?

Detective Spader had now given up on his theory that the murders somehow related to Barry Sumner and the men who had blackmailed his wife for years. I couldn't disagree.

The first two victims and Jankowitz had attended the same university at the same time in the same department. Both of those victims had matching tattoos on their upper thigh in their groin area. Did the third victim sport the same tattoo? And what about Jankowitz?

I checked the time. Even if Spader had gotten all forty of his winks last night, he was surely awake and working by now—because Spader is always working. And by now he'd most likely received a preliminary report on the third victim from the M.E.

I shot him a text: *Did the third victim also attend UC Berkeley? Did he sport the same unique tattoo on his groin?*

He immediately replied with two thumbs-up emojis.

Do we know if Jankowitz also had that tattoo?

I watched impatiently as the three moving dots in my text app signaled typing. Finally, a message popped up: *Today, when I learned the third victim had the same tattoo, I contacted the FBI. They did a strip search of Jankowitz when they booked him. Same tattoo. Same location.*

This was yet more evidence linking all four men. As I sat processing this new information, another text from Spader came in: *I can hear the wheels spinning in your brain.*

I sent him a laughing emoji, adding: *Is that cop ESP, or do you have a mini drone masquerading as a horsefly and peeping through my office window?*

I don't have the budget for mini horsefly drones. What are you thinking?

Not sure yet but one final question. Any word on what the tattoo represents?

Negative so far. Turns out there's no universal registration requirement for cryptocurrency. I've got someone continuing to search.

I gave Zack the news. He stepped away from his desk and joined me on the sofa, where he proceeded to study my laptop screen. "I know detective shows were big in the seventies, Sweetheart, but I don't see how you're going to tie fraud and murder into a craft project."

From his perch, Ralph squawked once before stating, "*Murder cannot be hid long. Merchant of Venice.* Act Two, Scene Two." He then took flight and landed on Zack's shoulder.

Zack rewarded him with a sunflower seed, but I scowled at the African Grey. "Nothing like a buzzkill bird smacking us with the reality of the situation."

"In Ralph's defense," said Zack, "Shakespeare probably didn't write many comedies where he mentioned murder."

"Probably not. Anyway, I take it you don't think crafters will want to decorate their walls with suspect boards?"

"Only the ones into true crime or conspiracy theories, but they probably already have all their walls plastered with suspect boards."

"Maybe I could convince them it's time for a decorating refresh. A suspect board spruce up. There's only one problem."

Zack raised an eyebrow. "Only one?"

"I don't think crime boards were a trope in seventies detective shows. Of course, my knowledge is based entirely on the few cable TV reruns I've watched of *Columbo* and *The Rockford Files.*"

He pointed to my keyboard. "One way to find out."

I asked Google. The oracle confirmed my suspicion and went on to state that shows of that era were more character-driven and less focused on visual aids.

"So, no suspect boards?" said Zack.

"I guess not."

Zack returned Ralph to his perch and settled back at his desk. I continued focusing on the timeline I'd created. As I stared at the events that had unfolded over the last three weeks, a thought began to form in my brain. The more I stared, the more the thought congealed.

Was it possible? My gut agreed with the idea now ricocheting around in my brain. I gasped.

Zack jumped out of his chair and was by my side in three long strides. "What's wrong?"

I continued to gape at my computer screen. "I think we've gotten it all wrong."

"Gotten what all wrong?"

"The murders. If I'm right, I know who committed them."

SEVENTEEN

"Explain," said Zack.

"We've all been operating under the assumption that Brad Jankowitz was kidnapped and murdered, probably because he picked the wrong person to scam. Likely some Mafia Nonna. Or maybe it had something to do with a drug turf war."

Zack nodded. "Either could explain a body dump in international waters."

"Except, we have no proof Jankowitz was murdered and his body dumped somewhere in the Atlantic. All we have is one video surveillance where he's being dragged out of his McLaren, restrained, then tossed into the back of the panel truck. A few minutes later, a second video surveillance camera at the docks shows him being forcibly dragged from the panel truck onto a boat."

"All evidence pointed to a kidnapping."

"Right, and it's certainly logical for the FBI to draw that conclusion, especially since they found no evidence of the boat ever returning."

"Are you suggesting the boat docked somewhere they didn't look?"

I shook my head. "No, I think the FBI was correct in assuming that another boat rendezvoused with them somewhere in the Atlantic and brought the kidnappers back to shore. I also agree that they scuttled the first boat to destroy evidence."

"But?"

"I don't think the second boat only brought back the kidnappers and the pilot of the first boat."

"Jankowitz?"

"Exactly. What if he wasn't kidnapped?"

"You're thinking he orchestrated a rescue to look like a kidnapping."

"I am. I also think the drivers of the panel truck, SUV, motorcycle, and both boat pilots weren't simply hired thugs. I think those men are his partners in the scamming operation. I also believe three of them are the dead guys who turned up in the garden across the street."

Zack thought about this for a moment. "We now know there's a definite connection between the first three victims and Jankowitz."

I ticked off the various threads that tied the five men together. "Close in age. Same major. At least three attended UC Berkeley. Most importantly, identical unique tattoos. Didn't Ledbetter say he believed Jankowitz was tied to similar scams across the country?"

"He did."

"Ledbetter thought Jankowitz was hopscotching across the country, but what if each of those guys had his own territory? Six men scattered across the lower forty-eight. Northeast, Southeast, Midwest, Southwest, Northwest, and California. Each pulling off similar scams in different cities, never two at the same time, and all choreographed to make it appear the crimes were being committed by one person."

"With each person immediately taking off for another city before the mark even knew she'd been scammed."

"When Jankowitz was arrested, I doubt he placed his one phone call to his lawyer. If I'm right, he called one of the partners who notified the others."

"You're suggesting they had a pact."

"Makes sense, doesn't it? They all flew into New Jersey to execute a prearranged rescue once Jankowitz was released on bail. No matter who was in trouble, the others would come to his rescue. Afterwards, it would be back to business as usually once they all assumed new identities. For all we know, this wasn't the first time they pulled off a rescue of one of the partners."

"Then why would Jankowitz all of a sudden start systematically eliminating the others?"

"Something within the group dynamic changed. Maybe he grew paranoid and thought the others were plotting to get rid of him."

Zack scrubbed his jaw. "Someone who thinks everyone is out to get him will quickly turn on the others to strike them before they have a chance to strike him."

"Exactly. Survival of the fittest. Kill or be killed. Then again, it could be as simple as a greedy man no longer wanting to share the fruits of their ill-gotten gains. What better way to divert suspicion from yourself than to make sure the authorities already believe you're dead?"

Zack shook his head.

"What? You don't believe me? It makes perfect sense."

"Oh, I believe you."

"Then what?"

"I'm not sure whether to worry about what goes on inside your head or be in awe of how your brain works. You don't think outside the box, Sweetheart. You've kicked that box to the curb."

Given the way Zack was staring at me, I wasn't sure that was a compliment. His brows knit together. "If you're right, you know what that means."

"He's not finished. We can expect two more dead bodies showing up in the garden across the street."

"Besides that."

I thought for a moment. Then it hit me. If Jankowitz was alive and eliminating all witnesses, my family and I were on his hit list.

Zack had pulled out his phone and begun furiously texting. After he hit *Send*, I asked, "Ledbetter and Spader?"

"Ledbetter and Spader."

~*~

I don't know exactly what Zack had texted, but both Spader and Ledbetter showed up at the house a short time later. After the four of us gathered around the dining room table, Zack first spoke to Ledbetter. "Anastasia has a credible new theory that pretty much upends your conclusion about the night Jankowitz was kidnapped."

Before Ledbetter could respond, Zack turned to Spader and added, "As well as your murder investigation."

Both men immediately turned their attention toward me, and I reiterated what I'd earlier told Zack. Neither spoke for a long moment after I finished laying out my theory, but their facial features told me they were giving serious consideration to my words.

Ledbetter was the first to break the silence. "If Jankowitz is alive, he's a mastermind of epic proportion. He'd need multiple skill sets, huge sums of money, and plenty of dedicated manpower to pull off what you're suggesting, Anastasia. We're talking about one man and a millennial at that. He might possess a high IQ, but he's no Lex Luthor. My limited interaction with him makes me highly skeptical he's capable of pulling off something this complex."

Zack stood up for me. "I don't know, Al. It's not beyond the realm of possibility."

Ledbetter grew thoughtful before nodding. "I'll give you that. Farfetched and highly improbable but possible."

"Still," said Spader, "like our other theories, it's all conjecture. Where's the proof? I'll grant you that it's likely all four men knew each other and possibly quite well, given those tattoos. Or not. UC Berkeley is a huge campus. We checked. The computer sciences programs graduate close to a thousand students a year. For all we know, those tattoos were a frat party stunt after a night of too many keggers. Maybe the B stands for beer."

When both men stared at me, I admitted, "I have no proof."

Ledbetter held out his arms, palms up. "Well, there you have it."

"But I know how to get the proof," I added.

Spader and Ledbetter executed simultaneous double-takes as they refocused their attention on me. "How?" asked Spader.

"Dory. If I'm correct, and Brad Jankowitz is alive, Dory interacted with him."

"Who's Dory?" asked Ledbetter.

Spader explained how we'd traced the purchase of the dictionary found on the lap of the first murder victim to the ShopRite bagger.

"Great!" Ledbetter pulled out his phone. "Text me her address. I'll pay her a visit this afternoon."

I held up my hand. "Not so fast. I'll do it."

Ledbetter scowled. "I appreciate the offer, Mrs. Barnes, but until you accept my invitation and complete training at Quantico, you'll have to leave the real FBI work to me and my team."

"Anastasia is right," said Spader. "She needs to contact Dory. By herself." Ledbetter opened his mouth to protest, but before he could utter a single syllable, Spader explained why. Ledbetter quickly backed down.

I'd learned the organization which had placed Dory at ShopRite didn't allow any of the young men or women in the program to work evenings or weekends. I knew I wouldn't find her bagging at the end of one of the ShopRite checkout aisles this afternoon. Most likely, she was at her group home or with her family.

I didn't know Dory's last name, the location of the group home, or her parents' address. However, I knew someone who could help. I place a call to ShopRite, setting the phone on speaker to allow Ledbetter and Spader access to both ends of the conversation.

As luck would have it, Gene Hoffnagel answered the office phone. After explaining my reason for calling, he at first hesitated to provide any of Dory's private information.

"I understood your reluctance, Gene, but Dory may be in danger."

"How? All she did was purchase a book for the guy. He never did anything inappropriate, and he certainly didn't try to lure her into his van. Besides, she only saw him that one time."

"Are you sure?"

"Absolutely. Dory is incapable of lying."

When I'd first contacted Gene Hoffnagel, at Detective Spader's request, I'd kept details to the barest minimum. I had never mentioned murder. I only asked to show Dory a few photos to see if she recognized any of the men. I didn't want to mention murder now and risk spooking the manager into refusing to cooperate.

"I only need her to look at one more photo and tell me if it's the man she called Mr. Johnny."

"I don't know. I'd like to help you, Anastasia, but what you're asking sounds to me like a violation of workplace privacy laws. I should probably speak to someone in corporate first, but given that it's a Sunday, I don't see that happening."

I sighed. "Gene, I'm currently sitting at my dining room table with both an FBI Special Agent and a Union County detective. I've convinced them I should be the one to speak with Dory. She knows and trusts me. But if you refuse to help, they'll just get a subpoena and show up at her door. You know how that's going to freak her out."

He quickly changed his mind. "Not without her parents' permission. Give me a few minutes. I'll get back to you."

I thanked him and disconnected the call. "I guess now we wait."

Ledbetter checked his smartwatch. "I'll give him fifteen minutes. We need to know if we're dealing with Jankowitz before he strikes again."

A killer who targeted twenty-something young men was scary enough. If I was right, and Jankowitz was behind the murder spree, I feared he had an even more lethal agenda than some random nut job with a gun and a grudge. He had a purpose, a plan, and the skills to succeed.

Gene called back in less than five minutes. "She's at her parents' home. They agreed to you stopping by to show Dory the photo, but they insist on being present."

Spader hadn't objected to Gene being present when I first met with Dory, but I had no idea how Ledbetter would react. However, when I glanced in his direction, he nodded. "That won't be a problem, Gene."

He then rattled off the address.

"I want you wearing a wire," said Ledbetter once I ended the call. "I'll have a team stationed near the house."

I had expected as much.

~*~

Less than an hour later, I stood on the wide front porch of the Belcourt home, one of the original northside Victorians which had survived the massive 1874 fire that decimated much of Westfield's downtown area. After greeting me at the door, Mr. Belcourt, a trim, cleanshaven man in his early fifties, led me down the hall to a modern kitchen bathed in sunlight.

I found Mrs. Belcourt and Dory working a simple jigsaw puzzle at a round clawfoot oak pedestal table, the one nod in the room to the home's past. Mrs. Belcourt was an older version of her daughter, although a little pudgier with gray streaks throughout her brown ponytail and minus the extra chromosome that gave Dory her unique features.

Dory showed no sign of surprise when she saw me enter the kitchen behind her father. Instead, her face broke out in a huge smile, and she waved wildly. "Hi, Miss Ana! We baked chocolate chip cookies. Would you like some?"

"Have a seat," said her mother. She rose from the table. "I made a fresh pot of coffee. Would you like a cup?"

"Thank you. I'd love a cup of coffee with one of Dory's cookies."

"Cream? Sugar?"

"Just cream, please."

Mr. Belcourt grabbed a plate of cookies from the island and offered me one before settling into a chair next to his daughter. Mrs. Belcourt returned with a mug of steaming coffee that she placed in front of me before returning to her seat on the other side of her daughter.

Dory watched with bated breath as I bit into the cookie. "Oh, Dory, this is delicious. Where did you learn to bake such yummy cookies?"

She beamed first at me, then her mother. "Mommy taught me."

"She taught you quite well." I took another bite. "Chocolate chip cookies are my favorite, and this is one of the best I've ever eaten."

The praise excited Dory to the point that she nearly jumped out of her seat. "Really, Miss Ana?"

"Really, Dory."

We continued making small talk while munching on cookies and drinking coffee. Or in Dory's case, using a straw to sip a glass of milk.

Eventually, Mrs. Belcourt turned the conversation to why I had arrived. "Dory, do you remember when you told us Miss Ana visited you at work?"

Dory's face glowed. "The day I met Mr. Johnny! He was so handsome."

A shadow passed across the faces of both her parents. I'm sure they hadn't been happy to learn a man had approached their daughter during her lunch break. Worse yet, they now knew law enforcement was trying to track him down.

I took the opening as my cue. "Dory, would you mind looking at one more photo for me?"

Her head bobbed up and down. "Sure, Miss Ana. I like helping you."

"Thank you, Dory. I really appreciate that."

I pulled up Jankowitz's booking photo, which I'd earlier cropped and altered to remove any indications that it was more than a picture of a twenty-something man.

Without saying a word, I handed my phone across the table to Dory. Her eyes took on a dreamy fangirl quality. "That's Mr. Johnny!"

EIGHTEEN

Dory's father placed his hand on his daughter's shoulder as he stared at the image on the screen. "Are you sure, Dory?"

"Sure, I'm sure, Daddy." She exuded sheer joy as she passed the phone to her mother. "See, Mommy? I told you Mr. Johnny was handsome."

"Yes, he's very handsome, dear." Mrs. Belcourt couldn't suppress a shudder as she took the phone from her daughter's hand and returned it to me.

"Thank you, Dory. You've been a really big help."

Mr. Belcourt rose. "Dory, it's nearly time for your movie. Say goodbye to Miss Ana."

"Could Miss Ana stay and watch the movie with us?" She turned to me. "We're watching *Finding Dory*. It's my favorite movie because the fish has the same name as me."

"Thank you for the invitation, Dory. Maybe another time. I have to get home to help Mr. Zack prepare dinner."

"Mr. Zack is very handsome, too," she told her parents. "Like Mr. Johnny. And Daddy. Don't you think my Daddy is handsome, Miss Ana?"

I smiled at Mr. Belcourt. "Yes, Dory. Your daddy is very handsome."

"Unfortunately, it's time for Miss Ana to leave." Her mother reminded Dory again to say goodbye, then added, "And you need to wash your hands before we watch the movie, Dory."

"Okay. Bye, Miss Ana."

As Dory raced to the powder room, her parents walked me to the front door. "Exactly what's going on with that guy?" asked Mr. Belcourt.

"Should we be worried for Dory's safety?" added his wife.

Being a parent, I knew how they'd react if she recognized the photo, even without knowing all the details. Spader, Ledbetter, and I had discussed how I should respond.

"I hope not, but I can't give you any guarantees. I was assured that someone in law enforcement will contact you later today to provide further information."

"Gene said both the FBI and the county police are involved," said Mrs. Belcourt. "What's really going on? Does this have anything to do with those bodies showing up across town?"

I had hoped they wouldn't connect that dot, but I couldn't lie to them. "It's possible."

Mrs. Belcourt gasped, and her eyes welled with tears. Her husband drew her into his arms. "They'll keep Dory safe," he said. Then he zeroed in at me over his wife's head and mouthed, "They'd better."

I certainly hoped so because I was just as worried for my own family's safety. And mine.

~*~

I returned home to find both Spader and Ledbetter still at the house. No surprise. I suspected they and Zack had spent the time strategizing next moves.

However, I didn't expect to find they'd called in a stringer. Yet, seeing Tino Martinelli typing away at his laptop shouldn't have surprised me.

The band had gotten back together: County Homicide, FBI, Homeland Security, and whatever alphabet agency Zack swore he didn't work for, all sat around my dining room table. Four men brought together by fate and a reluctant amateur sleuth lynchpin.

Tino, ex-Marine turned bodyguard turned Homeland Security cyber-sleuth exuded the quintessential Hollywood image of a Secret Service agent. Or a *Men in Black* cast member. However, being Sunday, he'd traded in his bespoke black suit and white shirt for black jeans paired with a black crewneck sweater.

His aviator sunglasses were currently perched backwards over his buzz cut. I suspected that rather than a fashion statement, the Ray-Bans concealed the eyes in the back of his head.

Tino's gruff, all business exterior disguised a teddy bear with a heart of platinum. If there was one guy who could figure out how to track down Brad Jankowitz, Tino Martinelli was that guy. More importantly, he'd take a bullet for me or any member of my family. Although, I hoped it never came to that.

"Mrs. B!" Before I'd even had a chance to hang up my coat, Tino jumped up from the table, nearly toppling the dining room chair behind him, and strode across the living room toward the foyer. A moment later, I was wrapped in a suffocating bear hug.

Once Tino released me and I caught my breath, I craned my neck to look up at him. "Are you on the clock? Or is this an unauthorized, off-the-books freelance gig?"

In the past, Tino had been known to take shortcuts or compromise ethics in the name of the greater good, both of which could jeopardize not only his job security but his freedom.

He nodded toward Ledbetter. "Inter-agency cooperation. I'm on special assignment."

I glanced between Ledbetter in the dining room and Tino, standing beside me in the foyer. They wore matching stone-faced expressions. Did Tino's bosses know about this inter-agency special assignment? I checked Zack for some hint of what was really going on, but his expression also gave no clue.

Tino did what Tino wanted to do, and what Tino *always* wanted to do was to right wrongs and keep the people he cared most about safe. I decided not to press the subject.

Instead, I hung up my coat and purse. After detouring to the bathroom to remove the wire, I joined the men in the dining room. Since I assumed they'd monitored my conversation at the Belcourt home, I nodded toward Tino's laptop and asked, "Learn anything new while I was gone?"

Tino looked first to Ledbetter, who nodded, before answering me. "This guy knows what he's doing. He hacked into all the security cameras on the street backing up to the garden and copied day and evening footage from each, all showing no activity on the street. Each time he came or went, he looped in the appropriate footage to mask his movements."

"That explains why he hasn't appeared on anyone's surveillance."

"Exactly."

Spader grimaced. "But Tino discovered something our tech missed. The killer was lazy. He repeated the same day and night loops each time, not factoring in changing weather patterns or phases of the moon. When Tino cross-referenced the footage with weather and the lunar calendar, he immediately spotted the discrepancy."

I turned to Zack. "Did he also hack into our cameras?"

"No. I've been monitoring them closely ever since the paintball incident."

"The killer took the trouble to shoot paintballs at our cameras before he posed the first body in the garden. Yet, he's made no attempt to disable our cameras since then. I think it's obvious that Nick was right."

Tino lifted his head from his laptop screen, his brows forming a questioning V. "You've lost me, Mrs. B. Nick was right about what?"

Apparently, Zack, Spader, and Ledbetter hadn't briefed Tino thoroughly enough on everything that had transpired since the first murder. "For one thing, about the word the first victim pointed to in the dictionary placed on his lap."

"Which was?"

"Joker. Was it just some random word in the middle of the dictionary? Or as Nick suggested, did it have deeper meaning?"

Ralph, having remained silent perched atop the china cabinet, made his presence known. *"Well guess'd, believe me; for that was my meaning. Braack! Henry the Sixth, Part Three.* Act Four, Scene Five."

Tino eyed Ralph as he said, "Batman's nemesis."

"Exactly what Nick thought. He suggested this was the first move in a game of cat-and-mouse."

"With you as the mouse."

I nodded. "A random killer with that kind of skill wouldn't keep leaving bodies where they'd easily be discovered unless he wanted them discovered. And he'd have no reason to taunt me with cryptic notes unless the bodies, like the notes, were messages directed specifically at me. He wanted me to find each body."

"At first," said Spader, "we suspected the killer was somehow connected to the former owners of the house that stood on the lot where the garden is now."

"The weird lawnmower guy?"

"That's the one. The wife had paid off blackmailers to keep them from filing assault charges against her husband. Once the husband was murdered, she stopped paying out the blackmail."

I picked up the thread. "After we eliminated that theory, we thought the killer might be a true crime podcaster out to make a name for himself by proving he's better at solving murders than I am."

Tino's smirk illustrated his skepticism. "What would he do? Turn himself in?"

I matched his smirk with one of my own. "More likely by framing someone else for his crimes, but it seemed unlikely that some rando podcaster could pull off what our killer was doing."

I glanced from Zack to Spader to Ledbetter to Tino. "Everything points to Jankowitz. Especially now that Dory has confirmed he's alive. He probably blames me for his arrest."

"Why you specifically?" asked Tino. "Why not Zack?"

"Because when Mama thought Jankowitz was Melissa Dugan's grandson, she probably complained to him about how I'm constantly getting involved in murder investigations. You know how she is. She doesn't worry about Zack. He's only a world-renowned photojournalist."

All four men chuckled. Were they laughing at my sarcastic comment or because they knew otherwise?

Zack placed his hand on his heart. "*Only?* You cut me to the quick, Sweetheart."

"You haven't been responsible for attempts on Mama's life. I have."

Zack got that pensive look on his face that told me his brain cells had kicked into overdrive. He walked over to the dining room windows and stared outside at the waning daylight hours. We all silently watched him as the seconds ticked by. Finally, he asked, "Anyone happen to have an RF detector?"

"What's that?" I asked.

"Radio Frequency Detector," said Tino. "They find hidden devices by locating unauthorized radio signals."

"You mean bugs? Like hidden cameras and listening devices? You think he's hidden them somewhere outside?"

"I think it's worth checking out."

"But if he has, won't he see you searching for them?"

"He'll only see us walking Leonard."

Ledbetter removed his watch and handed it to Zack. "Never leave home without it."

I stared gape-mouthed at the watch that was so much more than a watch. "That's a bug detector?"

As Zack strapped it to his wrist, he said, "If I'm right, Jankowitz called in the mass shooting at the movie theater because he saw the cameras being installed on the fountain and the stakeout on both streets. I think he's been spying on us all along."

"What happens when you identify the bugs?" I asked. "If you remove or disable them, won't he immediately know?"

"I'll deal with that," said Tino.

"How?"

"By turning the tables on him and beating him at his own game. Except, I'll adjust for weather conditions and moon phases."

"That still won't tell us where he's hiding," I said. "We need to find him before he kills again. There are still two other people who aided in his escape."

He'd continued typing away at his laptop throughout the conversation. "Working on it, Mrs. B."

Tino Martinelli was a white hat hacker, someone with mad hacking skills who used his talents to thwart black hat hackers, the ones who hacked for purely evil purposes, whether to create chaos, produce ecological disasters, foment political upheaval, or like Brad Jankowitz, scam unsuspecting individuals for profit.

While Tino continued hacking, Zack clipped Leonard's leash to his collar. After donning coats, we set out on our bug hunt.

"Pretend this is just a doggie pee break," said Zack as we left the house. "Don't scan the area as we walk, and don't look up at anything. We're just going to let the detector do its thing."

"Do you have any idea where he would have hidden the bugs?"

"Since he seems to be a master of disguise, as well as a car thief, I'm guessing he posed as a tree trimmer or cable guy and mounted them on branches or utility poles. I wouldn't be surprised to learn a bucket truck was reported stolen recently."

"It's scary how brilliant he is, but he's got to have help, doesn't he? Yet, if I'm right, he's killing off the very people who helped him escape."

"Maybe not all of them," said Zack. "There are at least two remaining so far. They could be the ones who have stayed loyal to the cause. It's possible there was an attempted coup within the ranks, and he eliminated the ones who proved disloyal."

I didn't know if his words or the plummeting temperatures caused me to shiver. Perhaps a combination of both. However, we didn't have far to go before Leonard picked a tree to do his business, and Ledbetter's watch started vibrating.

We kept walking, though. At the end of the block, we turned west. We walked north for a block, then looped around several blocks before making our way back toward the street that backed the garden. Zack wanted to make certain we wouldn't raise suspicion by only walking the two blocks where we expected to find bugs. In total, the watch buzzed six times, at the corners and midway between each of the two blocks.

~*~

By the time we returned to the house, Nick had arrived home and camped out at the dining room table next to Tino. I hoped Tino wasn't giving him hacking lessons.

I had a secondary worry, though. Mama still hadn't returned to the house. I did the math in my head. Most Sunday matinees begin at three o'clock. Shows run anywhere from ninety minutes to three hours. Not knowing which show she attended, she may have only recently left the theater. And I suppose, she and her date might have decided to stay in the city for dinner.

I kept telling myself not to panic, but myself ignored me. Zack had gone into the mudroom to fill Leonard's food and water bowls. "Would you check the tracker to see if Mama's on her way back to the house?"

My emotions were probably written all over my face, because he took one look at me and pulled out his phone. "She's at her condo."

My inner worry wart wasn't satisfied. I pulled out my own phone and sent her a text: *Mama, will you be back in time to join us for dinner?*

She immediately responded: *Not tonight.*

That wasn't good enough for me. How did I know Mama was really texting me and not Jankowitz or someone working for him? What if at this moment, Mama lay unconscious on the floor—or worse—while her assailant ransacked her condo?

NINETEEN

Even though I knew I'd risk having the wrath of Flora Sudberry Periwinkle Ramirez Scoffield Goldberg O'Keefe Tuttnauer descend on me, I called my mother. She was not happy, as evidenced by the way she ignored her own rules of etiquette when she answered the phone. "Honestly, Anastasia, I'm not a teenager."

No, she was a sexagenarian. Emphasis on the first syllable. I forced a light tone into my voice. "I just called to say I hope you had an enjoyable day, Mama. I'm sorry if I interrupted your dinner."

"Thank you, dear. I did. Now if you don't mind, I'd like to get back to my even-more-enjoyable evening."

She hung up before I could say another word, but when it came to my mother, I could read between the double-entendre lines. I now felt the need to take a scrub brush to a particular image that had settled into my brain. At least this time, she was in her condo and not participating in a horizontal tango in my spare bedroom.

Unfortunately, that image is permanently tattooed on my cerebellum.

Even though my own sleuthing had turned up zilch in the way of red flags on Franklin Bond, I wasn't satisfied. I walked into the dining room and tapped Tino on the shoulder. "Any chance you can pause what you're doing for a quick cyber-detour?"

"What do you need, Mrs. B.?"

"Verification. I'm worried my mother is in jeopardy. She's with a man named Franklin Bond. He's supposedly—"

"Franklin Bond from Rutgers?"

I stared wide-eyed at Tino. "You know him?"

"He was my economics professor."

Small world. However, given recent events, I was taking no chances. I pulled up the Scotch Plains Library website, scrolled to the description of his talk, and showed Tino the man's photo. "This guy?"

"Yeah, that's him."

"You're sure?"

"Absolutely." He cocked his head and grinned. "Let me guess, Flora's husband hunting again?"

"Isn't she always?" asked Zack, returning to the dining room.

"Then, he's legit?" I asked. "I was worried that someone had used A.I. to tamper with his website and the various clips of him on morning TV and cable news."

Ledbetter grimaced. "A.I. is turning us all paranoid. With everything going on, your worries are justified, Anastasia."

"But you don't need to worry in this case," said Tino. "That's definitely Franklin Bond, and the dude is one hundred percent legit. He's also a great guy." Tino winked. "And I'm not just saying that because I got an A in his course. I hope it works out for your mom this time. She could do a lot worse."

"She's already done a lot worse," I reminded him.

Even though Tino assured us he'd made considerable progress toward tracking down Brad Jankowitz, he hadn't succeeded by the time Ledbetter told everyone to call it a night. "We'll get a fresh start in the morning."

Tino shook his head. "No can do, man. I won't sleep until I find this guy. If necessary, I'll crash on the couch for a few hours while some of the programs run."

"Take the spare bedroom," offered Zack. "Flora is spending the night at her apartment."

"Did you plant the false footage in Jankowitz's spy cameras?" I asked.

"Not yet. If he's keeping an eye on the street, he knows we're here." He nodded toward Spader and Ledbetter. "I'll wait until these guys leave. After walking out with them, I'll move my car and return by cutting through backyards."

Once the three men left the house, I ordered Nick to bed. "You have school tomorrow."

"I'm getting a better education from watching Tino."

"That's what I'm afraid of."

Nick turned pleading eyes toward Zack but only got, "Listen to your mother."

A beat later, Nick uttered the quintessential teenage, "Fine," as he reluctantly trudged to his bedroom.

Since I had to be up early for work in the morning, I headed for bed shortly after Tino arrived back in the house, but Zack and Ralph stayed up to keep him company.

~*~

The next morning, I found Tino still camped out at my dining room table, working the keyboard with one hand while consuming a hearty breakfast sandwich of egg, sausage patty, and cheese with his other hand. Nick sat mesmerized beside him, watching every keystroke as he made short work of his own breakfast.

Zack emerged from the kitchen with two plates, placing them on the opposite side of the table. After a good morning kiss, I followed him back into the kitchen. While he poured two cups of coffee, I asked, "Were you and Tino both up all night?"

"It was worth it. We're closing in."

I wondered if that was the royal *we*. "What was your role?"

"Moral support and keeping the caffeine flowing."

Twenty minutes later, Nick grabbed his backpack and headed off to school. I left for work shortly afterwards.

My prior experiences had proven nothing ever good comes from strangers waiting to waylay me in our lobby. Therefore, when I entered to find a young woman nervously pacing the reception area, I shot off a silent plea to the gods and goddesses of reluctant amateur sleuths: *Please don't let her be here for me.*

They responded with hysterical laughter as they rolled around in the clouds.

The woman took one look at me and hurried across the lobby. Closer inspection revealed bloodshot eyes and tear-stained cheeks. Her designer stonewashed blue jeans and Taylor Swift sweatshirt needed a date with a Maytag and a Tide pod. Her cinnamon shoulder length curls screamed bed head. When she spoke, her voice trembled. "You're Anastasia, aren't you?"

I hesitated to answer. As previously mentioned, bad things usually come from people accosting me in the lobby. She reached for one of my hands and grasped it between both of her. "I'm sorry to barge in like this, but I had no choice. You really need to listen to me before someone else gets killed."

That caught my attention. "Who are you?"

Her eyes furtively scanned the lobby, landing on the receptionist intently watching us. Out of the corner of my eye, I saw our security guard stepping from the elevator. When he saw me with the woman, he picked up his pace and headed toward us.

The woman's entire body trembled. Her eyes telegraphed fear. "Please, is there somewhere we can talk?"

I held up my hand to assure the guard I was in no danger—at least I hoped that was the case—then led her to the seating area across the lobby. We settled into two chairs. She sat on the edge of hers and knit her fingers into a double-fisted knot.

When she didn't speak, I repeated my question. "What's your name?"

She chewed her lower lip. "I...I'm too scared to tell you. I turned off Locations and the Find My feature on my phone. I didn't drive. I took three buses and the train, using cash. I slept on a bench last night on the station platform, then walked over here. But he...he still might know where I am."

"He?"

"Jankowitz. Brad Jankowitz. He's crazy."

I stood and reached out my hand to her. "Come with me."

She hesitated. "Where?"

"Upstairs. You look like you could use some food and coffee. Then we'll talk."

As I led her toward the bank of elevators, the guard called out to me. "Everything all right, Mrs. Barnes?"

"We're good. Thanks."

Once upstairs, I asked, "Do you need to use the restroom?"

She shook her head. "I used the one at the station when it opened."

I then led her into the break room where I found Cloris pouring a cup of coffee. Before she asked anything, I said, "This is Effrayée, hoping Cloris remembered enough of her high school French not to ask any questions.

When she smiled and asked, "Would you like a cup of coffee, Effrayée?" I knew she understood.

While Cloris poured two additional cups, I showed the young woman my phone screen and said, "I'm going to check to make sure our conference room is available." I didn't want her freaking out when she saw me tapping my phone. She nodded.

After Cloris handed us both cups of coffee, I opened the large bakery box on the table. Cloris had provided an assortment of mini croissants today. "Help yourself."

She filled a napkin with three. On the way to the conference room, she asked, "Why did you tell your friend my name was Effrayée?"

"Because you wouldn't tell me your name. It's French for *frightened*. That way, she knew not to ask any questions."

I locked the conference room door behind us. "Take a seat."

We settled into cattycorner chairs at the near end of the conference table. After she downed half her coffee and one of the croissants, I said, "Now, take your time, and start from the beginning."

Her hands still shook. She clasped both in a death grip around her coffee mug. "My name is Margy May."

"How do you know Brad Jankowitz, Margy?"

"I'm his...was...his girlfriend."

"Was?"

She nodded. "He doesn't know that yet. I'm afraid of what he might do if I break up with him. He's changed."

"How?"

"He's grown increasingly paranoid lately, ranting on the phone about how he's not going to let anyone destroy what he built."

"Like me?" When she nodded, I asked, "Do you know his partners?"

She shook her head. "Just their names. They all live in different parts of the country. Everyone works remotely and travels a lot."

"Are Jase Everett and Bryson McGraw two of his partners?"

Her eyebrows shot up, and her jaw dropped. "You know them? How?"

When I told her, tears streamed down her face. "Dead? You think Brad killed them?"

"I do."

"I don't understand any of this. Brad was gone for several days and wouldn't say where he'd been, but he's been angry all the time lately. When he was home, he'd lock himself up with his computers for hours at a time. Go out at odd hours of the night. When I asked if everything was okay, he said I asked too many questions. He told me to shut up if I knew what's good for me. He'd never spoken to me like that before."

She inhaled a ragged breath. "A week ago, he said Jase flew in for a business meeting, and he was meeting him for dinner. He didn't return until three in the morning. I'd gone to bed, but I couldn't sleep. I watched as he pulled a gun from his waistband, stuck it in one of his boots, and placed the boots in the back of his closet."

"Did he know you were awake and watching him?"

"No, I pretended to be asleep. The next morning, it all seemed like a strange dream, but while he was in the shower, I looked in the closet. There was a gun in his boot. It totally freaked me out."

"What do you know about Brad's business, Margy?"

"Not much other than he's a computer genius with a knack for creating apps that make him and his partners a ton of money."

"Who besides Jase and Bryson?"

"Ryder Holden, Julien Sharpe, Gio Bianchi. They met during college through a gaming site for app developers."

"They all attended UC Berkeley?"

"I'm not sure. But after graduating, all six got together to form a company." Her brows knit together. "Do you think Brad plans to kill Ryder, Julien, and Gio?"

"He's already killed one other man. I don't know if the police have identified him yet. He may have plans to kill the other two, or they could be his accomplices."

Her lips started trembling again. "They were making a fortune working together. I don't understand why Brad would turn on them."

"Were you one of Brad's classmates?"

"No, I was at the local community college and worked parttime at a coffee shop near UC Berkeley. He was a regular, spending hours trying to figure out how to make it rich in tech. He wanted to create the next big thing that everyone had to have. That's what they all had in common." She frowned. "Then again, I suppose that's true of everyone in that field."

She took another sip of coffee. "Brad always flirted with me whenever he glanced up from his laptop. Eventually, he asked me out. One thing led to another, and we've been together ever since. Until now."

"Do you know where Brad is now?"

"Probably locked away in his computer lair."

"Does he know you're gone?"

"He may have seen me leave the apartment. He's got cameras everywhere. You wouldn't believe the massive computer setup he's got. A bank of dozens of computer screens that cover an entire wall, like something out of a spy or sci-fi movie. He's always monitoring them. That's why I took such extreme precautions to get here."

"How did you know about me?"

"I heard him yelling at someone over the phone. Said he's going to make you and your husband pay for all the trouble you've caused. He said some wannabe sleuth isn't going to kill his dreams.

I searched online for New Jersey amateur sleuths, and your name popped up. Then I read about bodies showing up on your street. I may not be a computer genius, but I can add two and two. I just didn't think he was killing his partners."

I opened the notes app on my phone. "What's the address of the apartment?"

She bit down on her lip. "What if he learns I ratted him out? If he's already killed three of his partners, he won't think twice about killing me."

"You give me that address, and he'll be locked away for the rest of his life."

She jumped out of her chair and began pacing the room. "What if you're wrong? What if the case against him gets dismissed on a technicality? Or the jury doesn't convict him?"

"That's not going to happen. He's killed three people and defrauded hundreds. Possibly thousands."

She stopped pacing. Her eyes bugged out. "Defrauded? How?"

"Through those apps he designs. Brad Jankowitz is wanted by the FBI for running a ring of scammers that prey on senior citizens. He steals their life's savings. That's how your computer genius boyfriend makes his money."

Her face showed shock and disbelief. "I...I...didn't know. I swear. Are you sure?"

"Positive."

"But he could still get off. It happens all the time."

"I know people who will protect you, Margy."

"I...I don't know." She continued pacing. I allowed her space to consider all that I'd said. Finally, she slumped into one of the conference chairs. "It's not just an apartment. He bought an entire building. The basement houses his computer setup and office, the top floor is our apartment. The other floors are empty."

"Where?"

"An industrial park near the docks on the border of Newark and Elizabeth." She then rattled off the address.

After typing the address into my phone, I noticed how Margy kept fighting to keep her eyes open. "You didn't get much sleep on that bench, did you?"

She stifled a yawn. "Hardly any. I was so scared Brad would find me, that I left without grabbing a heavy coat."

"Let's find you a place to take a nap while I make a few calls."

Panic overtook her. "Calls? Who to?"

"Relax, Margy. You're safe here. I'm calling the people who will protect you. You have my word."

She hugged her torso and took a few steps away from me. "Who are these people?"

"My friends. One is a county detective. The other is an FBI agent. You can trust them."

"I guess I have no choice, do I?"

"Of course, you have a choice. You can go back to the apartment and wait until it's raided."

She laughed. "Not the best of options. I'll take you up on that nap, but you have to promise me your friends won't tell Brad how they found him."

"You have my word. Besides, they may already know where he is and have made an arrest."

"How?"

"Brad might be a computer genius, but he's no match for someone else I know."

I led her to my supply closet and arranged some quilts and pillows on the floor for her. "Lock the door behind me. No one will disturb you."

As soon as I got back to my cubicle, I sent Zack, Spader, Ledbetter, and Tino a text.

"Everything okay?" asked Cloris, crossing the corridor from her cubicle to mine.

"It will be shortly."

"I suppose you can't say more than that."

"Not right now but you'll be the first to know as soon as I can. Meanwhile, our guest has a date with Mr. Sandman in our makeshift guest room. I'm running over to the deli to get her a decent meal."

"You mean you're running out for some craft supplies, right?"

"Isn't that what I said?"

"I'll cover for you."

My phone chimed an incoming text from Zack as I stepped into the elevator: *Tino succeeded. Ledbetter sending in a team.*

The elevator arrived on the ground level. When the doors opened, I stood face-to-face with Brad Jankowitz. And his gun.

"Where is she?" he demanded.

I stared down the barrel of a gun pointed at my head. Rather than my life flashing before my eyes, all I could think about was how I had a huge tell that flashed like a neon sign across my face whenever I told a lie. Yet, if ever I needed to harness my inner actress, this was the time.

I virtually crossed every digit as I locked eyes with Jankowitz. "She who?"

"Don't mess with me. You know who. Margy."

How had he discovered she came here looking for me? Had his mad hacking skills enabled him to observe every keystroke on her phone as she typed? I'd once seen that in a TV show, but was it even possible in real life? If so, he'd seen her search history. Turning off Locations and the Find My feature on her phone hadn't protected her. Or me. Or anyone else in the building. My coworkers were all sitting ducks.

Jankowitz had known exactly where to find Margy. He'd probably followed her from the comfort of his office the moment she fled the apartment yesterday. No doubt, he even knew she'd spent the night on a bench at the train station. Maybe he'd parked behind our office building and continued to track her until she'd entered the building before he made his move.

I stood my ground, not that I had an escape route. There was only one way out, and Jankowitz currently blocked it. I certainly wasn't about to back up and cower in the corner. I stood with my legs locked, planted in the middle of the elevator. Gritting my teeth, I glared daggers at him. "I don't know anyone named Margy."

The elevator doors began to close. Jankowitz repositioned himself at the elevator threshold to keep them open and waved the gun at me. "Out. Unless you want to die here. Your choice."

He'd already killed three people in cold blood. For all I knew, he'd killed more. No matter what, I couldn't let him see through my lies. Above all, I couldn't let him head upstairs.

I needed to buy time until the cavalry arrived. The moment Ledbetter discovered Jankowitz wasn't anywhere in his building, he'd know where to find him—assuming he'd read my text. But even if he hadn't, Zack, Spader, and Tino should be on their way.

However, no one would arrive anytime soon. Even with lights flashing, sirens blaring, the impossible unicorn of no traffic, and pedals to the metal, they'd still have to travel twenty miles to get from Westfield to our cornfield on the outskirts of Morristown. That took time.

I had no choice but to do as Jankowitz demanded. As I stepped in front of him to exit the elevator, he grabbed my left arm and yanked me into the lobby. Using my body as a shield and with the gun pressed against the back of my head, he marched me through the lobby toward the exit.

My steps faltered as I approached the reception area. Where were the receptionist and the security guard? Had Jankowitz killed them, too? I saw no evidence of a struggle, no pools of blood, no bodies. Only a strong, pungent odor that clung in the air surrounding the counter where they normally sat.

I sniffed. Odor is supposed to trigger memory. Even though on more than one occasion, I'd smelled the aftermath of a discharged gun, this smelled unfamiliar. Did different weapons and ammunition give off different odors when fired? Yet another hole in my database of criminal knowledge.

But if Jankowitz had killed the guard and receptionist, someone would have heard the shots. Like many other businesses, we had active shooter protocols in place. No alerts had gone off, not in the building nor on my phone. That gave me hope that both the guard and receptionist were still alive.

However, once Jankowitz got rid of me, he'd stalk each floor in search of Margy. Our building would become the site of a mass casualty event.

I didn't for a moment believe the gun pressed against my skull was his only weapon. Most likely, the backpack strapped across his shoulders was stuffed with an arsenal of death, not granola bars and trail mix for a hike in the woods.

He jabbed the gun hard against my head. "Keep moving."

When we reached the door, he pushed me against the glass, forcing me outside. A gust of wind caused the cold, crisp morning air to smack me in the face and made my eyes water. Or maybe that was my fear. When I blinked, several tears streamed down my cheeks.

The low rumble of a freight train sounded in the distance. The roar grew deeper and louder as the train drew nearer until it surrounded us on all sides and vibrated the ground beneath our feet.

I suddenly realized, this was no approaching freight train. This was an earthquake, and it was growing more intense by the second. A massive flock of blackbirds flew up from the surrounding cornfields as the stalks snapped and flattened.

Across the street at the train station, I watched the corrugated metal overhang that sheltered passengers snap away from the roof, crash onto the platform, and tumble onto the tracks. Cars in the parking lot rocked back and forth.

Jankowitz had frozen on the small patio in front of the entrance to our building, but he clamped down even tighter on my arm.

My chances of surviving had taken a nosedive. You'd think a guy who went to school at UC Berkeley would be used to earthquakes, but his actions suggested otherwise. I sensed from the way Jankowitz was breathing that he was in full-blown panic mode.

The hand holding the gun against my skull trembled. At any moment his uncontrolled quivering might cause the gun to discharge. Or he could decide whatever he'd planned to do with me wasn't worth the effort. He might shoot me here before fleeing. Either way, it wasn't looking good for me living to see future grandchildren.

New Jersey rarely experienced earthquakes. When we did, they were usually mild, the kind most people sleep through. But not always. This was one of the rare ones that ranked higher on the Richter Scale. And that meant, at any moment my coworkers would stream out of the building.

I sensed Jankowitz had come to the same conclusion. He suddenly shook off his panic and started dragging me toward the side of the building. We'd only taken several steps when a huge boom erupted. The force caused him to lose his grip on my arm.

I wrenched out of his hold, throwing him off balance as I tripped. I landed in one of the flowerbeds that surrounded the building, the mulch and fallen leaves cushioning my fall.

The ground ceased rumbling. I pushed myself to my knees and spied Jankowitz several feet away. He'd landed on his back on the concrete. He winced as he rolled to his side.

Our eyes locked on the gun at the same time. It lay halfway between us. I scampered to my feet, ran toward the gun, and scooped it up a split second before he reached me.

He latched onto my wrist with one hand and squeezed hard enough that I feared my bones would snap. His other hand tried to wrest the gun from my grip. I grasped onto it with both hands and every ounce of strength I could muster as he twisted my body, forcing my torso backwards.

One thought took over my brain: If Jankowitz pried the gun from my hands, my life was over. And maybe the lives of countless others.

As we continued tussling for control, I twisted my torso sideways, fell to my knees, and sank my teeth into his wrist as a shot rang out.

TWENTY

Jankowitz collapsed on top of me.

A moment later my coworkers began streaming out of the building. Everyone froze. No one said a word as they focused on the scene sprawled on the patio.

I shoved Jankowitz's lifeless body off me. As my adrenaline subsided, I pushed myself to a sitting position. Although the ground vibrations had ended, I didn't trust my legs to hold me upright should another tremor occur.

I glanced at my coworkers. Their collective stunned gaze traveled from a small pool of blood collecting around Jankowitz's head to the weapon still in my hand.

I stared at the gun. It wasn't smoking. I grasped the barrel with my left hand. It felt cool to the touch. The bullet that had felled Jankowitz hadn't come from the gun in my hand. But if I hadn't shot him, who had? The security guard?

I slowly turned from the body at my feet and the silent throng of dazed and confused coworkers and scanned the area. That's when I saw Zack, Tino, and Spader racing toward me. Three good guys with guns. One of them had taken out Brad Jankowitz. My guess? The good guy with the most to lose.

I was grateful I hadn't killed a man. However, if one of them hadn't beaten me to it, given the chance, I would have pulled the trigger. I'd made up my mind. I knew if I didn't kill him first, he'd kill me. I wasn't going to let that happen. Not if I could help it. I'd have a clear conscience, knowing Jankowitz would never kill again. That alone would have allowed me to sleep at night.

Zack lifted me to my feet and enveloped me in his arms. Behind me I began to hear murmuring voices. Someone started clapping. Others joined in until everyone was applauding. Some even cheered.

Spader and Tino had joined us. I wriggled out of Zack's embrace and into a side hug, then stared at my coworkers. "Why are they cheering and applauding?"

"They think you single-handedly took down a serial killer," said Zack.

That made no sense to me. How could they possibly know? The press hadn't yet learned that Jankowitz was alive. We'd only connected the dots hours ago. I scanned the crowd. Cloris stepped from the scrum, pulling Margy forward with her. When Margy saw Jankowitz's body, she must have said something to Cloris that others overheard.

I handed Spader the gun I still held. "I never fired it."

He glanced toward Zack, confirming my suspicion. "We know."

"I would have. I wasn't going to let him harm anyone else."

Tino winked at me. "We know that, too, Mrs. B. You're one badass amateur sleuth."

I corrected him. "*Reluctant* amateur sleuth."

"Sure. If you say so."

Margy gingerly made her way toward us, pulling Cloris with her. She stopped a foot away from Jankowitz's body. "Is he dead?"

I nodded. When I pushed Jankowitz off me, he'd landed on his back. Where the bullet had entered his body wasn't obvious to anyone staring down at him. But I knew.

My husband had given Brad Jankowitz a taste of his own medicine. That shot added one more mark in my Zack-is-a-Spy column. They don't teach shooting skills like that at the Boy Scout riflery range.

Margy pulled her gaze away from the body and spoke to me. "You saved my life. He would have killed me."

"He would have killed both of us," I said.

"I don't understand any of this. He was brilliant. He could have been the next Steve Jobs. I thought he was, not a thief and a killer." Her eyes welled with tears. "Why?"

"Greed," I said.

She shook her head. "What an incredible waste."

Spader and Tino had herded the other employees away from the body but ordered them not to reenter the building or leave the area until other law enforcement arrived. Within minutes, the Morris County police, CSI, and the medical examiner converged on the scene.

When the FBI arrived a short time later, Tino and Detective Spader pulled out their badges and approached the agent who had immediately taken charge. Zack, Margy, Cloris, and I remained several yards away, out of earshot of the conversation going on between the three.

The FBI agent, a fiftyish stocky woman of medium height, with a salt-and-pepper ponytail, occasionally nodded as Tino and Spader spoke. But at the same time, she repeatedly cast a sideways glance in our direction.

"Do you know what's going on?" I asked Zack.

"I assume Tino and Spader are filling her in on what led to the shooting."

Worry gripped me. The longer they spoke, the tighter the grip. Worry morphed into fear. My husband had done more than shoot a man. He'd killed him. To protect me.

I glanced up at Zack. How could he look so calm? Even though I'd told myself I could live with killing Jankowitz, would I really be able to walk away free from the emotional turmoil? "Do you think this has something to do with you shooting Jankowitz?"

"Probably."

"Are you worried?"

"Not in the least."

We locked eyes. Had Zack just confirmed every one of my alphabet agency suspicions? I wish I could get into his head the way he's able to get into mine, but mindreading is his superpower, not mine. "Well, I am."

He pulled me closer. "Don't be."

Easy for him to say. If Tino or Spader had shot Jankowitz, I doubt the FBI agent would look at either man with the same hardened features and narrowed gaze she directed our way.

Another couple of minutes passed until Tino called out, "Zack," and waved him over.

After a short exchange between Zack and the agent, she secured an evidence bag from one of the officers. Zack removed his gun and dropped it into the bag.

"Why did Zack hand over his gun?" asked Cloris.

"I think it's standard procedure." At least it was on TV crime shows. I told myself the same would have happened if either Tino or Spader had shot Jankowitz. I hoped I was right.

Eventually, all three men and the agent walked toward us. Zack introduced her as Agent Rhonda Sinclair. She zeroed in on me. "Are you injured, Mrs. Barnes?"

"A few bruises and some soreness. Nothing major."

"You should still get checked out when you're cleared to leave."

"When will that be?"

"Special Agent Ledbetter is on his way. He'll be in a better position to answer questions about timing. However, we first need to determine if the building sustained any structural damage. The county structural engineer is on his way to check it out. If he deems it's unsafe to enter, we'll have to move everyone to a different location before we proceed with interviews."

I nodded toward my coworkers, all of whom were growing increasingly restless. "They don't know anything."

She raised an eyebrow. "How do you know that?"

"Jankowitz didn't interact with any of them. He never got beyond the lobby." I explained how we came face-to-face when the elevator arrived on the ground floor, and the doors opened, adding, "By the way, the security guard and receptionist are missing."

I then mentioned the strange odor in the air where both were normally stationed. That caught her attention.

She removed a small notepad from her jacket and asked for descriptions of both individuals. When I finished, she ordered a search of the grounds, including every vehicle in both our parking lot and the train station lot.

They began with our lot, with all employees ordered to pop their trunks. By process of elimination only three vehicles remained—those of the guard, the receptionist, and one other vehicle. Two were SUVs with visible storage areas, both empty. The third was a black panel van.

Spader snapped a photo of the license plate, then told Sinclair, "The victim had a history of auto and license plate theft." Sinclair nodded to an officer who used a gadget to unlock one of the doors, but no one was found inside.

By the time the search of our parking lot had ended, the engineer had concluded his inspection and deemed the building free of structural damage. Agent Sinclair ordered law enforcement to head indoors to continue their search before checking the vehicles in the train station parking lot. Within minutes, one of the officers stuck his head out the front door and shouted, "Found 'em!"

The guard and receptionist were discovered gagged and trussed up on the floor under the reception counter. Jankowitz had overpowered them with bear spray, probably because he hadn't wanted to risk someone hearing gunshots and alerting the police before he found Margy. The EMTs checked them out, administered first aid, then whisked them off to the hospital for a more thorough evaluation.

By then, Special Agent Aloysius Ledbetter had arrived. He briefly conversed with our publisher, Hugo Alsopp-Reynolds, before all staff were ushered back into the lobby. Those closest to the entrance grabbed the few seats in the reception area. Everyone else was forced to lean against a wall or settle on the floor while Ledbetter explained the interview process.

"Various conference rooms and offices throughout the building will be used for interviews. Officers will escort you to and from your interviews. Everyone will use the stairs, not the elevators, in case we experience aftershocks."

A member of the production staff asked, "Are we free to leave after our interview?"

Ledbetter deferred to Hugo. "Unless you've been told otherwise by law enforcement, everyone is free to take the remainder of the day off."

Naomi Dreyfus, Hugo's longtime partner and *American Woman's* editorial director, added, "A counselor will be onsite tomorrow for anyone who needs to speak with a mental health professional."

"It's good to have Hugo back at the helm," whispered Cloris.

"In more ways than one." Several trauma-inducing events had occurred since Trimedia, our former overlords, had moved our offices from Manhattan to a building surrounded by New Jersey cornfields. However, not once had Trimedia offered to spring for counseling for anyone.

Ledbetter took Tino and Spader up on their offer to aid with interviews to speed the process along. Most of the interviews took less time than the trip from the lobby to an interview room and back. Since Jankowitz had never made it beyond the lobby and had interacted with only the security guard, the receptionist, and me, as I'd told Agent Sinclair, none of my coworkers knew anything. Still, "t"s needed crossing, and "i"s needed dotting.

Not surprisingly, Ledbetter had decided to interview me himself. The moment I took my seat, I began peppering him with questions about what he'd discovered at Jankowitz's lair, beginning with, "Did you capture the two remaining guys who helped Jankowitz escape, or did he also kill them? What about the money he scammed? Have you recovered any of it or figured out where it is?"

He leaned back in his chair, crossed his arms over his chest, and cut me off with a chuckle.

"What's so funny?"

He pointed to his chest. "Me, interviewer." Then, pointed toward me. "You, interviewee. For someone who refuses to join my team, you certainly act as though you're already a member of the Bureau."

"I have a vested interest in this case. The guy tried to kill me."

Ledbetter huffed out his frustration. "I'll tell you what I can tell you when I can tell you, Anastasia."

"Which tells me absolutely nothing."

We sat across the table from each other and engaged in a glaring contest until I blinked first. "You could at least tell me if I need to worry that my family and I are in danger."

"We won't know that until we identify the third victim and find the two other men."

"Ryder Holden, Gio Bianchi, and Julien Sharpe."

His face registered surprise. "How do you know their names?"

"Margy told me. They weren't in the warehouse building, but you know they're alive?"

"No one was in the warehouse. We won't know if they're alive until we find evidence one way or the other, which is why I don't want you leaving this building yet."

I mulled over his words. "So, we don't know if they're accessories in a triple murder or additional victims."

Ledbetter nodded.

"And we don't know if they even know the fate of the three other men. If they do, they could be in hiding, fearful they'll become his fourth and fifth victims. Or they could be lying in wait to carry out his vendetta."

"That about sums it up."

"Do you know anything new at this point?"

"We know Jankowitz is dead, thanks to your husband."

"Who took him out before Jankowitz killed me."

"Not saying I disagree with Zack's action."

"Good to know."

"Bottom line, we won't know more until the tech team combs through the massive amount of computer files found on his server."

"From the setup Margy described, that could take days."

"Or longer. But we already have a team working on it."

Ledbetter rose, walked to the door, and opened it. "The officer will escort you back to the lobby."

As I walked past Ledbetter, I said, "I want good news the next time we meet."

"I hope I can give it to you."

As I was escorted downstairs, I passed Zack and another officer heading upstairs. I wondered if Ledbetter knew more than he let on and would be more forthcoming with Zack. However, I sensed he'd told me far more than he initially planned to and possibly all that he did know at this point.

Margy had been one of the first people taken upstairs for questioning. Unlike all my coworkers, her interview dragged on. She hadn't returned before I was escorted upstairs. However, I found her seated in one of the reception area chairs when I returned from my interview. Besides Margy and one remaining officer, the lobby was empty.

I settled into a chair next to her. "They aren't letting you leave?"

She shook her head. "That woman FBI agent told me they want to put me up in a hotel for at least a few days. They might want to question me further. Also, to protect me. She suggested Ryder, Gio, or Julien might try to kill me. A week ago, I would have laughed at that. But last week, I would have laughed at anyone suggesting Brad was a killer."

"Have you given any thought to what you'll do once this is over?"

"Head back to California. I want to put Brad and all of this behind me and finish my degree."

"Do you know anything that can help them track down Brad's other partners? Or find where they hid all the money they stole?"

Margy shrugged. "I told them everything I know. I hope it was enough. I do know they all routinely traveled throughout the country."

"All were here the end of last month. They staged a fake abduction after Jankowitz was released on bail."

Margy's eyes widened in disbelief. "Brad was arrested? For what?"

"Fraud. He tried to scam my mother. That's how my husband and I got involved in this. They made it look like the Mafia had grabbed him and dumped his body in international waters. We all thought he was dead until he got too cocky, and I started connecting the dots."

"You? Not the FBI?"

I shrugged. "I'm a bit of a reluctant amateur sleuth."

"That's some superpower."

I offered her a sheepish grin. "I'd prefer being able to fly. Traffic is a nightmare in New Jersey."

After she laughed, I asked, "Do you know anything about the money?"

She snorted. "The money I thought they made through a legitimate business? I know they invested it all in crypto."

"I don't suppose you know how to access Brad's account."

"It's not his. It's theirs. One joint account."

"They all had access to the account?"

Margy shrugged. "I guess so, but I don't know for sure. Brad never talked much about the business."

With those words, Margy had uncovered Jankowitz's endgame. I read it in her eyes even before she asked, "Are you thinking what I'm thinking?"

I nodded. "Why settle for one-sixth the profit when you can take all of it?"

She shuddered. "Do you think that was his plan all along?"

"Maybe."

Once again, her eyes filled with tears, and her body gave off an involuntary shudder. "How did I not see what a ruthless scumbag he was?"

I reached out and gave her hand a squeeze. "Don't beat yourself up. It happens to the best of us."

When she eyed me in a questioning manner, I added, "Long story, best left for another day."

EPILOGUE

Although Mother Nature's hissy fit had lasted less than a minute, for those of us unused to powerful earthquakes, it had felt far more violent than the official 4.8 recorded on the Richter Scale. More importantly, no deaths, severe injuries, or property damage had been reported across the tri-state area.

However, my frayed nerves didn't fare as well. The longer the last two scammers remained at large, the jumpier I grew. Lack of sleep, coupled with massive infusions of caffeine to keep me functioning, certainly didn't help.

The only good news was that no additional bodies appeared in the Memorial Garden. Then again, the killer was dead, and even if the others were his accomplices, it seemed highly unlikely one would try to kill the other.

However, Zack still insisted on driving me to and from work and Nick to and from school until the two remaining men were apprehended. Since no one knew if they were plotting any retaliation, Morris County posted officers at the entrance to our office building, while Union County officers kept an eye on our house and Mama's condo. With a new man in her life, she'd refused to return to our spare bedroom.

Zack received a phone call from Ledbetter on Saturday morning while he, Nick, and I stood tackling a week's accumulation of fallen leaves. After he placed the call on speaker, Ledbetter said, "I'm finally at liberty to release information about the case. I'll trade you answers for one of your gourmet meals."

"You're on," said Zack.

"Should we expect the two other Musketeers?" I asked.

"My next two calls."

"What about my mother?"

"I'll leave that up to you," said Ledbetter.

Once the call ended, I asked Zack, "Any thoughts about including Mama?"

"Your call."

I didn't need to ponder the pros and cons very long. The last thing I wanted was Mama bringing my newest potential stepfather along for the meet and eat, even if he was an expert on elder fraud. I'd prefer my initial introduction to Franklin Bond under less serious circumstances and with fewer people present. "Let's give her the CliffsNotes version afterwards."

"Smart woman."

~*~

Ledbetter, with Spader and Tino in tow, arrived at six-thirty. Ledbetter carried a sheet cake-sized bakery box.

I'll be the first to admit to a gargantuan sweet tooth, but even I had my limits. "I hope you're all planning to take doggie bags home with you if we can't freeze the leftover cake."

I then went to lift the lid, only to have Zack quickly move the box out of my reach. "No peeking."

"Are you just saying that, or do you have some inside knowledge about the contents?"

"Wouldn't you like to know?"

In truth, there was a lot I'd like to know. The dessert was the least of my many questions. I shook my head in defeat.

Tino and Spader each held two bottles of wine. The Three Law Enforcement Musketeers appeared to have grown exceedingly chummy since first meeting. I suspected Tino and Spader already knew everything Ledbetter planned to impart this evening. For that matter, I assumed D'Artagnan, AKA my husband, had also previously been briefed. Tonight's performance was for an audience of one. And possibly the budding teenage crimefighter-in-training.

After we gathered around the dining room table, but before we feasted on a dinner of coquille St. Jacques, asparagus, and mashed potatoes, Ledbetter said, "We have a press conference scheduled for Monday, but some of what I'm about to tell you will be withheld from the press."

He then raised his wine glass. "Before I begin, though, a toast to Anastasia for her uncanny ability to see beyond the obvious and think outside the normal law enforcement box. Once again, you've aided us in immeasurable ways."

The others raised their glasses, and added, "Here, here" and "To Anastasia." Except for Nick who raised his apple cider and toasted, "To Mom!"

Once I'd stopped blushing, I speared Ledbetter. "Exactly what are you planning to withhold from the press?"

He winked at me. "Your involvement," and after a pause added, "And Margy's connection."

When I raised an eyebrow, he continued, "Yours for obvious reasons and Margy's to keep her from being hounded by the press. Right now, she prefers total anonymity, and we saw no reason not to grant her request. Not only is she completely innocent, in some ways, she's also one of Jankowitz's victims."

I raised my wine glass. "And for that, I raise a toast to Special Agent Aloysius Ledbetter."

After a repeat of raised glasses, Ledbetter said, "Now, back to our regularly scheduled case update." He nodded toward Spader. "First, the New Jersey Crime Lab fast-tracked the DNA on our third victim and identified him as Ryder Holden. On Wednesday, with that information and continued interagency cooperation, Tino tracked Gio Bianchi to an apartment in Denver and Julien Sharpe to one in San Diego. Neither received bail. Once they were both behind bars, we allowed Margy to return to her parents' home in Berkeley."

"Were Bianchi and Sharpe accomplices to the murders of the other three partners?" I asked.

Ledbetter shook his head. "Turns out they had no idea the others were dead, let alone that Jankowitz had killed them."

Nick eyed Ledbetter with extreme skepticism. "Are you sure? What if they're only saying that to angle for lesser sentences?"

Spader chuckled. "Like mother, like son."

"Both are fully cooperating," said Ledbetter, "but we have proof that neither returned to New Jersey after participating in Jankowitz's fake abduction."

"Was Jankowitz planning to kill them as well?" I asked.

Ledbetter nodded. "He summoned the other three to New Jersey, one at a time and instructed them not to mention the meeting to the others."

"They blindly followed his orders?" asked Nick.

"His game. His rules. In theory, the six were equal partners, each having a territory around the country, as your mom initially hypothesized. However, since the idea for the elder scam and the apps came from Jankowitz, he insisted on calling the shots. Because the scam worked so well, none of the others questioned the hierarchy."

"What changed?" I asked.

"Jankowitz's obsession with seeking revenge against you."

"I'm guessing my mother shared her worry over my involvement with dead bodies and law enforcement."

I turned to Zack. "That's probably why he looked so surprised and uncomfortable when he came to pick up Mama." My mother had never mentioned if she'd met with Jankowitz in person or had only spoken with him on the phone prior to his arriving at our house.

Zack nodded. "Since she hadn't filled out his questionnaire at that point, he'd have no reason to check that the address she gave him wasn't her home."

"He should have walked away at that point," said Ledbetter. "But his greed was too overpowering. During questioning, both Bianchi and Sharpe mentioned he blamed you for his arrest. You became an overpowering fixation."

"Zack and I were responsible for his arrest." All those red flags, coupled with Zack's instincts, were what had led him to text you the evening Jankowitz showed up at our house.

"His need for revenge led to his eventual downfall," said Spader.

"Dumping the bodies in the memorial garden was all about getting even with my mom?" asked Nick. "That's sick."

"Ego played into it," said Ledbetter. "He thought he could outsmart law enforcement while toying with your mom before making her his final victim."

Tino spoke for the first time. "But he grossly underestimated Mrs. B."

"And Zack," added Spader, both men confirming my earlier suspicions.

"Jankowitz is dead," I said. "How do you know all this?"

"Once again, because of his enormous ego," said Ledbetter. "He documented everything. We've uncovered a terawatt of electronic evidence."

"Everything?"

"Everything," he repeated. "Every scam, every victim, every amount stolen, down to the penny. The meticulous planning of his phony abduction. How he managed to keep from getting caught. His plot to defraud and kill his partners. Even the tattoo."

Ledbetter nodded toward me. "You were even partially correct about that. The V symbol with the horizontal lines is from a petroglyph symbolizing wealth."

"And the B?" I asked.

"Not an obscure cryptocurrency. It represented the billions Jankowitz claimed they'd make through their various elder scams. Or so Sharpe and Bianchi thought."

"I'm guessing that wasn't the case?"

"The B stood for Brad. An inside joke because all along, Jankowitz's endgame was to kill the others for their shares. Something else you suggested."

"What about the money?" I asked. "Will his victims recover any of what they lost?"

"All and then some. Even though the six of them spent lavishly, crypto has skyrocketed in value since the inception of the scam."

"Margy suggested they all probably shared access to the crypto account."

Ledbetter shook his head. "Only Jankowitz held the passkey. Funds from the scams were immediately deposited into the crypto account. Jankowitz paid all expenses for the group and doled out whatever additional money anyone requested."

"And the others readily agreed to that?" I asked.

"He convinced them he'd already made a killing in crypto while still in school, making him the ideal person to handle the funds."

"Had he?" asked Nick.

"Probably not," said Ledbetter. "He bragged in his cyber-diary about the ease of manipulating the others."

When Ledbetter had finished updating us—or more accurately—updating me and Nick, and everyone had finished dinner, Zack stood. "Nick, if you'll clear the table, I'll bring in the dessert."

Nick turned to Ledbetter. "What's for dessert?"

Ledbetter shot a quick glance in my direction before answering. "Something very special."

A few minutes later, Zack returned to the dining room and placed a large cake in front of me. In true interagency one-upmanship, Ledbetter had commissioned a badge-shaped cake.

Not just any badge, though. An almost exact replica of a gold FBI badge, complete with an eagle on top and blind justice in the center of the emblem. However, in place of the Department of Justice wording at the bottom, this badge read, *Anastasia Barnes, Official Secret Asset.*

Ledbetter turned to Spader and said, "I'll see your Black Forest taser cake and raise you a personalized chocolate Chambord FBI badge cake."

"Chambord?" asked Nick, his disappointment written across his face. "Isn't that alcohol?"

"No worries, Nick. I was assured the alcohol burns off in the baking process," said Ledbetter.

Ralph had silently observed dinner from his perch atop the china cabinet. He chose that moment to contribute to the conversation. *"Braack! I will be assured I may; and that I may be assured, I will bethink me." Merchant of Venice.* Act One, Scene Three."

ANASTASIA'S
EMBROIDERED HEART BOX

As the crafts editor at *American Woman*, Anastasia designs quick, easy, and inexpensive craft projects that leave her readers with a sense of pride over the finished product. This embroidered heart box can be made from Valentine candy boxes or heart-shaped inexpensive papier mâché or wooden boxes found at craft stores.

Materials: any size heart-shaped box; thin marker; acrylic spray or brush-on primer and paint in your choice of color; paintbrush (optional); four pieces of felt in complementary colors; four skeins of embroidery floss in complementary colors; embroidery needle; scissors; small, medium, and large heart-shaped cookie cutters smaller than box lid; fabric glue.

1. Using the box lid as a template, trace the lid onto a piece of felt. Cut out the heart shape.
2. If using a heart-shaped Valentine candy box, skip this step. If using a papier mâché or wooden box, spray or brush a coat of primer onto the box. Allow paint to dry. Repeat with the chosen

paint color. Apply a second coat if necessary but allow the first coat to dry completely before applying the second coat. Note: If using spray paint, it's best to apply several light coats of paint rather than one heavy coat to avoid drips.

3. Using four strands of the embroidery floss color of your choice, backstitch around the large heart, approximately ¼-inch from cut edge. Set aside.

4. Trace one each of the three cookie cutters onto the three remaining colors of felt.

5. Using four strands of the floss colors of your choice, blanket stitch around the large and medium hearts. Use a running stitch approximately ¼-inch from the cut edge of the smallest heart.

6. Using the fabric glue, glue the largest heart to the top of the lid, then glue the large, medium, and small cookie cutter-shaped pieces of felt in that order on top of the lid.

A NOTE FROM THE AUTHOR

Dear Readers,

If you read *Seams Like the Perfect Crime*, the fourteenth book in my Anastasia Pollack Crafting Mystery Series, you know that Anastasia's deceased neighbor was inspired by a neighbor who lived across the street from my husband and me many decades ago. However, the real-life inspiration for that character was never murdered (as far as I know,) and the home was never razed to build a memorial garden with a life-sized bronze statue of the man and his lawnmower. That all sprang from my quirky imagination.

However, the elements of elder fraud and cryptocurrency crimes in the plot of *Embroidered Lies and Alibis* were both inspired by recent events, neither of which are unique. On the day I finished writing the book, I saw an interview with yet another victim on the evening news. She was one of the lucky ones, though. A good Samaritan, who was in the right place at the right time, prevented the woman from losing her life's savings.

Unfortunately, Internet and phone scams against the elderly continue to grow, with A.I. making it even easier for hackers and scammers to defraud people out of their savings. Financial losses each year now run into the billions (yes, that's billions with a B!)

However, those figures only represent the crimes that have been reported. It's feared that thousands more go unreported every year because the victims are too scared or too embarrassed to tell anyone. In addition, the psychological and mental toll on the victims and their families is immeasurable.

Education is the best defense against these crimes. Make sure your family members know what to look for to prevent becoming a victim. You can find information online at reputable government sites and AARP.

My books are written to entertain readers, but I hope with *Embroidered Lies and Alibis* I also educated you and prevented you or a loved one from becoming a victim.

If you've enjoyed reading *Embroidered Lies and Alibis*, please consider leaving a review at your favorite review sites.

Happy reading!
Lois Winston

ABOUT THE AUTHOR

USA Today and Amazon bestselling author Lois Winston began her award-winning writing career with *Talk Gertie to Me*, a humorous fish-out-of-water novel about a small-town girl going off to the big city and the mother who had other ideas. That was followed by the romantic suspense *Love, Lies and a Double Shot of Deception*.

Then Lois's writing segued unexpectedly into the world of humorous amateur sleuth mysteries, thanks to a conversation her agent had with an editor looking for craft-themed mysteries. In her day job, Lois was an award-winning craft and needlework designer, and although she'd never written a mystery—or had even thought about writing a mystery—her agent decided she was the perfect person to pen a series for this editor.

Thus, was born the Anastasia Pollack Crafting Mysteries, which *Kirkus Reviews* dubbed "North Jersey's more mature answer to Stephanie Plum." The series now includes fifteen novels and three novellas. Lois also writes the Empty Nest Mysteries and has written several standalone novellas. Other publishing credits include romance, chick lit, and romantic suspense novels, a series of romance short stories, a children's chapter book, and a nonfiction book on writing, inspired by her twelve years working as an associate at a literary agency.

Learn more about Lois and her books at www.loiswinston.com. Sign up for her newsletter to receive a free Anastasia Pollack Crafting Mini-Mystery.